BLOOD RIBBONS

For May,

[signature]

BLOOD RIBBONS

LIN LE VERSHA

This edition produced in Great Britain in 2024

by Hobeck Books Limited, 24 Brookside Business Park, Stone, Staffordshire
ST15 0RZ

www.hobeck.net

A CIP catalogue for this book is available from the British Library.

ISBN 978-1-915-817-731-0 (ebook)

ISBN 978-1-915-817-732-7 (pbk)

Cover design by Jayne Mapp Design

https://jaynemapp.wixsite.com

For Mary

ARE YOU A THRILLER SEEKER?

Hobeck Books is an independent publisher of crime, mystery, thriller and suspense and we have one aim – to bring you the books you want to read.

For more details about our books, our authors and our plans, the chance to enter competitions, plus to download *Crime Bites*, a free compilation of novellas and short stories by our authors sign up for our newsletter at **www.hobeck.net**.

You can also find us on Twitter **@hobeckbooks** or on Facebook **www.facebook.com/hobeckbooks10**.

PROLOGUE

THE RHINE GLIMMERED in the morning light as Pieter cast his line with a wide smile, expecting a catch. Pike had been plentiful over the summer, especially in the polders. Although pike still lurked among the reeds in late October, waiting to snatch their prey, he suspected today he'd have a better chance of landing some perch.

Actually, it didn't matter what he caught – even if he caught nothing. He drew a deep breath down to the bottom of his lungs and slowly exhaled, content with his world, which shimmered as the day developed. One of those glowing autumn days, which felt full of promise, as if anything was possible.

Pieter adjusted his feet on the narrow promontory – a grassy finger poking into the river – ensuring he wouldn't slip on the mud. Standing on the very edge, he felt privileged to be sharing this perfect moment with the motionless heron on the far bank, fishing with deadly accuracy. At least one of them was having some success!

An impatient car hooter intruded on his peace as the frantic rush to work started behind him. It was a relief not to have to join them – he grinned, celebrating his newfound freedom. The novelty of his retirement from the surgery a month ago was still shiny and new. Although he'd loved working with his patients, the world had turned, and he found it frustrating to spend so much time on the mass of paperwork now required of him. And anyway, he'd lost his appetite to keep on top of the latest research.

A few white clouds interrupted the solid blue, and the slight breeze he'd felt at dawn, which rustled the crispy leaves on the trees, had disappeared. It must be time for the breakfast he'd packed in the well-worn knapsack, stowed on a hump of grass behind him. His stomach rumbled on cue, so he wound in his line, unfolded the low canvas stool and unzipped his bag.

Relishing his ham sandwich, which always tasted delicious out here, he delved into his bag for the flask of strong black coffee, when a slight movement to his right made him jump. Not a rat?

Horrified, he leaped up, slipped, lost his balance and toppled over. He was annoyed that his new jacket would be swathed in a layer of sludge. Wiping the gunk out of his eyes, he rolled onto his right side and levered himself up with his elbow. Panic swept through him, and he gasped out loud.

In front of his face was a grey-white hand, tangled in the weeds at the edge of the bank. As Pieter slithered to his feet, the back of a head bobbed up, and further down, caught in the tidal flow, the legs appeared to be kicking – treading water. It was a man, face down in the water. Could he still be alive? No. Pieter knew a dead body when he saw one.

CHAPTER ONE

STEPH COVERED her ears with her hands, attempting to block out the searing noise of the screaming engines. She frowned across at Hale as she gave up trying to lip read what he was saying. The bench below her shook her so violently that her teeth crunched together, and she had to grip onto the metal frame beneath her thighs to keep herself steady. The clouds whipped past the tiny portholes on the grey metal wall opposite, making her feel dizzy and seasick.

'Go! Go! Go! Now!' The screamed order, far louder than the engines, made her jump, and, feeling slightly wobbly, Steph pushed herself up and through the gap that opened behind her.

She stepped into a field, relieved to be away from the throbbing engines. Her ears buzzed after the assault on them. Hale stood beside her, gazing at the surrounding cyclorama of hundreds – no thousands – of parachutes, gently floating to the ground from a clear blue sky. A sight far too magical to be the next killer move in the war.

'Impressive.' Hale looked back at the fuselage from which

they'd just emerged. 'Certainly gives you an idea of what it must have felt like.'

'That noise for hours – dreadful! Just imagine it.'

They stepped onto a narrow path, which led them through urban carnage with the most horrific destruction on either side. The devastation made it impossible to imagine what the street must have looked like before it was destroyed.

They picked their way through the rubble of bombed buildings, alongside ragged walls threatening to collapse into more piles of bricks. A slice of bedroom, the iron bed clinging to the jagged edges of the floor, tottered above them to the right, and domestic debris was scattered all around them.

Battered pans, broken crockery and rags, which might once have been clothes, had exploded from the gutted houses and emphasised the impact of war on those whose lives had been wrecked. That was if they'd survived the onslaught. The air was pierced with the sound of screaming babies, barking dogs and the unanswered cries of pain from the wounded, hidden from sight. Steph shuddered.

The first shot made her jump; instinctively, she ducked. Hale took her arm and led her through the nightmare of destruction, where jagged glass clung to window frames and anything flammable was consumed by darting flames. Although she knew the constant shooting was only noise, Steph found it difficult to stand upright and crouched down as the rattle of gunfire followed them down the path.

Scraps of net curtains hung limp in front of the exposed interiors of half rooms, which no one could ever live in again. The relentless firing warned of snipers, and in front of them, the sudden explosions of mortars and grenades threatened annihilation. She was aware of her heart racing as they reached the end of the path.

Ploughing through the wanton destruction was depressing enough, but they were thrust further into hell when they emerged into dark silence. In the gloom of the escape path, she gasped as she made out the shapes of bodies strewn on the high bank, left to lie where they fell, alone in the mud. No such thing as a good death here.

Blinking, they stepped into bright autumn sunshine and returned to the twenty-first century. Steph took a few deep breaths to calm her panic, surprised at her extreme physical reaction to the installation.

'Ah! The loo. Won't be a moment.' She opened a door on her left with the universal image of a female – why did they always wear dresses? She rolled her eyes at her own stupidity, pleased she hadn't asked the question out loud. Catching sight of herself in the mirror, she paused to brush her hair and re-do her lipstick.

Gerard, her new hairdresser, had done a great job persuading her to have it cut shorter, so her blonde curls framed her face, making her blue eyes appear bigger and emphasising her cheek bones. She'd been concerned that the style was too young, but now she was used to it she was pleased she'd let him have his way.

As ever, when faced with a mirror she sucked in her stomach and turned to the side, checking her light blue shirt was tucked in. Her long legs looked good in her new jeans bought especially for the trip, and as she pulled herself up to her full five foot nine inches, she smiled back at herself – not bad for mid-fifties. Despite longing all her life to be thin and petite, she had at last accepted she was what people called 'big boned', and consequently, as she aged she benefited from nature's Botox so had few wrinkles. Well, apart from a deep smile line, but that didn't count, did it?

As she emerged, Hale held out his hand and grinned at her, and they wandered towards the cluster of tables around the outside coffee bar.

'I hope the kids make it down to the basement – that was really something.' Steph glanced back at the Hartenstein Museum, originally the Oosterbeek Hotel, which had been the HQ for the Germans, then the British during the battle for Arnhem Bridge.

'Coffee?' Hale, holding onto her elbow, steered her towards a table under an enormous green and white striped umbrella and pulled out a chair for her. As he leaned on the counter placing their order, she admired her partner, Chief Inspector Philip Hale – known as Hale by everyone. Taller than her and as thin as when she'd first worked with him, he had the most beautiful smiley eyes and crinkly grin; she was lucky to be with such a lovely man – sexy too. He flicked back his hair, which constantly flopped across his forehead, and although it was now more grey than brown, it suited him, and he was aging well. He winked and grinned at her as he walked towards her.

Hale stopped to let a man pass with a large black dog on a lead – was it a labradoodle? A picture of her dog, Derek, a black and white collie cross, pushed its way into her head, and for a moment she felt lost without him beside her. It was the first time she'd gone away and left him since rescuing him three years earlier. Surprised by the acute pang of loss, she sighed, then smiled as she thought how much her life had changed for the better since Derek and Hale had appeared in it.

Steph tugged her pullover off, suddenly too hot in the sunshine, and slung it over the back of her chair. 'An impressive collection of guns and military stuff, but that experience – wow! That was a real taste of what it must have felt like – and only a few minutes. Imagine days of it!'

6

'Just relieved we've never had to sign up for that.' Hale brushed a stray blonde curl back behind her ear and placed his hand on her shoulder, gently massaging it.

'Look, I'm still hyper.' She held out her hand, which shook slightly. 'And it was only pretend.'

Sipping their coffee, gazing at the dark red leaves against the clear blue sky, they watched a small group of subdued students help the veterans, some wiping away tears, towards the tables in the cafe.

'And to think they had to live it.' Hale nodded over at two of the veterans being guided to seats by their carers and, Steph was pleased to note, a couple of students who were listening to them intently.

Some loud shouts to their left attracted their attention. Six of the students were playing army games like little kids around the tank on the front lawn, clambering over it and shooting their fingers at one another while making machine gun noises. They had been so well behaved on the long coach journey the day before, and although they were simply letting off steam, she hoped they wouldn't upset the veterans, some of whom were frowning at their antics.

At that moment, one student, Amy, a tall girl with black goth hair and a long swishing skirt, swept towards them. She stood beneath the turret and spoke to the group, who listened to her in silence. Then, glancing sheepishly at the tables of veterans, the boys climbed off the tank and sauntered towards the café. Steph was impressed that this girl could sort them out with so little fuss.

The tallest veteran had taken off his maroon beret and was wiping his eyes with it. Zoe, another of the students, after helping him to sit down and handing him a cup, appeared to be concentrating on what he was saying. His mate sat with his elbows on the table and his head in his hands, eyes down, staring at the ground. He was saying nothing, apparently overwhelmed. It was bad enough being reminded what it was like in the battle by the stuff in the glass cases, but to be transported back to the reality of living it must be devastating.

Seeing the horror on the two men's faces, Steph wondered if it had been a good idea to return them so effectively to the reality they must have spent years burying since fighting in the battle for Arnhem Bridge.

It was the first full day of their trip to Arnhem with students from Oakwood Sixth Form College and veterans from the battle for *A Bridge Too Far*. Steph, a former police officer, now college receptionist and PA to the Principal, had been asked to join her great friend Caroline, the Head of Art, who was running the project. The Principal was thrilled when she asked if Hale could accompany them too – an extra hand was always welcome.

A charity for the Arnhem veterans had commissioned the art, English and history departments in the college to produce a book to commemorate the seventy-fifth anniversary of the battle. A small group of veterans, most of them in their early nineties, had returned to the town, the woods and the cemetery with their carers and the students to produce the text, photos and drawings.

A river cruise company had lent them a boat due for re-fit for their brief stay on the Rhine and their trip back seventy-four years. It was a generous gesture by the Dutch company that owned the boat, and it gave their project high status. On three floors, the rooms, or cabins, were well planned and decorated like first-class hotel rooms, and at first glance, the boat didn't appear to need a re-fit. Steph supposed that cruise passengers demanded high standards, but the large dining room and the lounge bar, both with excellent views of the river through their glass sides, were luxurious.

Caroline had planned a full programme, including visits to Arnhem, the war graves cemetery and the landing zone, followed by two days in The Crown, a posh hotel back in Suffolk, where they would finish their book in time for it to be published for the seventy-fifth anniversary celebrations.

It had felt such a good idea, but was it? There had already been hints of animosity and unresolved tensions on board, and when she'd heard someone shouting, 'You'd better watch out – it's payback time!' in the bar last night, she wondered what on earth she and Hale had signed up for.

CHAPTER TWO

ZOE WAS ON A MISSION, so she ignored the phone until it rang for the third time. Whoever was phoning was being persistent or irritating. She sighed, gave up resisting and answered it.

'Hi, Amy ... Yes, I'm coming to the bar before supper. I need a while to finish something ... Yes, my black skirt and white top. You? ... No, I don't think that's too dressy, and you always look so dramatic in your dark green dress ... See you later.'

Opening the wardrobe, she pulled out a short black skirt, which made her waist look thin, and a designer ivory silk blouse, a birthday present from her gran. She must be careful not to splash red wine down it.

Pulling her hair up with two copper slides, she checked herself in the mirror, pleased that she hadn't sliced it off as Amy had suggested. Her boyfriend, Ollie, said he was relieved she hadn't, as he loved her long hair. Before coming away, she'd put red highlights through her brown curls, which emphasised her green eyes and flawless complexion. Her gran told her to keep out of the sun, as she was lucky to have such good skin, and not to ruin it.

She had a couple of hours before Ollie was coming to collect her for supper. Opening her safe, she pulled out a padded envelope and, bringing it over to the desk, slid out an old notebook wrapped in greaseproof paper. With great care, she flattened it on the desk, tilted the angle-poise lamp so it was in full beam and started reading.

Actually, she almost knew it by heart, but reading it in the place where he'd written it might throw more light on what had happened. The familiar copper-plate style of writing, initially in ink and then pencil, placed it firmly in its age and told the story of one man's Arnhem.

She hoped that bringing her great grandfather's diary of his nine days in the battle might give her some clues about what had happened to him. How he'd died. Her gran had entrusted it to her a couple of years ago and urged her to take it with her on the trip to Arnhem. Gran was eager to find out how her father had died, as she'd always blamed the war for her miserable childhood, spent in an orphanage after pneumonia took her mother away two years after her father's death.

Zoe was also seeking answers to explain her own fractured life, and for a while this book helped, but now she needed the full story. She had shown it to Caroline, who became excited, saying it was just what they needed to bring the battle alive, and suggested they could use it at each of their evening sessions.

The first part had been photocopied and left in each room, as Caroline had asked her to read the next section at their first meeting that evening. She'd better read through the introduction again in case anyone asked questions. It wasn't the reading that worried her but the questions, as she knew her so-called mates could take the piss out of her as they had with other speakers back at college. Would they be kind to her? Now she felt sorry she'd agreed. Oh well, she'd done it now. Zoe set her phone alarm and started reading the familiar words.

Duncan Shaw. The Battle for Arnhem 1944

I knew when I signed up it wouldn't be constant action, but I wasn't prepared for these long periods of doing nothing. Just waiting and watching.

One minute sitting against a wall, dozing (never proper sleep), the next, pushing hard into a wall beside a broken window, to shoot at shadows and muzzle flashes in the houses opposite. Never sure if I've hit anything until silence convinces me that he's bought it and hopefully I've survived.

It's the third day since I landed here in Holland, and, finding this child's school exercise book in the house we're holed up in, I've decided to write about the battle we're fighting. Having never experienced war before and only coming in at the end, it will provide excellent material when I return to teach my history classes. It will be history in the making. Perhaps I can use it to write a book, a first-hand account of this battle, which our commanders think will end the war.

So, back to the beginning. Although teaching is a reserved occupation, I decided I'd waited long enough. No one else my age appeared to be left at home and I wanted to do my bit, so I joined up.

After training, I joined the Paras and got selected for the 21st Independent Parachute Company. A crack company supposedly full of the best. By the time they got to me, I think they must have been scraping the bottom of the barrel. Our job as pathfinders is to parachute into the drop or landing zone (DZ/LZ) and clear it (military euphemism for killing any enemy in the vicinity), then mark it for the mass drop thirty minutes later.

We spent days stuck in our barracks, cleaning our equipment, receiving instructions and using maps to become familiar with the terrain around our target. Letters to loved ones were written but wouldn't be posted until after the top-secret operation was underway. The generals were convinced that after the success of the Normandy invasion, the Germans were on the run, and with this final push, it would all be over by Christmas.

Day 1 Sunday 17th September

At last, on Sunday 17th September, the order was given to stand to. I tied my kitbag (packed and ready for days) to my right leg and attached the parachute to my back.

The silent, excited crocodile of men, well prepared and ready for battle, shuffled its way up into the Stirling aircraft. I sat beside my new pals on benches along the sides of the fuselage. Opposite, I grinned at Bill, who nodded and winked. Action at last had lifted our spirits, and weak jokes stimulated nervous laughter. I joined in and felt lucky to be with such a grand bunch of men, but wondered if anyone else felt the annoying tremors in their stomach I was experiencing.

Through the open door, I could see the oaks still crowned with green leaves at the end of a dazzling yellow field of corn. A breeze cut through it, making gentle waves. It was ready for harvesting, which was late this year. I wondered if I'd be back in time to see the trees turn rusty and take a walk along the path through our wood at home with Mary, sharing the rich reds of the autumn.

The door shut tight, and I switched my thoughts to the task

ahead. In the gloom, I could see Bill opposite was yawning and sweating, a sure sign of nerves. He was feeling it, too.

It wasn't the most comfortable ride I'd ever had. We were in the Stirlings, twenty of us paratroopers crammed in like sardines, with the other battalions following in American Dakotas. They would have the luxury of bucket seats, not benches.

It was a bright sunny day when we were dropped around noon, sixty miles behind German lines, or what had been the German lines before they retreated. There would be no darkness to hide our arrival. From the maps, the DZ was eight miles from the target, Arnhem Bridge. It had been decided this was the safest place to fly in the men and heavy equipment for the biggest airborne battle in history. History in the making and I was part of it.

At last, the order 'Prepare to jump' was given and the red light came on. Hypnotised, we stared at it, waiting for it to go green.

Floating down, it felt like another exercise. Luckily, we met no resistance and there were no injuries. After all, we were the 'crack' brigade. We collected our chutes and extracted our guns from our packs, ready to fight, and headed for the woods.

A group of men set out enormous white letters as guides for the Dakota and glider pilots, while we took positions at the edge of the wood to protect them from enemy fire.

Half an hour later, we could hear the whines first. Then the dots in the sky turned into fighters. They were clearing the way for the Dakotas and the hundreds of gliders that carried thousands of men, jeeps, motorcycles, anti-tank guns and heavy equipment needed for battle.

As the first chutes hit the ground, the brr-brr-brr of a German Spandau floored several of our men.

Unfortunately, the thirty minutes gap since we'd arrived had given the Germans enough time to get in the way. Our return fire by Brens soon stopped them and we gave our attention to the gliders.

The enormous number of gliders, landing at fifteen second intervals on the soft ground covered in heather, didn't make it easy, and too many failed. It was appalling to watch. We stood helpless, as many of them crashed into each other or got their noses buried in the sandy soil then turned over, crushing their pilots. I can still hear the screams of those men.

As the men found their platoons, they were sorted into sections and led off into the woods over the railway line or marched down the road to Arnhem. Sarge tried one of the radios but got nothing. It must have broken when we landed. We dug our foxholes with our entrenching tools, had a brew, ate some of our ration pack and settled down for the night, ready for the next drop.

CHAPTER THREE

Zoe finished reading and returned the book to the safe. She had been allocated a lovely room, which should probably be called a cabin, but then, as the boat hadn't sailed since they'd arrived, it felt like a floating hotel that swayed around a bit with the tide.

She pulled a chair over to the balcony door and opened it so she could see Arnhem Bridge. Apparently it had been re-built, so it looked exactly like the one that had been destroyed. The grey structure on thick girders resembled a cage with open sides, topped with struts bent into a banana shape. And had that battle really been for this? But it wasn't, was it? They thought this would be the final push at the end of that dreadful war, which would end it by Christmas.

According to her watch, she had well over an hour until Ollie arrived to collect her for supper. She loved spending time with him, but she knew he needed space to be with his mates and she didn't want to be clingy. She drew in a deep breath and scanned the wharf. It would be good to have a walk before supper. She could do with the exercise, or to 'stretch her legs' as

Gran would say, and she could make it to the bridge and back in time for dinner.

She logged herself out on the card reader at the Reception desk and walked down the gangplank and along the path beside the boat. Even though the boat wasn't moving, it felt strange to be on firm ground after the gentle swaying of the river.

Caroline had suggested they should use Duncan's account to structure the commemorative book and that she could illustrate it. The silhouette of the bridge gave her the idea of using it as a shadow behind the text with a line of little bridges to divide the days. The open construction would be ideal beneath the text and remind readers what the battle—

'Zoe.'

She turned when she heard her name but couldn't see who it was. Must have imagined it. Stepping lightly, she became aware of steps behind her.

'Zoe – you got a minute?'

She gasped as a dark shape enveloped her. Panicking, she sidestepped towards the high wall away from the river and fished in her pocket to grab her phone. Would she have time to use it? How stupid to have come out here alone!

'Didn't mean to scare you – it's all right, love.'

Zoe didn't feel it was all right at all. 'Who are you?'

As she stopped, ready to run, she recognised the man from the queue waiting to get on the coach at Oakwood the day before. He must have picked up her fear, as he stepped back, well out of her personal space.

'I'm Ken, Jim Craddock's carer – on your coach, remember? Just wanted a word.'

She relaxed her hand and allowed her phone to drop back into her pocket. 'Really? What about?'

'Nothing much. Just a little chat.'

She glanced back towards the boat, then towards the bridge. The wharf was deserted. He grinned at her. Keeping her voice steady, she did her best to sound confident. 'Let's go back to the boat, then.'

As she spoke, she tried to go round him, back towards the boat. He stepped in front of her, blocking her way. His hand reached out and touched her arm. She flinched and stepped to the side, this time further towards the wall, out of his reach.

'No need to be worried. I just want a word – in private.' He came in closer. Her nose crinkled as she tried to stop breathing in his cigarette breath.

'We can talk on the boat.' Zoe made herself as tall as possible, but heard her voice a little higher than normal, despite her struggle to sound unconcerned.

'Not about this, we can't. It's about your great grandad – Duncan Shaw. Let's sit down on this seat for five minutes. I'm sure you want to hear what I've got to say about him.'

His hand on her elbow, he nudged her further towards the bench by the wall. She resisted his touch and shrugged her arm away from him, trying to swivel round to side-step him and get away, but the pressure from his hand became more urgent.

'Just five minutes, love.'

The backs of her knees touched the wood of the bench, so she sat. She didn't want to appear hysterical or make a fuss. After all, he was with the group and they were in sight of the boat, and she was sure she could outrun him if he tried anything. His beer gut suggested he hadn't spent much time at the gym. She shuffled to the end of the bench and put her left hand on it between them, a little way away, so he would have to sit on it if he came any closer. If he knew something about Duncan, it might be worth listening to him.

'That's better, love.'

Ken sat down at the other end of the bench, clearly in an attempt to re-assure her he wasn't going to make a move on her, and gave her a broad smile. He needed to find a dentist – and soon.

'So, what do you want to tell me about my great grandfather?' She tried to sound in control, as if he was trying her patience. Even she wasn't convinced it worked.

He paused and fiddled around in his pocket, bringing out a crumpled packet of some Dutch make of cigarettes, which he held out to her. She shook her head. She'd never smoked and wasn't starting now.

'Mind if I do?'

She said nothing and waited while he sparked up the blue disposable lighter and took a deep drag on his cigarette.

'Well?' Tilting her head so she didn't have to breathe in his smoke, she could see his profile – his thin, pointed nose, narrow lips and the most enormous bags under his eyes. She estimated he was in his fifties and although his face was a bit saggy now, his high cheekbones and cheeky grin would have made him good looking when he was younger. But she was amazed that someone wearing designer clothes hadn't bothered to get his teeth fixed.

'I want to talk about your mum.'

'What about her?'

He threw the half-smoked cigarette away, trailing an arc of sparks through the air; it landed several feet away and smouldered on the black asphalt.

'Did you know your mum and me were friends? Very good friends?'

'No.'

Her stomach tightened. He grinned at her, showing his stained teeth again, the front one chipped and going bad.

'Well, we were. As I say, we were great friends. We even shared a flat for a while – several years, you know.'

They sat in silence while a boy of about twelve, being pulled by a small black poodle wearing a pink collar and lead with a pink bow on the top of its head, passed them on his way towards the bridge.

'Jo said she never put your father on your birth certificate. You could well be sitting next to your father right now – just think of that.'

Zoe thought of it. She shuddered.

'Maybe we could do one of those DNA tests to make sure.'

The horror of this was percolating through. She felt sick but said nothing.

'You see, your mum and me were together so long because we had a shared interest.'

'Oh?'

'A shared interest in food.'

'Sorry?'

'You know, food... Come on, love – a girl in this day and age must know what I mean by food?'

Puzzled, Zoe frowned. 'No – apart from what you eat.'

The grin got wider as he lit up again and took another deep drag on his cigarette. She held her breath to avoid breathing in the plume of smoke.

'You know what skunk is? Charlie? Weed?'

'Of course I know. They're names for drugs. Why?'

'Your mum and me spent many pleasant hours off our heads, stoned out of our minds, in la-la land – perfectly happy we were.'

Zoe sat in silence. Could this be true?

'You didn't know, did you, love?'

Again, she didn't answer.

'Course, she'd left your snotty gran by then. Edith had thrown Jo out and wouldn't let her near you.'

Again Zoe didn't reply, but pressed her lips together, keeping her face straight. Repelled but fascinated, she remained stuck to her seat, wanting to know more, yet dreading what he might say.

'Edith told you she'd gone away to find herself, or some such crap, but your mummy was the other side of town, a few miles away, and that bitch wouldn't let her see you.'

He stared at Zoe for a few moments, making her feel uncomfortable under his glare. 'And that's only the beginning of what I know.'

CHAPTER FOUR

ZOE FORCED herself to remain sitting beside him, despite the urge to run away or smash out at his grinning face.

'Yeah, Jo and me, we were together for years, living the high life...' He nudged her with his elbow. She leaned further away. 'High life, geddit?'

He chuckled, clearly thinking he was a brilliant comedian.

'Look, I'm going now. Thank you for telling—'

'Sit down, girlie, I haven't finished yet.' He shoved her back into her seat. Her head hit the wall. Ken slid up the bench so they were both perched at one end; Zoe clung onto the side of the seat to stop herself from toppling off.

'No, you're going to sit here and listen to me until I've finished, right?'

She froze as she saw the glint of metal in his left hand. A knife! What had she got herself into? The wharf was deserted. Would anyone hear if she screamed?

'That's right. Calm down, girlie. All I want to tell you is I was your mum's friend, and we had a non-stop party for years.'

With her right hand, Zoe squeezed the wooden slats hard.

22

She shifted her left hand to her right thigh, as far away as she could get from him, and stared hard at the river, saying nothing, pretending she wasn't terrified.

'Well, your mum was a good-looking woman – a good-time girl. A party animal. Know what I mean, girlie?' He leaned in, almost touching her face, and spoke slowly as if to a child. Disgusted, she squirmed.

The knife came closer. 'She was on the game, a woman of the night, a prozzie, the Oakwood bike – understand that, do you?'

Zoe nodded. Bile threatened to erupt. She swallowed and breathed through her mouth.

'As I was saying, she and I shared a past. A past your stuck-up gran lied about.' His voice dropped to a menacing whisper, his mouth beside her ear. 'But the past has a way of coming back to haunt us. Just like all the crap we're doing in this place now. We either dig it up, which is what those old fuckers are doing, or it comes along and smacks us in the face. Well, this is your wake-up call, love.'

Zoe's stomach lurched; she was convinced she'd throw up. She couldn't bear to look at him or breathe in his filthy breath. And there was the knife. She spoke to the river. 'What do you mean?'

'What I mean is you and I are joined. Joined by my past with your mum, and we have a future together. I'm probably your long lost daddy.'

'That's where you're wrong.' Her voice, suddenly strong, pierced the silence.

'Oh, I don't think I am. Your mum may have gone away, but her past life hasn't and neither has your future. Look at you. A bright girl off to uni, posh boyfriend from that rich

23

family. You thought you had it all planned out, didn't you? And guess what? You've now got me as a bonus.'

Zoe tried to stand, but he grabbed her arm, squeezing it hard, forcing her back down – the hand holding the knife got closer to her stomach. She screamed. She felt the point prick her side and stay there.

'Now, let's not have any more hystericals. You haven't heard what I want, yet. It's nothing really. Just a little help. Can I take this away?'

Zoe nodded, and the knife moved back to rest on his lap.

'That's better. Now all I want is for you to put a little present in your luggage when we leave this godforsaken place. It'll be all wrapped up nicely. Then you give it back to me when we get back home. That's all I want. Simple, eh?'

Horrified, Zoe gasped. 'You want me to smuggle drugs!'

'Not drugs. It'll be a souvenir of your visit to Holland for your gran, that's all.'

'I'm not smuggling drugs. If I get caught—'

'You won't.'

'You can't say that! I won't do it!'

The tip of the knife against her side made her freeze. If she did it and got caught, she'd go to jail. How could she get out of it?

'Oh, I think you will.' His lips touched her ear. She closed her eyes, trying to cut out the nightmare whisper. 'If you don't help me, I'll tell your gran all about the bits she doesn't know about your mum – the really exciting bits.'

'Do it. She can cope.'

'Really? You think so? A shock like that could give her a heart attack or a stroke and finish her off, and it would all be your fault, wouldn't it?'

'That's not true.'

'It will be if you don't help me, and then there's your posh friends in Southwold. I'll tell them what I've told you, but I'll sex it up a bit, so they get the full technicolour picture.'

'They won't be bothered.' Was it best to show she didn't care or crumble and give in?

'I think they will. They won't be too keen on having their precious boy go out with the daughter of a drug addict who opened her legs for anyone who'd give her enough for her next fix.'

This was a nightmare, wasn't it? Zoe opened her eyes, hoping. But no – there was the river. Why had she left the boat?

The whispering continued. 'Not sure if it got passed down to you, they'll think, and we don't want our little boy getting contaminated, do we? So, it's bye-bye, little Zoe. And then, there's this Caroline woman. I wonder what she'd do if she found out and spread it round that college of yours. Who would have thought it of our little goody-goody?'

Disgusted, she felt a gobbet of his spit land on her cheek, but she refused to let him see her wipe it off. He moved back a little and his voice got stronger. 'Now, you know what you have to do. Just one teensy thing and I'll keep my mouth shut and keep well out of your little charmed life.'

He leaned back and appeared to be waiting for her to respond. She was numb and didn't know what to say. 'Unless you'd like us to celebrate Father's Day together? Now there's an idea.'

Swallowing hard, she stared ahead. She was trapped. What was she going to do?

'I need your answer now. Are you going to take it or not?'

The prick of the knife hurt — was she bleeding? She had to

get away from him. If she agreed now, maybe she could think of a way of getting out of this mess later.

'Right. I'll think about it.'

The point of the knife penetrated further.

'All right, I'll do it! Now let me go back or they'll become suspicious.'

'There's my good girl. Now, give me your phone.'

She obeyed – she was too scared not to. He passed it back so she could put in her passcode, and he punched in a number. The theme tune from *The Godfather* burst out from the phone on his thigh.

'You've got my number and now I've got yours. See? We're friends.'

He held out her phone. She wanted to disinfect it.

'I'll walk back with you, keep you safe.'

'No, you will not.' Hearing her voice, she surprised herself by its strength. 'You stay here – wait 'til I'm on the boat.'

'Whatever you say, love. I'll be in touch, and don't worry – I'll not be far away.'

This time he let her stand, and, trying hard not to wobble despite feeling faint, she walked as briskly as she could towards the boat. Concentrating on placing one foot in front of the other, she forced down the sick that kept threatening to gush up from her stomach. Could he be telling the truth? Could he really be her father?

Gran had said her mother had had a sort of breakdown and left Zoe with her, and that was all she'd known and accepted. She'd felt rejected, especially after parties or sleepovers when her friends were picked up by their mums, but she'd got used to it. Now the news that her mother had been a prostitute and a drug addict living a life a few miles away had thrown Zoe sideways.

Was she still there? Had he said where her mother was now? Why hadn't she asked him? Suppose she was still living in Oakwood. If she was, it appeared she hadn't wanted to meet Zoe up to now. More to the point, would Zoe want to meet her?

How she regretted going for that walk and being thrust into this messy nightmare. How could she get out of it? If only she hadn't met Ken. Perhaps he'd disappear after she'd done what he asked, but she knew from TV that blackmailers don't let go. If only he could disappear. Or he'd never existed... and supposing he was telling her the truth about being her father?

Who could she talk to? Caroline or maybe Steph? Steph looked as if she'd been around, and she'd been in the police, so she might know how to deal with it. Zoe sighed and her head drooped as she watched the river current rushing past.

Some deep breaths learned in yoga calmed her a little. She wiped the bottom of her eyelids in case her mascara had run, pulled back her shoulders and walked towards the boat.

As she neared the gangplank, a shadow moved into the light at the top of it.

'Zoe, where have you been? I was starting to get worried. Are you OK?' Ollie walked down to meet her and gave her a big hug. She relaxed into his arms. He and his family wouldn't care about who her mother or father were... Would they?

CHAPTER FIVE

ZOE FELT a little queasy sitting at the front of the lounge beside Caroline. Her mouth was dry, and she'd eaten little of her dinner, as the food stuck in her throat. She hoped her deliberate smile would spread to the rest of her, as she'd heard that it released some chemical – dopamine, was it? – that made you feel happier and more confident. At least, that was the theory.

She looked around, but she hadn't seen Ken at dinner and he didn't appear to be here now. Her tense shoulders relaxed. Sitting at the front table, Ollie grinned at her, giving her confidence, and making her feel safe. He looked as though he could be her brother – the same brown hair with reddish bits and the same greenish hazel eyes.

They had been together since the first week of college, well over a year ago now. She'd been at Oakwood School and Ollie had come from Framlingham College, where he'd been a boarder. His parents, who lived in an enormous Edwardian house in Southwold, decided that he'd stand a better chance of getting into a Russell Group uni if he took his A Levels at a state sixth form college rather than an independent school.

She had got on well with his parents and his two sisters from the first time Ollie had taken her home to meet them, and they involved her in all their family events. She'd loved going on holiday to Tuscany with them last August, and she was always invited to their frequent parties. Her gran got on with Ollie and was pleased that Zoe was being accepted into what she called 'the right set'. She and Ollie simply worked and talked about a future together. Both planned to go to London after A Levels – he was applying to study history at UCL and she was going to Central St Martin's art school.

Her eyes moved from Ollie to scan the room full of students and veterans, who stared back at her. Most of them were dressed up for dinner, enjoying a few beers at their tables. Well, some of them were. Caroline had taken the students aside and told them that only those who were over eighteen were allowed to drink alcohol – she knew who they were and anyway the barman would be asking for ID. There were a few groans but she said they were guests of the Dutch government and they needed to respect their laws and this trip was a privilege and not to embarrass her.

Once again, Zoe was relieved that there was no sign of Ken. Amy looked brilliant in her dark green dress with its handkerchief hem and scooped neckline. Jon, the star of the rugby team, was spending a lot of time looking down it, while Amy was consciously ignoring him. No doubt by the end of the trip they would get off – they were both up for it and fancied each other like mad.

Flashes of light glinted off the rows of medals on the veterans' chests and transformed them from old men with memories to proud soldiers with stories to tell, like her great grandfather. They sat up straight and walked with more confidence when the medals were displayed across their chests. If only Duncan could have been here – she would have loved listening to his memories and knew she'd enjoy spending time with him. Her gran, who felt deprived of her father, would have had a whole store of tales to tell her, but even the few words she owned told of a bright, lively man. How different to that slob Ken, who presented himself as her father. Surely not?

Caroline's voice interrupted her 'if only' dreams. 'Welcome, veterans, carers and students to this exciting project. I thought we'd wait until this evening for our first formal meeting about our seventy-fifth celebration of Market Garden and the battle for *The Bridge Too Far*.'

Caroline paused, and glancing around the room, Zoe saw that all eyes were fixed on her great teacher, with several people smiling and nodding. She looked so cool in a long grey, floaty dress, which complemented her mass of grey curls, with an Indian pink silk scarf flung over her shoulder.

As usual, she had no notes; Caroline never appeared to need them but knew how to hold her audience with her low but strong voice. Fingers crossed that Zoe could do the same when it was her turn. Beside her, Caroline took a deep breath and continued.

'I hope you all had a good journey yesterday. Although it was long, we thought it better to stay on a coach rather than clambering on and off trains or boats. And several of you have told me how much you enjoyed the drive through the French countryside.' Once again, she paused and smiled around the room, clearly checking that everyone was with her. They were.

'Today we visited the Hartenstein Museum, which took many of you veterans back over seventy years. Tomorrow we will honour our dead at the Commonwealth War Graves' cemetery. On our final day we will visit the common, where most of you landed in September 1944, and have a tour of

Oosterbeek, Arnhem and the bridge, which as you can see has been re-built – or replicated, I should say, so if you did make it to Arnhem you should recognise it.'

In this pause there was a slight mumble from some tables, and she could hear a few of the men's comments – 'Expect Oosterbeek has been re-built after the mess Jerry made of it', 'We made a mess of it too!', 'Jesus Christ, that first landing was easy – then look what happened!'

What would she do if they started talking over her? A movement at the back of the room alerted her to someone entering the room. It was Ken. Panic swooshed over her. He grinned, nodded and leaned against a wall at the back, directly in her eye-line, and did that salute thing that cowboys do in films. Now she was really nervous and hoped she wouldn't need the loo.

Caroline swept the room with her eyes, waiting for the murmuring to die down before she continued speaking. 'Today is 20th October 2018 and we have until the end of the month to get our book with your memories and our research, drawings and photographs sent to the publishers. It usually takes about twelve months to publish such a complicated book, but our publisher has agreed to get it printed by August 2019 in time for the seventy-fifth anniversary memorial here on 17th September. So, we need to get—'

The theme tune from *The Godfather* blasted out from someone's mobile phone. Caroline stopped until it finished and looked around to see who owned up to it. Several students snickered as Ken raised his hand in apology and turned it off. 'What a dickhead!' came from Jon, sitting in front of a mass of empty glasses. Caroline threw him a hard stare and his head went down.

Resuming her smile, Caroline continued. 'I understand

that Prince Charles has already accepted the invitation to attend, and he has asked to receive our book before he comes.'

Several of the men nodded and, looking impressed at this announcement, murmured their approval, but it was met by puzzled glances from a few of the students. Obviously, appreciation of royalty increased as you got older, or maybe it was a generation thing? Zoe tuned back in to listen to Caroline as she heard her name.

'...Zoe has kindly allowed her great grandfather's diary to be duplicated, and the first instalment was delivered to your rooms earlier today. Now she is going to read the next section to us. Over to you, Zoe.'

Caroline gestured with her hand that Zoe should stand in her place. Caroline had not needed the microphone, but they'd decided that Zoe would use it, so Caroline pulled it in front of Zoe, who stepped up to it. All she could see was Ken grinning at her. The metallic taste of blood stopped her from biting the soft inside of her cheek and she shifted her position, hoping to block him out. It didn't work. Why had she volunteered Duncan's account? Why wasn't she sitting safely at one of the tables with her mates? Too late now.

CHAPTER SIX

STEPH FELT FOR ZOE, who was looking at the mic as if it was a cobra or some other venomous creature. Although she had made many presentations in her years as a police officer, particularly when asked to talk to kids in schools, she wouldn't like to be in Zoe's shoes, speaking in front of her friends. It was always easier to speak to strangers.

Seeing Zoe pause and her smile disappear, Steph followed her eye-line to see a well-dressed man standing at the back, lounging against the back wall, whisky in hand, grinning at Zoe. Now why would he be putting her off? He winked at Zoe and grinned. Steph saw her lower her head, adjusting it to the left, apparently to get a pillar between them.

Who was he? Steph closed her eyes to envisage the queue waiting to get on the coach, where she knew she'd seen him before. He'd been with one of the veterans, called Jim Craddock, who had stayed in his cabin since they'd arrived. Thinking back, he'd introduced himself as Jim's son – Ken, was it? Whoever he was, he had certainly unnerved Zoe, who appeared to have frozen.

Concerned that Zoe had been thrown somehow by this man, Steph started clapping and nudged Hale to do the same. Their applause rippled through the room and several of her friends whooped and cheered her. Zoe gave a tense smile and cleared her throat. Despite the red rash moving up her neck, a sure sign of her nerves, Zoe took a deep breath and was about to start when Steph saw Amy, looking less Goth this evening, waving her hand in the air. Now what?

'Please, Zoe, I've read the first bit, but it doesn't read like my diary – I mean I write notes about what I've been up to.'

There were whoops and 'Oooh' from some boys, which distracted her for a moment, but Amy ignored them.

'I mean, I write my thoughts, impressions – but this reads like an essay.'

Caroline raised her eyebrow and looked towards Zoe, posing the silent question. Zoe nodded and stepped closer to the mic. Before she spoke, she nervously checked the back of the room again, where Ken appeared to be listening intently and smirking at her. Zoe looked anxious and shifted even further to the side, presumably to get out of his stare. What on earth had been going on to unnerve her like that?

Zoe cleared her throat. 'Duncan was a history teacher, and he said at the start that he intended to make a record of the battle to teach his pupils and to write a book when he got home. So, I suppose this is less of a diary and more of an account or... memoir.'

'Thank you. It makes sense now.' Amy smiled at her friend.

Once again, Caroline's glance raked the room, but as there were no hands raised, she smiled across at Zoe, who began to read, appearing to be more confident now she'd said something.

Day 2. Monday 18th September 1944.

I woke before dawn, forgetting where I was and wondering why I couldn't feel my hands. I was freezing in the trench, but I was grateful for the dry weather. I looked around and saw that several others had also been disturbed by firing from the south. Jerry was getting closer from the sound of it. I hoped he would stay away for the second drop, due at 10.30 hours.

At about 09.30 hours, a few chaps from the recce group brought in two German POWs. The good news was that the 2nd Paras had reached the bridge at Arnhem and captured the north end. But the bad news came from the POWs we caught, who were from the Waffen SS, a crack unit, not the odds and sods we thought were left behind. General Urquhart had gone up to the front line. The radios weren't working, and word was the COs had to run around in jeeps to find out what was going on.

When we got to the DZ about 10.00 hours, the resistance from Jerry was much greater than the day before, and they started firing as soon as we appeared. Suddenly, I heard a sound like a cricket ball hitting a bat and Jock fell beside me. He folded over, his guts ripped out, and blood seeped out around him on the ground. A surprised expression was frozen on his face. At least it had been quick.

Sarge checked he'd gone, picked up Jock's gun and ammo and ordered me to leave him. Grabbing my Denison smock, he pulled me away so violently I nearly fell over him. I obeyed and joined the next group lying on their stomachs waiting to get a shot at Jerry. It felt wrong leaving Jock lying out there, unburied on the pine needles.

A Spandau rattled up from the trees opposite, making us push our heads down further into the ground as the surrounding trees were split by the bullets and we were showered with sharp missiles of bark and heavy branches. It stopped. Someone had put him out. Four tanks lumbered to the edge of the wood and sheltered under the trees. It was difficult to make them out in the shadows. They hadn't all gone back to Germany then.

Zoe looked up and appeared to notice a boy wearing a navy baseball cap with his hand up. She glanced at Caroline, clearly asking for help. Caroline indicated with her eyes that Zoe should respond.

'Yes, Jamie?'

'What's Spandau doing there? My dad has some of their CDs.'

Zoe looked lost, as if he was speaking a new language.

Caroline butted in. 'Sorry, Zoe, you probably don't know what Jamie's going on about. Spandau Ballet was a pop group during the 1980s. Would any of the soldiers like to explain what a German Spandau was, please?'

Tom, broad shouldered and well over six feet, constantly wore his beret as if it was glued onto his head and had an extra wide collection of medals across his chest. He waved one of his two sticks in the air and spoke – or rather shouted – in a deep, resonant voice. 'I can, miss.'

Those on the tables in front turned to see who was speaking and didn't need the mic. 'It was called MG42 – or machine gun 42. It was reliable and could fire over one thousand rounds a minute – about twice as many as our Bren guns. They were heavy and often mounted on jeeps.'

'It was known as Hitler's buzz saw because of the sound it made.' Another veteran called Ron added to Tom's clear explanation. He was one of the elegant old soldiers – the sort who could appear in adverts on daytime TV selling toffees or funeral plans. Silver-haired, spotless white shirt, knife-sharp creases down his grey trousers, he spoke with quiet authority.

Tom made a 'humph' sound and plonked himself down in his seat, apparently not impressed by Ron's supplementary information. Steph realised it was Ron she had seen sitting with Zoe outside at the museum. She had enjoyed her chat with him earlier and been impressed by his old-fashioned manners and calm, intelligent appraisal of the fighting in which he'd been involved. More gentle, and indeed genteel, than Tom, he cut a dapper figure with his smart navy blazer and permanent beaming smile, which he directed towards Zoe, who returned it.

'Thanks for that. Any more questions?' Caroline scanned the room.

Amy put up her hand. 'What you've read is a lot so far. How did he have time to write it all when he was in a battle?'

Zoe opened her mouth, and she jumped as a deep voice boomed out once again – it was Tom. Steph wondered if he went to bed in his beret, as he never seemed to take it off. 'That battle wasn't like you see on the films, my dear.' He swivelled round so he could see Amy. 'We were stuck in those houses for days. Trapped on either side by Jerry. It was flipping boring sitting and waiting for action, I can tell you, holding a gun in case they came at us down the street.'

Caroline smiled at him. 'Thank you for that helpful comment, Tom. I'm sure we were all wondering the same thing.' She nodded at Zoe to continue.

The Eureka transponder guided the aircraft in, and we threw smoke bombs to give cover to the landing parachutes. Several men were shot, and the mortar bombs hit some gliders as they landed.

However, the smoke worked for the majority, and they mustered behind us in the wood, ready to march off. We watched, impotent, as the last three Horsa gliders were set on fire and several Hamilcar gliders, carrying jeeps and anti-tank guns, got their noses dug deep in the heather and overturned. No one got out. Our equipment was lost.

The DZ was finally clear. We were ordered back to Oosterbeek and told to hole up in the houses along the main road. When we arrived, the Dutch thought we'd come to liberate them and we were mobbed as heroes by deliriously happy crowds, desperate to celebrate their release from occupation.

Their euphoria didn't last long. As the firing followed us and came closer, the disappointment on their faces showed the realisation that the brief moment of hope and freedom had passed, and they were now on the front line.

Most moved out of town, pushing prams with cases and a few belongings, their faces downcast as they said goodbye to their homes and handed them over to us. A few stayed and sheltered in the cellar of the largest house near the Hotel Hartenstein, which was our HQ.

A gentle old lady passed me, panting as she pushed her belongings in a wheelbarrow down the path. She stopped, looked back at her house, smiled, wished me good luck, and told me to do whatever was needed to free them once more. I waited until she was out of sight before entering her neat and tidy house with my muddy boots to smash the glass out of her front windows with my rifle butt.

In the street, Sarge barked some orders at a group of men, but I couldn't hear him properly and kept my head down, hoping he hadn't noticed me. He had taken against me when he knew I'd only just joined up – called me Johnny after that film *Johnny Come Lately*. All through training he had insisted if he needed a model to show unarmed combat, or wanted to pick on someone to humiliate, he'd choose me. I think he must have had a tough time at school, as he wasn't the sharpest knife in the drawer, and when he found out I was a teacher, he wanted to exact his revenge.

At first, I thought I was being oversensitive, but even the others noticed and jollied me along, saying he'd stop when we got over here. He hadn't and went out of his way to give me the dirty jobs. It didn't help when Jock bought it. He'd been a good friend who'd kept me going ever since we'd been in the same barrack block, waiting to fly over here. Strange how you make such firm friends so quickly in war.

The door flew open. In pranced Tug and Lefty, one behind the other, imitating music hall sand dancers, their hands and arms held stiffly in front and behind like Egyptian hieroglyphics. It must have been them that Sarge was ordering into the house.

Lefty is much younger than me and left school a term early so he could choose which service to join. Tall, with an athlete's body and dark, matinee idol good looks, makes him popular with the girls. He's always smiling, whatever's going on. He has a natural authority and Sarge never bullies him. Tug's shorter, blonde with sparking blue eyes, and takes a great pride in his appearance – one of the Brylcreem boys. He can't keep still for a moment and reminds me of a robin as he darts around.

It didn't take us long to turn the old lady's house into a battle station. We dragged the polished mahogany table to the centre of the room for the Bren, which faced out of the front windows. We pushed her heavy brown furniture to the sides of the room to provide cover.

Lefty told me to go to the loft, knock some slates off the roof, and set up a perch as a sniper. I was sad to be up there by myself away from the lads, but it could have been worse. Sarge must have been distracted earlier, or he'd have insisted I should be in the wettest fox hole.

Tug and Lefty had also been christened by him. Lefty was a Roman Catholic or left footer and came in for much unholy leg pulling, and Tug? Apparently, that's what men with the name Wilson are always called. It's after an incident in some nineteenth century sea battle or other where a man called Wilson saved the day in a tugboat. The military is a fascinating world of its own making. When I get back home from this, I think I'll do some research into it.

I took a mattress off one of the beds, leaned it up against the hole to lie stomach down and made myself comfortable. I rested my rifle between the hole in the slates and aimed it at the crossroads. The air outside was warmer than in the loft, which smelt of damp wood and something else pretty vile. Dead mouse, that was it. You can't forget that pungent, disgusting smell, and once it gets in your nose, it's stuck there. I searched around but couldn't find it.

For once, all was still. Painfully still. Not even the sound of a bird. Clever creatures, birds. Lucky too. They could fly away from the noise and carnage of a battle while we had to go the other way. I stopped myself from thinking too much. After all, I had signed up for this.

A brew with the others and another feast from our ration pack stopped my rumbling stomach and my melancholy wandering. That is the positive element of this fighting lark – your mates. They watch your back as you watch theirs. Despite their jokes and banter, my mind drifted back to Jock lying out there on the pine needles in the late evening. The sun would have dipped behind the pine trees, and it would get cold. Sarge wouldn't let me near him when we knew he was gone, not even to close his eyes. They were wide open. At least it had been quick.

CHAPTER SEVEN

Zoe's pause was met by a stunned silence. Steph knew her simple but thoughtful reading had captured the imagination of the room. The sly grins from some of the students had disappeared as they lived alongside Duncan through his words, and Steph saw several veterans close their eyes.

At first, she thought they'd nodded off and hoped they wouldn't snore and upset Zoe. But they appeared to be listening intently and murmured or nodded in agreement as they re-lived the memories Zoe's great grandfather was stirring up.

Caroline handed a glass to Zoe, who thanked her and immediately began sipping the water. 'Zoe, that was mind blowing and beautifully read. Before we go on to the next day, has anyone got any questions or comments?'

Steph scanned the room. No one wanted to be the first to ask a question. Several of the men had their heads bowed, clearly affected by the description Zoe had read. Caroline had deliberately put out the right number of chairs around the tables and mixed up students and veterans with their carers.

But Steph noticed a space on the table to her left. Two students sat beside empty chairs. Whose were they?

Of course, Jim Craddock and his son, Ken. She wasn't sure why Jim had come on the trip, as he didn't appear to want to take part. He'd missed the visit to the museum and had moaned constantly. Caroline said Jim wanted dinner in his room, and a steward had taken him a tray, but surely, he would have come to the bar afterwards? Obviously not.

And there was Ken, lounging against the wall at the back, texting on his phone. He raised his head and winked at Zoe again. Her head dropped immediately, and she appeared to avoid looking in his direction. Steph wondered what on earth made him wink at her.

There were still no questions and Zoe appeared uncomfortable, so Steph put up her hand. Caroline nodded towards her. 'This is a question for some of the gentlemen rather than Zoe.' Clearly relieved, Zoe sat down. 'Could someone explain why the radios didn't work, please? It sounded from Duncan's diary as if it was a general problem.'

Ron, on a table at the front, turned towards her and started talking. 'Speak up, chum!' Steph craned forward to see it was Tom under the beret. These uninhibited men certainly called it as it was. Caroline rushed over with the mic and handed it to Ron, giving him an encouraging smile. He cleared his throat.

'Can you hear me now?'

'As clear as a cracked bell!' Tom's powerful voice jeered him. Who else? He was the grumpy know-all and made a good pair with the moany Jim. He certainly didn't need the mic to make himself heard.

Ron faced Steph to answer her question. 'The problem was that we landed eight miles from the target and had radios with a range of about two to three miles, so they were useless.'

'Why did you take them then?' One of the rugby boys – Jon, was it? – with his arm draped across Amy's shoulders and almost on her chair, slurred his words slightly as he yelled across the room. He was one of the over-eighteens who was pushing it. A poisonous glare from Caroline made him lower his head to avoid her gaze.

'Good question, lad, and one we asked many times over those few days. The situation we landed in was bad enough but made much worse with no efficient or effective way of communicating. The generals had ordered radios, and we were stuck with the ones that were sent and we had to get on with it. There were no mobile phones, no wi-fi or internet and our technology was primitive and not too reliable.' Ron sat down and Alistair, sitting beside him, patted him on his arm. Alistair was another gentle giant and made a natural best friend for Ron.

'In the first part you gave us, it said your great grandad was in a reserved occupation – what's that?' The student who spoke, Sam, was the shortest student in the group, and his gigantic, black-rimmed spectacles earned him the nickname Brains. Steph knew he had a reputation among the students as a swot, but she was pleased he'd made such an impressive contribution to the discussion.

Zoe started to answer but stood open-mouthed as she was interrupted once again by Tom. 'They were jobs that allowed the lazy buggers to avoid fighting.'

Sam swivelled in his chair. 'What were the jobs, please?'

Tom's scowl was replaced by a look of surprise at someone challenging him, but Sam adjusted his glasses and continued to stare at him, waiting for his answer. Tom's carer, Judy, a thin woman with short grey hair, put her hand on his arm to calm him. Clearly irritated, he shrugged her off.

'Well, son, teachers, doctors, dentists and such like.'

'But those men in public service jobs weren't lazy, were they?' Sam would not let it go – good for him.

Ron, still holding the mic, joined in. 'No, Sam, of course they're not. But I'm sure you can see it was difficult for those of us who were living in hell out here to think of others our age, safe back at home, avoiding the war. Some men did see it as a way of getting out of fighting.' Ron darted a look towards Tom, obviously intended to shut him up, but it missed its target.

'For most it was a heaven-sent excuse to skive, son. They was as bad as the conchies.' Tom spat out his words, his contempt obvious.

'Oh, do you mean the conscientious objectors, sir? Surely, they were brave, standing up for what they believed in? Shouldn't we admire their strong integrity when so many of them were reviled and punished, rather than conforming?'

The tension in the room was becoming solid, but before Tom could reply, Sam persisted. 'But Zoe's great grandad was older, and he chose to leave his job to fight. You can't call him lazy, sir.' His use of 'sir' was inspired. Steph was pleased to see Sam defending his argument and nodded her encouragement. She'd had several chats with him in Reception at college and knew he had strong principles.

Ron, clearly sensing that this discussion should be ended, switched on the mic again and stood up to make his point. 'You're right, Sam. Zoe's great grandad was a brave man. He didn't have to fight and could've stayed at home teaching but chose to join up, which, in my opinion, makes him doubly brave. By-the-by, I think all teachers are much braver than soldiers, facing you lot day after day.' He waited for the students' groans and the adults' laughter to die down.

Ron turned to face Zoe. 'But Tom's right, the rest of us

didn't have much choice, but Duncan did, and you should be proud of him, my dear. Isn't that right, Tom?'

Once again, he directed his challenge at the grumpy man, who was now frowning, apparently struggling to follow Ron's argument. The row of empty glasses on the table in front of him hinted at the reason. Judy, who must be Tom's daughter from the similar shape of their noses, nudged him and mumbled something in his ear. He scowled back at her, but she nudged him again – this time harder. He shrugged his shoulders.

'If you say so, Ron.' With that, he sat back in his seat.

Amy put up her hand, and Ron passed the mic to the next table. 'That bit about his friend being shot and dying beside him was dreadful. Did they really leave men where they died and not bury them?'

Ron was apparently becoming the veterans' mouthpiece, as once again he held out his hand for the mic. Steph could see the others listening to him in respectful silence. 'In a battle, Amy, I'm afraid you don't have time to live your normal life. Your job is to stop the enemy, and if one of your friends gets killed, you hope there'll be a time later when the fighting stops and you can return to bury him. If he's injured, that's another matter. Then you do everything you can to get him out of the firing line and stretchered away to the medics.'

Steph was impressed that Ron appeared to know most of the students' names, and they listened closely to what he had to say. Yes, Ron was a real hero. She was a little surprised that Caroline had stayed silent throughout this exchange, even during the sticky bits, but Steph trusted she'd have a plan.

Caroline rose to her feet again. 'Thank you for those stimulating questions and comments. War, as we all know, is a complex subject and I'm pleased we're exploring that.'

From the thoughtful expressions on the students' and veterans' faces, it appeared Caroline had managed to get them to move away from the black and white perceptions of war and into the grey. They looked at her expectantly as she spoke directly to Zoe.

'Thank you so much, Zoe, for sharing your great grandfather's incredible writing, which has brought the experience to life for us.'

Zoe's head jerked up from checking her phone when Caroline mentioned her name and she acknowledged the comment with a faint smile. That girl was really upset or distracted by something.

'Tomorrow, we visit the war graves, so please meet in Reception at ten o'clock and get on the same coach as today please.' Caroline paused and scanned the room. 'Now, students, you have a short session with Mike Simpson, setting up the trial we'll present on our final night. I wish you all a very good evening and thank you for your attention.'

Having done her duty, Caroline slumped down in her chair as people began to leave the room.

'Thank goodness that went all right.' She reached for the large wine glass containing a rather good Merlot that she'd left earlier and gulped a couple of mouthfuls. She let out a deep breath and relaxed back in her chair. 'Oh! That's better. How do you think it went?'

'Very well. They were all entranced by Zoe's reading. She has such a clear voice and conveys Duncan's story so well. And you were great!'

'You should be really proud of what you are creating here, Caroline.' Hale held up his glass and saluted her.

In her peripheral vision, Steph saw Zoe disappear through the glass doors to Reception, in the opposite direction to the rest of the students. Through the frosted glass she could see two figures – Zoe and a larger shadow that resembled a man, then both disappeared.

'Won't be a moment.' Curious, Steph left the table and came into Reception to see Zoe and the man going down the gangway.

He appeared to be herding her, as she was dragging her feet and looking back over her shoulder. What on earth was going on?

CHAPTER EIGHT

STEPH BOUNCED DOWN THE GANGWAY, then stopped. Where had they gone? She searched the empty pools of light thrown by the streetlamps. From her right, *The Godfather* ringtone was carried on the wind. She spotted them as they turned into the brightly lit café on the wharf, about a hundred metres away from the boat. Almost jogging, she could see Ken open the door for Zoe to go in, then he followed her. At least they were in a public place – much safer than the deserted, shadowy wharf.

Steph wove her way through the maze of outside tables, filled by a noisy group of Dutch sailors. They were downing beers at a frantic rate and laughing uproariously at a large man in full uniform balancing on a metal chair telling a funny story.

Opening the door, Steph stepped into a wall of noise. She walked along the line of drinkers standing at a marble-topped bar towards a glass case, housing a few dried up cakes. At the end of the counter, she stood on tip-toe, searching the crammed café for Zoe's copper slides or Ken's gelled dark hair, but they weren't at any of the tables.

To her left was a flight of stairs, and climbing up a few

steps, she heard music so assumed there must be more tables up there. As she reached the top of the stairs, the solid techno beat hit her. Through the gloom she saw a small dance floor, crammed with dancers bouncing as one to the insistent rhythm.

Two enormous speakers threw out the sound, which made the floor vibrate and forced the black fabric covering their front to pulsate in and out with the beat. Along the walls, a line of metal bistro tables and chairs could be seen in the gloom, with the only light coming from the flashing bulbs at the front of the DJ's decks and the yellow neon sign flashing 'BAR' above a small kiosk in the corner.

Standing against the wall, Steph raked the room, but couldn't find them at one of the tables or on the dance floor. Anyway, this would be a stupid place to hold a conversation, unless you were good at lipreading.

Heading back to the ground floor of the café, she noticed some concrete steps painted gloss red that appeared to go down to a cellar – the loos? It was worth a look. At the bottom of them were three doors; two led to the toilets and the third, which was ajar, was apparently the storeroom. Eureka! She could hear voices inside.

About to push the door open, she stopped as she heard her name.

'—that Steph woman – you know she was a cop, don't you? And her boyfriend is an inspector or something. If you go near either of them, I'll make sure they find what they're looking for and you'll be inside as soon as look.'

Peeping through the crack of the door, Steph could see Ken's back, his arms outstretched with his hands caging in either side of Zoe's head. Backed up against the wall, she looked terrified.

Ken's face moved in closer to hers. 'Now, the day we leave—'

'Can I help you, lady?' A waiter balancing a tray of dirty glasses came up behind Steph and, as he spoke, kicked the door wide open and walked in, evidently heading towards a dishwasher.

Ken swivelled round, clearly shocked to see Steph standing in the doorway. For a moment, she was struck dumb, and Ken too appeared to be taken aback, but Steph got in first.

'Zoe, what are you doing down here?'

A look of relief flooded Zoe's face. At the same time Ken lowered his arms and, smiling, strode towards Steph. 'Two friends having a drink.'

'Oh? I don't see any glasses?'

'Couldn't hear ourselves think upstairs, so we came down here where it's quiet.' He was now uncomfortably close to Steph, whose instinct was to step back, but she forced herself to hold her ground and his stare. He lost, lowering his gaze, pretending to find something in his pocket.

Steph, her confidence boosted, stood in his way. 'Please do not ask one of our students to leave the boat again. There is a programme of our activities on the noticeboard in Reception, and Zoe should be in a session with the other students, not out here alone, with you, in a bar.'

Ken said nothing but sneered at Steph. As he pushed past, he ensured his arm brushed against her, before stopping and turning to Zoe. 'We'll have our little chat later, OK?' With that, he took the steps two at a time and disappeared.

By the time Zoe and Steph were outside the café, there was no sign of him or indeed the carousing sailors. Steph indicated an empty table at the side. 'Would you like to sit here for a few minutes?'

'No thanks. I'd like to get back to my friends.'

They started walking towards the bright lights of the boat.

'What on earth were you doing with him out here alone?'

Zoe looked embarrassed. 'I'm not sure, really. He texted me and said he needed to tell me something urgent – about Duncan – away from the others. Sorry, it was stupid to come out here with him.'

'And was it?'

'What?'

'Urgent – what he had to tell you?'

'I don't know – he didn't get that far.'

At the bottom of the gangway, Steph blocked Zoe's way, so she was forced to face her. 'Look, I've no idea what's going on here, Zoe, but it didn't look right – in fact, you've looked scared stiff all evening. Do not let him talk you into going anywhere alone with him again. If he asks you, come and find me or Caroline. Understand?'

Zoe nodded, her voice a whisper. 'Yes, Steph.'

'And if you ever want to talk about anything, we're always ready to listen. Whatever it is. Do you hear me?'

'Yes, Steph, thank you. Now I should get back to the others.'

'Yes, off you go.'

Steph watched Zoe climb up into the boat and go through Reception. Then she took a few steps back into the dark shadows of the wharf trying to spot Ken, but he was nowhere to be seen. She was convinced there was something going on – maybe Caroline could have a chat with Zoe and get it out of her. Whatever it was, it didn't look good.

CHAPTER NINE

'AND WHERE HAVE YOU BEEN?' Hale sounded worried, while Caroline looked it.

'I saw Zoe leave the boat with Ken Craddock and followed them to the bar along the wharf.'

'What?' A horrified expression turned to panic on Caroline's face and showed them how tense she was about the responsibility of running the trip, despite her apparent calm exterior.

'Jim Craddock's carer?' said Hale.

'Yes. That's him. But he's hardly done much caring, has he? Been away most of the time as far as I can tell. Anyway, I found them in the café cellar, where he appeared to be threatening her. As soon as they saw me, he left, and I brought her back with me.'

'Did you find out what was going on?' Caroline looked alarmed.

'No, she wouldn't give anything away. Something about information he had on Duncan, but I didn't believe her. I also noticed him standing at the back staring at her while she did her reading, and she appeared really spooked by him.'

'I'll have a quiet word and see what I can find out. We must make sure she's safe.' Caroline placed her empty glass on the table.

'And I'll keep an eye on Ken and warn him off when I get the chance,' said Hale.

'Thanks. We can't have him going off alone with a student.' Caroline appeared relieved by Hale's suggestion.

Hale stood and pointed to their empty glasses, and after they both nodded, he went to the bar to order three brandies. Caroline looked as if she needed it.

Chief Inspector Hale had been Steph's boss when she was in the Suffolk police and worked with Mike, her late husband. When Hale arrived at the college to investigate a murder, he soon signed her up as a Civilian Investigator, and they started a relationship that was still going strong after three years.

Steph relished this second chance at love, and they were comfortable in each other's company. He still kept his flat, but actually lived with her. Both were happy with the arrangement. He was a couple of years older than her and fit, in all senses of the word. A few more grey hairs, slightly deeper smile lines in his sculpted face, and intelligent eyes that gave her goose pimples when he fixed them on her.

'What did you say the students are doing?' Hale scanned the elegantly decorated deep blue and beige lounge, as he passed them their glasses and resumed his seat.

Caroline took a sip. 'Thanks. With Mike, discussing the historical facts of the case. He's setting up a court case accusing the generals of knowingly sending in thousands to their death on a gamble. We thought it was a good idea to get them occupied and away from the temptation of the bar after Zoe's reading.'

The head of the history department, Mike Simpson, was another popular teacher, and his A Level results were always outstanding. Having heard stories from his students about how he brought history alive, Steph wasn't surprised they did so well.

'And the defence? Is there any?' Hale licked his lips, savouring his brandy.

'Lots, apparently. Arguments like taking the bridges over the Rhine could have been the final push that made the Germans retreat.'

'Good job Tom isn't in there with them. He was spitting feathers earlier and would be a star witness for the prosecution.' Steph felt Hale rubbing his foot against her leg under the table. This holiday – or rather college trip – was doing them both good.

The lounge door opened, and the captain beckoned to Hale, who didn't notice him until Steph gave him a nudge and hissed, 'You're wanted.' At this, Hale jumped to his feet and strode off into Reception.

Those on the tables around Steph craned their necks, fascinated by what was going on. But as they couldn't see anything through the frosted glass doors, they soon returned to their chat and drinks.

Caroline and Steph waited for a few moments, but as Hale didn't return, they chatted about the visit planned for the next day. They were just about to order another round of drinks when Hale re-appeared. 'We're all needed in the captain's office.'

His serious expression didn't bode well as he ushered them along the corridor and into the office. As Hale opened the door, it appeared little more than a large cupboard, dominated by a desk with three chairs squashed in a line in front of it.

Sitting on one of them was a man who could have been taken for a young George Clooney, with designer stubble professionally cut around the edges to give him a well-defined jaw and deep blue eyes. His pale blue shirt topped tight denim jeans, while his expensive-looking leather jacket was casually draped over the back of the chair. He'd certainly made himself at home and knew how to dress, too.

As they entered, he grew and grew from his seat. He must have been well over six feet six and was forced to stoop when his head met the ceiling. His broad smile made him even more attractive, and Steph became aware of Hale bristling – he must have picked up her appreciation of this handsome man-mountain.

'Inspector Hendrik Bakker, meet Caroline Jones, the leader of the tour, and Steph Grant, an ex-police officer and now a Civilian Investigator – and my partner.' Steph was surprised to hear the possessive 'don't even think about it' tone in his voice. He'd never done that before. She felt a prod in her back from Caroline and a provocative 'Mmm...' which she hoped none of the men could see or hear.

Hendrik extracted a black wallet from his trouser pocket, which he flipped open and held out to her. It was his badge – a more elaborate affair than the British warrant card. She leaned back so Caroline could see it before he slotted it back in his pocket and squeezed on the end chair by the wall.

Caroline nudged Steph into the seat beside Hendrik. For a moment they touched thighs until both squiggled so there was a decent space between them. Grinning, Caroline slipped into the third, while Hale leaned against the door, frowning.

'I am pleased to have such an important English detective

on our team – the captain tells me you are a Chief Inspector.'
Hendrik grinned at Hale.

'Hang on, Inspector Bakker—'

'Henk, please.'

'Henk, you must understand I have no jurisdiction or formal powers in Holland. I am here with my partner and don't even have my warrant card with me.'

'But you have your professional eyes and ears and along with your lady here – what did you call her? Your "Civilian Investigator." partner — you can keep me up to the minute and go places I cannot go.'

'As long as you understand this is informal, then? OK.'

Hendrik gave a thumbs-up sign in agreement.

Meanwhile, Captain Dimitrov sat at his desk, his pen hovering over the open notebook in front of him, already with several lines of writing on the page. Silver grey hair, about sixty, with a ramrod straight back, he had a natural authority, and Steph had been impressed by his calm confidence and his distinguished appearance. He nodded towards the Dutch detective. 'Please Inspector, tell us from the beginning.'

'We've worked with your Metropolitan Police for some months. We have been following the movement of large quantities of drugs to England, where they are sold to buy guns to be used in crimes in both our cities. And now we believe they are smuggling diamonds too.'

He paused and cleared his throat. Steph was impressed by his fluent English, spoken with the lilt of an American accent, picked up no doubt from films. 'As you know, the use of guns by gangs is increasing both here and in your country, so there is always a demand. The Eastern European gangs, most from Romania and Albania, control the traffic of people and they smuggle drugs.'

Hendrik took a sip of water from the glass on the desk in front of him. Captain Dimitrov stopped taking dictation and frowned at him. 'Romanians? Albanians? Inspector, how are we involved in this? We have no Romanians or Albanians on our crew.'

'But you do have a smuggler.'

Shocked, the captain sat up straight, as if he'd been called to attention.

Before he could speak, Hendrik continued, looking across at Hale. 'We believe your tour is being used as a cover to smuggle drugs, or possibly diamonds, from Antwerp to the UK.'

Caroline leaned across Steph so she could see Hendrik properly. 'You're not blaming our students, are you? I'm sure our students wouldn't get involved in anything like this.'

Hendrik sat back to avoid the force of Caroline's passionate defence of her students and raised his hands as if protecting himself. 'No, ma'am, it is not one of your students, but an adult who we believe has hidden among them. This is his photograph.'

He handed a passport-type photo to Steph, who shared it with Caroline. Hale raised his hand – he had obviously seen it.

'That's Ken Craddock, isn't it?' He was a few years younger, and despite his smile, Steph was sure it was him.

Hale's voice made her look up. 'Yes, it's him. I've told Hendrik – Henk – and the captain that his father, Jim Craddock, has participated very little in the tour so far and appears to be here for the ride.'

Hendrik frowned. 'These are ghost men. We know they are there. We can see their crimes, but they disappear before we catch them.'

'How did you know he was here?' Steph turned to him; she

found their faces almost touching and caught a whiff of his citrusy cologne. She sat back.

'A blue notice when his passport was checked at customs in Newhaven. We have been following him ever since with the cooperation of your police and the French.'

Caroline leaned forward once again. 'We've hardly seen him since we arrived. I think he went to the Hartenstein Museum on the coach, then he disappeared, but—'

'I have just seen him in the bar along the riverbank.' said Steph.

'Tell me, what was he doing there?' Hendrik gave Steph his full attention.

'Ken was in the lounge this evening, listening to Zoe, one of our students,' Steph explained to Hendrik. 'I saw him leave with her and followed them to the cafe, where I found them in the cellar. He appeared to be threatening her, and she certainly looked scared.'

'What were they doing?'

'She told me some story about Ken having additional information on Duncan, that's her great grandfather who died here in the war, which is why she went with him. That bit may be true, but she wouldn't tell me what was going on or why she looked so scared.'

'I would like to interview this Ken and his father.'

Caroline leaned forward once again. 'Surely you don't think Jim's involved in international smuggling – a man over ninety?'

'Would you think to search an old man returning from a battlefield trip for drugs or diamonds?' Steph was the first to respond.

'Exactly right.' Hale nodded across at her. 'These gangs are clever and will go to any length to avoid being caught, and as you say, he's not been a part of the tour so far, has he? He could be here as a smuggler and not for your project, Caroline.'

Letting this news sink in took a few moments of reflection, broken by the captain's pen tapping. Hendrik sat up straight. 'I would like to be here, on your boat, to see what happens with this man, Ken, and his father.'

Caroline leaned across Steph once again. 'And how will we explain you joining us, Henk?'

'Simple. I'm a representative of the Dutch government and a part of your excellent project.'

A loud knocking on the door silenced them. Hale opened it to reveal the second officer, a concerned expression on his face, who said something that sounded urgent to the captain in Dutch. The captain pushed his chair back to join the officer outside, from where they could hear an anxious mumbling, which Hendrik must have understood, but his face remained impassive.

The captain edged past Hale. 'I think we all need to go up to the Reception, as Jim Craddock has just reported his son, Ken, as missing.'

CHAPTER TEN

STEPH AND CAROLINE, followed by the three men, walked into Reception to find an irritated Jim Craddock, shouting his story to the duty manager.

'He told me he was just going to do some shopping in town and not to worry, he'd get back later.' Jim wobbled on his stick and Caroline moved a chair for him. He sat down with an enormous sigh.

Steph stepped forward. 'What time did you say he left you?'

Jim looked her up and down. From the moment she'd met him, she hadn't taken to him. There was nothing she could put her finger on, but whenever he was close to her, she felt the hairs on the back of her neck stand up. From the look on his face, the feeling was mutual. He turned to Caroline to answer Steph's question.

'When you lot left at ten this morning, Ken went off by himself and now it's close on eleven and he's not back.'

Steph leaned towards the red-faced Jim. 'But he was in the lounge this evening, and I saw him about an hour ago in the bar close to the boat. He didn't come back with me, but it's a bit soon to decide he's missing. He's probably stayed there for a drink.'

Jim threw her a poison glance. 'He's missing, I tell you. He may well have come back to the boat and gone off for a drink, but he told me he'd see me before bed and he isn't here. Now you tell me where he is, missus!'

'We can look at the films on the boat's cameras,' the captain offered. Hale nodded at Hendrik, and the two men followed the captain down the corridor to his office, leaving a vexed Jim frowning.

Steph hadn't been too keen on Ken either, even before what she had witnessed at the bar. Her thirty years in the police force had given her a sixth sense to suss out conmen and liars, and she was convinced that Ken was both. He had that cocky look she'd seen so often, which his oily charm didn't quite cover. He was Jim's son and his carer for the trip and certainly a chip off the old block. And then there was Zoe, who appeared scared of him in the lounge and terrified in that bar. Something was going on all right, and she hoped for her sake, Zoe wasn't involved.

Jim was one of those old people who hadn't mellowed with age. His face was dominated by frown lines and his mouth was frozen in a permanent downturn, and she had yet to see him smile. He moaned about everything and nothing pleased him. It sounded as if he was complaining so that he could make a case for compensation when they returned home, but since all this was free, he'd not get far.

He had been a total pain on the coach, grumbling about the length of the journey and that there were not enough stops. The air con was too cold, then predictably when the driver turned it off, he was too hot. Since they'd arrived, he found the bed uncomfortable, the food foreign and untouchable and the chat in the bar too loud.

He hadn't mixed with the other veterans, sneering at their camaraderie. Those who heard him moaning rolled their eyes but said nothing. Jim didn't appear as well-heeled or smart as some of the men with his shabby blue blazer, shiny grey trousers and grey-white shirt complete with frayed collar. Maybe he had real money problems. But Ken, top to toe in designer gear, including the stubble, certainly flashed the cash at every opportunity and made sure everyone saw it.

Caroline, who had been on the other coach so not fully exposed to his moaning, crouched down to Jim's eye level and smiled up at him. 'Let's not panic yet, Jim. Ken will probably be back before long. Now, would you like a nice cup of tea?'

Steph smiled inside, as she had never seen this side of Caroline before. She was one of the most popular teachers, but no pushover. Her students respected her despite the hard boundaries she set, and she was the ideal leader for the project.

Helping Jim to his feet, Caroline steered him to the small table and chairs off Reception and arranged for a cup of tea and a plate of shortbread to be brought to him.

'What did you think of the museum, Jim?' Caroline was clearly attempting to distract him from the worry that was making him chew his bottom lip and glance nervously out of the window and at the sliding door leading to the gangplank.

'Didn't bother going. Knew it would be a random collection of guns and uniforms and they'd have whitewashed it.'

'Really?' Caroline's tone of voice suggested even she was losing patience with him and seeing the real Jim at last. But now he had his audience, he was in full flow.

'Like in the fourteen–eighteen war – lions led by donkeys. Total fuck up, that's what Arnhem was.'

'Oh?' Caroline was clearly taken aback by his piercing voice and raw aggression.

'Yeah, we went in there like lambs to the slaughter. Not sure what the generals were thinking about, but it wasn't us or those poor buggers at the end of the bridge.' He slurped his tea and scowled. 'I was lucky to get out along with the others here.'

He flapped his hand towards the bar, from where they could hear the veterans' lively chatter and laughter. 'Tomorrow you'll see just how many comrades we lost. That lot lying beneath Dutch soil was a brave bunch who gave their lives for what? That's what you've got to get your kids to ask, miss – what the fuck was it for?'

From his tone of voice, Steph knew there was no good arguing with him or putting forward a different view. Caroline appeared taken aback by the venom of the old man so stopped trying to cheer him up.

'I'm sure Ken will be back later.'

Jim grunted, frowned, and gave Caroline a vicious look. 'Right, well if you're not going to do anything, miss, I'll take to my bed.' Placing his hands on the arms of the chair, he levered himself up and reached for his stick, which Caroline held out to him.

'Will you be all right getting to your room? Do you need any help?' Steph half rose as she offered her help.

'I'm not a cripple yet, missus.' Jim angrily jabbed his stick down hard to the floor and stabbed Steph's big toe in her Birkenstock sandals. She winced but managed not to yell out.

'You need to move your foot out of the road, don't you?' She was sure she saw him smile as he walked off.

'Ouch! Did you see that? I'm sure he meant to do it. And it hurts! I bet it'll be bruised in the morning.'

'Ooh! Looks nasty! He's not the cheeriest of souls is he?'

'You can say that again.' Steph massaged her big toe then sat up trying not to make a fuss. 'The trial that Mike's running sounds fascinating. A really clever way of getting them to think through the arguments.'

'Yes. He's a great teacher. It will be interesting to see if the veterans hold the same views as the students.'

'Will he involve them?'

'I think he wants to suss them out and find a couple who might be prepared to give some evidence to support the students' argument on both sides.'

'Ron and Alistair would be good, wouldn't they? And how different to Jim!'

'Good night, sleep well.' Caroline smiled and waved at Sam who was on his way to his cabin. 'What a lovely chap he is. Talking of which, is Hale OK? This is hardly a holiday for him is it?'

'Perhaps not the holiday we planned but I think he's intrigued by it all. A shame the drugs and diamond smuggling have brought him back to his world. I think he was enjoying living in yours.'

'He's very good with the kids and would have been a great teacher. You've done well there, Steph.'

Steph sighed. 'Yes, I've been lucky—'

Steph stopped as she felt a hand gently squeeze her shoulder. Hale, returning with Hendrick from viewing the CCTV, bent down, kissed her cheek and winked at Caroline. Steph, a little taken aback at this public show of affection especially in front of Hendrik, smiled and felt herself blush as he sat in Jim's seat with Hendrik opposite.

'Who's lucky?'

'Certainly not Jim!' Caroline grinned at Hale. 'But you have to admit he sounded really worried.'

'He's going a little over the top. Ken may not have gone to see Jim, but he was here on the boat and in that cafe only an hour ago.' Hale looked at his watch. 'He's not missing, just late and not at Jim's beck and call.' Steph bent over to rub her sore toe.

'But if he's not back by tomorrow morning, Hendrick, we ought to report him as missing.' Caroline sighed then, clearly trying to look in control, stood and walked towards the large lounge. 'How about a nightcap?'

Hale cleared his throat. 'Sounds like a plan. While you were talking to Jim, the captain took us to Ken's cabin, but we found no one there.'

Hendrik nodded. 'Captain Dimitrov got his deputy to search throughout the boat, but your Ken Craddock, he is nowhere to be found. And we have gone through the boat's film, and it is as you say, Steph, he left in front of you and has not returned.'

They all waited, as it was clear he hadn't finished. 'I got permission from my boss to stay on board to talk to him when he returns. The captain has offered me a cabin close to Ken's.' He patted Hale on the shoulder. 'Now, shall we have that drink?'

CHAPTER ELEVEN

A LOUD KNOCKING INTERRUPTED Steph's dream of sunbathing beside Hale on a deserted sandy beach. She glanced at her watch – eight twenty-five? What day was it? Sunday. A late start.

Rubbing his eyes, Hale sat up, but she was already out of bed and opened the door a crack.

'Henk?'

'May I?'

Before she had time to reply, he had deposited a tray holding three mugs of coffee on the small table by the window and sat in one of the chairs. 'I have news. I thought I would bring some coffee with it.'

She was pleased now that she'd brought her new PJs that weren't too revealing, in case of disturbed nights dealing with student mishaps. She passed Hale his coffee and sat opposite Hendrik. Dressed as they were and dishevelled from sleep, it was a bizarre meeting.

'We have found a body and we think it could be your Ken.'

Hale frowned and his tone was formal; he was clearly irritated at the suggestion that he owned Ken. 'When and where?'

'I have come quickly from the river. This morning at the start of the day, a fisherman saw a body floating in the river, upstream. We think he had been dead for a few hours and is the right age, but the water has changed him. We need to identify him.'

'And you think it was an accident or was he murdered?'

Hale appeared happy to leave the conversation to Steph and to sit up in bed, sipping his coffee.

'He had nothing in his pockets to tell us who he was. We will know more after the autopsy but we think he may have been beaten.'

'Oh?'

'Bruises on his face and—' He rubbed his wrist. 'His wrists.' Hendrick looked across at Hale. 'When you are ready, we will search his cabin.'

'Right. I'll be out in about ten minutes.' At last, Hale spoke and climbed out of bed.

Hendrik turned back to Steph. 'What will the students and soldiers do today?'

'Presumably this has nothing to do with any of them, so I suggest we continue with our plans.' Steph also stood up.

'Your plans?' Hendrik replaced his mug on the tray and looked up at her.

'We'll visit the Commonwealth War Graves cemetery at Arnhem this morning. A coach will collect them at eleven. Then back for lunch at one thirty, free time in the afternoon and a meeting after an early supper.'

Hendrik stood. 'Then continue. Will you two be able to stay back here and help? We must talk to the father.'

Steph went towards the door. 'That's fine. We can wait

until the others have left. Jim Craddock doesn't appear to want to go to anything, so should be in his cabin as usual.'

Hale pulled the curtains and revealed three police cars and an ambulance. He then moved towards the shower, clearly hinting that Hendrik should leave. 'And how do we explain the number of police cars and officers out there?'

Hendrik followed his gaze out of the window. 'Tell them the truth. A fisherman found a body in the Rhine, and we are investigating.'

Steph placed the empty mugs back on the tray. 'May I tell Caroline why we will not be joining her on the trip?'

'She can keep a secret?'

'Absolutely.'

'Then do it. I will wait outside Ken's cabin for you.'

Steph phoned Caroline to tell her about the latest drama and to check she could cope without them. Moving Mike Simpson to Steph's coach was the obvious move, so the two of them could manage the visit between them.

Hale had appeared irritated since Hendrik had arrived and invaded the first few days' break he'd had for ages. While Steph was getting dressed, she could hear him make phone calls to his contacts in the Met and his boss in Suffolk, and both confirmed they were liaising with the Dutch police in an attempt to stop the smuggling.

Potter, his mate in the Met Regional Organised Crime Unit (ROCU), had actually met Hendrik when he'd visited London a few weeks earlier. He said Hendrik had earned a reputation for downing a few and warned Hale that Hendrik could drink him under the table.

Half an hour later they arrived at Ken's cabin and found Hendrik waiting for them, key card ready, which he inserted as soon as they reached him. When they had put on the nitrile gloves and plastic overshoes Hendrik handed to them, he opened the door.

They stepped into the gloom. The curtains and blinds were drawn, and they breathed in a heady smell of a musky cologne. Hendrik turned on the lights. 'Keep the blinds down – his cabin looks onto the bank.' Hale nodded his approval.

Luckily, the cabin had yet to be visited by the cleaners, and it was obvious Ken had left in a hurry the night before. Jeans, tee shirt and a blue hooded bomber jacket were flung over one chair, while his boxers and socks had fallen off the pile and lay on the floor. The table held a small open notebook, a biro and two marked-up maps of the land around the Rhine.

Hendrik and Steph checked the wardrobe and drawers, which held a collection of expensive designer gear and trainers – most of them new. Hale concentrated on examining the map. 'Look, the circles show the places we are visiting on our trip, and the crosses are close by. Meeting points?'

Hale, careful not to touch the map, moved back so Hendrik could take a photo. From his expression it was clear Hale was impressed by the thoroughness with which Hendrik took photographs of all the items they found in situ.

'Could be meeting places.' Hendrik, who had moved to the safe in the cupboard by the door, had come prepared with the opening kit – a master key and passcode. Steph peered over his shoulder as he pulled the door open. Inside was a wad of twenty-pound notes – several thousand pounds at a rough estimate, and an even larger pile of Euros.

Hendrik put all the notes in a plastic bag. 'About twenty thousand euros here or perhaps more—'

'And about ten thousand pounds in English money is my rough guess,' said Steph.

'A very rich man, this Ken.' Hendrik squatted down so he

could see inside the safe. 'Ah ha! What is this?' He tugged away at the black rubber mat, which covered something at the very back of the safe. Before he pulled out a black drawstring bag, he took a photo of it in the safe, then he went over to the table to open it, emptying the contents bedside the maps.

A pile of pea-sized irregular stones was scattered alongside the maps, ranging in colour from pale yellow to those tinged with a muddy brown.

Hale gasped. 'Henk, you've hit the jackpot!'

'Jackpot?'

'It means a special prize. Are those uncut diamonds?' Steph gasped.

'Yes. A fortune.'

For a moment they stared speechless at the hoard, until Hendrik took photos with his phone of the pile of stones with the bag beside it. 'It was as we suspected. They have moved onto diamonds now. Please place them in the bag.' Steph did as she was told while Hendrik returned to the safe.

'I have a feeling there is more... Ah! And here we have it.' Delving deeper into the safe, he took another photo then pulled out a small block, about the size of a paperback book, covered in black plastic. Bringing it over to the table, he removed the Sellotape from one end to reveal another plastic bag, this time transparent and holding a white block.

'Coke?' Hale peered at it. 'Cut this and it would be worth at least forty or fifty thousand pounds on the streets.'

'And easy to bring home in an old man's bag. Could be a book.' Steph took Hendrik's phone and clicked several photos of the brick and a couple of close-ups to indicate the scale.

'Drugs and diamonds! Your intel was correct.' Hale pointed to the maps. 'Maybe these crosses are where he made the pick-ups?'

'I think the diamonds came from Antwerp.'

'Really?' Hale peered to locate it on the map.

Hendrik leaned over and pointed to it. 'It's a couple of hours from here. Someone could have brought them to one of those places.' Hendrik looked closely at the marks on the map. 'Your Ken could visit them all in the time you are here – an English tourist in a taxi. You say he hasn't been much with the group?'

Steph shook her head. 'No, he missed everything yesterday, including meals – well, apart from appearing in the bar last night.'

Picking up the maps, Hendrik counted the crosses. 'Possible. I will get our team to check the CCTV in those places, although we do not have as many cameras as you English have.'

Hale closed his lips together, clearly resisting the temptation to respond to this dig.

Hendrik took a deep breath. 'Will you let me suggest something?'

'Go for it!' Hale frowned, his expression at odds with his words.

'We suspect we have a murder to investigate, and it may be your Ken or it may not. It is a man of the right age, but that is all we know. If it is him, he is dead, and we are no closer to bringing down the smuggling ring.'

Steph had an idea what Hendrik was about to suggest and glanced at Hale to see how what he had said so far was going down. He was listening intently, the frown fixed. 'Today is Sunday and you will be back in the UK on Tuesday. We have not identified the body – there was nothing in his pockets to help us say who it is – so we say he is missing still.'

Hale's frown deepened, and his eyes narrowed as Hendrik continued. 'You could give the diamonds and drugs to his

71

father in a sealed bag with Ken's other property, pretending you don't know what's in it. Ken will be missing still.'

'Are you sure we shouldn't use fakes? This would destroy the chain of evidence in our country.' Hale's tone of voice hinted to Steph that he wasn't happy, but Hendrik didn't appear to have picked up the vibe.

'To allow the drugs and gems to run has been authorised.'

'And when do you plan to tell Jim Craddock his son may be dead?'

'As soon as we identify the body as Ken. Why upset an old man making him see a body that may not be his son?'

Hale said nothing as he appeared to accept that Hendrik's argument was logical, and he waited for him to continue.

'Ken is gone. Disappeared. If he is our body and Jim identifies him, it is all over. We have the drugs and diamonds, but our line is cold. We have to start again.'

Hale listened thoughtfully and frowned as Hendrik warmed to his theme.

'Yes. If the body is Ken, we identify him and that is that — our operation is over. He was our one link. If we leave him disappeared for a few days, I think we may get the ring leaders this way.'

Before either Steph or Hale could speak, Hendrik continued, each word emphasised, and he was very persuasive. 'We do not know it is Ken. All we know is a fisherman at dawn was in the right place and found a body before it drifted down river. It could have been days before the body was found if he had not been fishing up here.'

Hale threw a glance at Steph before he took over. 'Do you have any evidence that Jim Craddock is involved?'

Hendrik nodded. 'We think he's being used as a mule. But no, we have no firm evidence... yet.'

The ticking clock on the wall measured the tense silence while they considered Hendrik's suggestion.

He looked from one to the other, appearing to assess their reaction to his controversial idea. 'Don't look so worried!' He grinned. 'I will consult with my boss and tell you what she says. It will be kosher. Do not worry.'

Hendrik laid a re-assuring hand on Hale's shoulder. 'If she doesn't agree, we'll take Jim to see the body. If she does agree, we'll make a plan.'

Steph knew only too well the frustration of having a long-term investigation kicked into the long grass; if this was Ken's body, many of the lines of investigation would be closed, and Hendrik was right, he'd have to start again. Hale looked resigned. He, too, understood the hard grind it took to build up a case and collect the evidence, and clearly realised the resources already expended in both countries would be wasted.

'You have no objection to me contacting my boss in Suffolk, as this appears to be getting serious?'

'Not at all, Hale. They know me in your Met – what do you call it? The Regional and Organised Crime Unit?'

'ROCU – yes.'

Steph moved to the door. 'Right. Breakfast everyone.'

As they reached the door, Hendrik spoke. 'And on our cameras, I have seen a young lady from this boat who was with Ken twice yesterday. She sat with him on the bank by the bridge and then later going to the café with him, as you said.'

'Really?' Steph shut the door and turned to face him.

'Yes, a girl with long dark hair wearing black and white. She talked with him for quite a while. I hope she is not involved.'

CHAPTER TWELVE

ZOE HEARD herself gasp as she walked through the wrought-iron gates and saw the rows and rows of identical white grave-stones filling the massive field as far as the distant shadows in the dark wood beyond.

The notice at the gate stated that 1,754 soldiers, sailors and airmen who had lost their lives in hostilities around Arnhem were buried there, with the majority involved in Operation Market Garden.

They lay in precise, regimented lines, with the headstones rooted in a narrow strip of earth running down the length of each row, in which a variety of small shrubs and flowers had been planted to create splashes of colour between the identical bleached stones. Perfectly mown grass corridors between them created an air of ordered calm. So different from how these men must have faced their deaths. Meticulously clipped grass edges – not a blade out of place – illustrated the care taken in maintaining a memorial to the sacrifice of these men.

It was only when Zoe walked between the rows she saw that, although the stones appeared to be identical, each one told a different story. Etched on each headstone was the name, regiment and the regimental badge of the man lying beneath the soil, along with the date of his death. Several had inscriptions at their base, which she assumed must have been chosen by their families. She stopped at one stone commemorating a soldier who had not been identified and whose stone bore the simple title 'A soldier of the 1939-1945 war'. A cross filled its centre, under which was the inscription 'Known Unto God'.

'Sad that, isn't it?' Ron stood beside her in the bright sunshine, which, although pleasant, seemed wrong somehow. It should be grey and overcast in this place, not sunny and warm.

'Yes, it is.' Her voice was just above a whisper. It felt appropriate to move slowly, almost tiptoeing between the soldiers' graves, and to speak quietly not to disturb them.

'He fought and died for his country, but we don't know who he was. His family cannot mourn their son or father in his resting place, but they've done their best here, haven't they? Given him dignity at least.' Ron stood to attention and bowed his head like she'd seen the Queen do at the Cenotaph on TV, and she copied him.

A week ago, she would have thought herself bonkers to do something like that, but here a spell had been cast that pulled her in to the sad, silent reality of war.

'Do you recognise any of the names? You know, of your comrades?' She felt she might be intruding but felt compelled to ask.

'A few. Strange, I find I'm using our regimental badge to look for them. You see, we rarely knew each other's full name – just a first name or even a nickname. Our full names were printed on our ID tags. That's how most of these men would have been identified.'

Zoe stepped along to the next grave and read the inscription out loud. 'Winds of Heaven blow softly here where lies sleeping those we loved so dear.'

'Beautiful, isn't it?'

'And look, there's an identical one next to it.' Zoe pointed out the writing and Ron bent down to get closer. 'That one is Claude and this one Thomas. Same surname. They must've been brothers.'

'Even twins.'

'How awful for their family to lose both of them.'

In silent contemplation, they stood side by side until Ron spoke first. 'Well, your family certainly understood the impact of loss, from what you've told us. Is his grave here?'

'No... Well... it might be. If it is, I think it'll be one of the unidentified ones. We know he died near Arnhem, possibly near the hotel or museum as it is now, but we've not found him on any of the lists.'

'Let's go and sit over there, for a moment, shall we? My old legs need a rest.'

They walked past the subdued veterans, their carers and the students accompanying them, creeping respectfully through the graves and reading the inscriptions. No talking or laughing in this place, which really was a 'corner of a foreign field'. When she'd studied that poem for GCSE, it had only been a poem to be dissected, but now with so many men lying in this particular corner, she felt a little faint and overwhelmed.

They sat, basking in the sun shining through the tips of the trees, flashes of yellow among the green leaves starting to rust. Zoe was grateful that Ron turned aside while she blew her nose and wiped her eyes. She had wanted so much to come to this place to breathe the same air as Duncan and to get some understanding of how he had lived and died, but she was surprised how much it hurt.

Ollie had gone off with his mates after they got off the coach and left her to walk through the graves by herself. He must have realised this was her mission, and she needed to do it alone.

'How did you get his writing, Zoe?'

'My gran gave it to me. Her mother, Mary, his wife, told her it got sent home with a letter from another soldier saying that Duncan had died near Arnhem and this book was found in his pocket. The book got sent back with his watch and his pen.'

'How did his friend know where to send it?'

Zoe blew her nose again. 'It was the most amazing coincidence. He was found by one of his ex-pupils. He was a history teacher, you know. Anyway, George Dickson, he was called, found Duncan's body, took his belongings and sent them to his old school then they sent them to Mary, his wife.'

'Did she get his dog tags?'

'She had one of them. I suppose the other must have been lost and wasn't on his body when they found him. I've searched all the data bases but he's not on any of them.'

Zoe looked back at the rows of white stones, many of them now in shadow as the sun moved round behind the tops of the trees. 'Maybe he's in one of the unidentified graves over there.'

'So, you don't know how Duncan died or where his body's buried then?'

'I know it sounds crazy, but I'd hoped to find him and somehow thought it would help.'

'Not crazy at all.' Ron paused and frowned. 'Help what?'

'Me, sort out my life. You see, from what Gran said, all was fine until he didn't come back. It all went so wrong after.'

'Really?'

77

'Yes. Mary died a few years after him, from pneumonia, leaving Edith, my gran, an orphan.'

'How sad.'

Zoe shivered. The sun had been hidden by solid grey clouds, and it was cooling down. 'Yes, it was. Very. She had the most dreadful time in the orphanage, from the stories she's told me.'

'But she's got you now. You sound close.'

Zoe took her jacket out of her knapsack and, with Ron's help to pull her right sleeve out, put it on. 'We should be. You see, she brought me up.'

'Oh, I see.'

'Gran's convinced our family went wrong after Duncan died. She says if he'd come back home, it would all have been different. I thought if I could find out what happened here, at least we'd know what it had all been for. But now I'm here, there are so many others who also suffered, I'm not sure I'll ever find out what happened to him.'

She was aware of Ron examining her, so she turned to face him. 'Thank you for listening.'

'No, my dear, thank you for telling me.' He placed one hand on the right arm of the bench and the other on the seat beside him, breathing out and emitting a little groan as he levered himself up. Zoe held onto his elbow and helped him to stand. 'Oh, don't get old, Zoe. There's not much to recommend it! Oooh! That's better.' He stretched his back and pulled his shoulders back.

'We ought to be getting back to the coach. Look, I think most of the others are on it already.' Zoe pointed to the almost full coach and the row of faces peering out at them.

'And there's your friend Ollie, waiting for you. Such a nice lad.'

They walked down the gravel path towards the bright blue coach, which looked out of sync with the green sculptured lawns with their spotless stones. 'I'll tell you what, my dear, I'll ask around. Your memoir may have already jogged a memory or two – let's see if I can find out anything more about your Duncan Shaw. This might be our best chance.'

CHAPTER THIRTEEN

ZOE STEPPED up to the mic with greater confidence than earlier, now she knew her mates wanted to hear her great grandfather's story. The murmuring in the room dissolved into total silence as everyone waited for her to continue.

Day 3. Tuesday 19th September

On guard in my perch, keeping an eye on the road and listening to the shooting that was getting closer, when Tug shouted up the stairs, 'Stand to, Sarge coming!' I decided to stay where I was in case he accused me of leaving my post.

The mumbling downstairs became louder, and his tinny shouting cut through the two floors. He was certainly upset about something. The thump of boots stamping up the stairs told me I was doomed.

His shadow fell across the room as he peered up through the loft hatch. When he saw my face, he spat out, 'Flippin' heck, are you deaf, Johnny? Get down here now!'

I slid down the rickety ladder and stood to attention before him.

'About time too. Not got all day. There's a war on, you know. Took you long enough to find it though, didn't it?'

'Sorry, Sarge, didn't want to leave my post.'

He made a 'Humph' sound. 'Just doing the rounds. Checking all's well. The other two skivers will tell you the latest. Jerry's getting closer. You hold your position here and don't sleep on the job!'

He must have seen the mattress. 'Anyway, what do you think this is, a ruddy school holiday?'

After he'd gone, I went downstairs to see Lefty and Tug. News was, General Urquhart had got back. He'd been stuck in a house for twenty-four hours on the outskirts of Arnhem with a Jerry tank parked outside the front door. He managed to get out through the back garden and got to HQ with the news that Lt. Col. Frost's men were holding the north end of the bridge, but the German tanks had come across from the other end and pinned them down in a few houses.

Our men couldn't get into Arnhem to reinforce them from the other side of the town, as the Panzers had brought in tanks to destroy the houses and root them out. Lefty kicked at the edge of a rug that had ridden up and said, 'They're stuck there like Spam in a sandwich – poor beggars.'

Sarge had also told them to go easy on the ration packs. We were expecting a drop, but not to bet on it. There was no water in the house and nothing in the kitchen cupboards. No idea what the old lady had lived on. I hadn't seen her carrying any food away in her wheelbarrow. A brew was all I wanted.

As we talked, the shooting that had been coming in bursts ever since we'd moved into the house was suddenly louder and much closer. I went back up to the loft, as I could hear rumbling up the road.

As I lay down on the mattress and poked my head out, I saw a

Jerry helmet bobbing up over a wall in a garden at the crossroads. It disappeared before I could get a fix on him. Then a rumble. A tank appeared, its turret turned towards the end house, and instead of a shell, a flame burst out – a flame thrower! I could feel the heat from where I was. The front of the house crumbled under the force of the flames, and the tank moved on.

One of ours screamed as he ran out from the garden, his hands trying to protect his face, now a red mass and his camouflage smock alight. He rolled on the ground in agony, trying to put out the fire. A shot rang out. He lay still and silent. The Jerry helmet must have taken pity on him, but I couldn't make out where he was. No one else appeared from inside the house or from behind the tank.'

I saw a movement behind the wall of the house opposite. It was one of our lads holding the end of what looked like a washing line. As the tank rumbled past, he pulled on the line and an anti-tank mine, which looked like a flat frying pan with a lid, slid across the road under the tank.

The men in the tank wouldn't have seen the explosion that tore through the metal, but we felt the furnace heat. Poor beggars, trapped inside that tin can. Flames as high as the houses and black smoke covered the gardens. The smoke stung my eyes as I squinted from my eyrie, searching for any survivors or Jerries creeping behind, using the tank as cover.

At last, all fuel consumed, the smoking wreck slumped to the ground, blocking the road. It would need a hefty shove to move that out of the way.

I joined them downstairs for a brew. They'd found some water in a bucket in the garden. We didn't say much, and no one mentioned our chap turned into a Roman candle. Then I came back up here, and before the light goes, I'm writing this.

The sound of firing comes in bursts from the woods. Spandaus and mortars mostly. There is the most beautiful sunset behind the trees with the streaky clouds lit from beneath with a deep crimson light. I wonder if Mary can see the same sunset?

For a moment I close my eyes and cut out the whining mortar bombs and the waves of the battle and return home to our walks along the River Blyth, down to the sea in the early evenings. I can hear the gentle chug of Dave's boat, setting out to sea to fish for the night and I see his son John, who waves excitedly as he recognises us. One day, when I'm back, we'll take the nipper on that walk with us.

I can see that bench by the river and us sitting on it, gazing across the fields at Walberswick church tower with the sun sinking behind the trees. So peaceful. Peace. Will we ever see it again? Will they? The mothers and wives of the men in that tank don't know yet.

Silence followed her last words, broken by a boat's siren in the distance and laughter from the bar along the wharf. Still, no one spoke as they allowed Duncan's story to sink in. It was as if Duncan had been in the room with them. His story had moved them back seventy-four years, and Zoe realised Caroline was using this personal account of one local man to get them to understand the history of the battle and to experience the complexity of war.

CHAPTER FOURTEEN

SURPRISED BY THE SILENCE, Zoe dropped into her seat. No doubt Caroline would let them have free time. She didn't want to bore them, but at the same time, she wanted to share Duncan's story.

Caroline stood. 'Wow! That was certainly something. Up for another episode?'

Murmurs of 'Yes, please', 'Want to hear what happened', and general noises of approval rippled through the room.

'OK, Zoe, off you go.'

Zoe, feeling thrilled by the impact Duncan's writing was having, moved up to the mic once again.

Day 4. Wednesday 20th September

Last night I dozed rather than slept. The mortars and shooting came in bursts. I lost count of how many times we stood to, ready to protect our house and street against the creeping shadows aiming to hit us first.

No breakfast and a few mouthfuls of water from two saucepans left out to catch the rain in the back garden. At dawn, as I went to collect them after the rain had stopped, I looked across the desecrated garden, which showed signs of having been a vegetable plot. The old lady must have dug up all the food to survive the occupation. Will that soil ever be tilled again? It's fertile enough.

The three of us shared the remnants of our ration packs. The few crumbs didn't touch the bottom of my stomach or stop the gnawing hunger pains. We sat, our backs against the walls. Time dragged. We were trained for action, not for spending acres of time doing nothing.

Forced to wait with nothing positive to do, my other training kicked in. History, particularly that of warfare, had taught me that no plan ever survives contact with the enemy, and I've begun to suspect that's exactly what's happening here.

As I write this, I close my eyes and think back to a Wednesday in my classroom. Are the Lower Third up to Richard II yet? A difficult reign with peasants revolting, and his death, which, appropriately enough, could have been from starvation or was it murder? I smile as I see my pupils' bright faces, amazed at the tales of cruelty and power from our past, and wonder how this war will be written up. Will pupils in the future learn about the desperate fight for survival we are experiencing? I hope my writing will make a contribution to that story.

My wanderings were interrupted by Sarge and his grating voice. If only I'd been up in my perch. As soon as he saw me, that was it. He ordered me to go out to the DZ with him and some other poor sod he'd volunteered, to send out the tracking signal from the Eureka set and mark the field for the supply drop from Blighty. Lefty and Tug were to hold the house.

It was a grey, grim day with an insistent drizzle, but not enough to collect anything much to drink in the saucepans. Parched and hungry, I marched with Sarge and Bob to the woods and the DZ. The burnt-out tank blocked the road, and we saw no sign of Jerry on the move, but we passed the bodies of a few of ours and even more of theirs.

We found an abandoned Jerry jeep with a mounted Spandau and about ten belts of ammo. Sarge grinned. This would be useful. Bob, the tallest of us, pulled the dead driver to the side of the road and Sarge told me to drag his partner's body to join him. He was a weight. I avoided his face, or what was left of it, and pretended I was dragging sacks of coal into the coal hole for us at home. It helped.

I felt dizzy as I climbed into the jeep and was relieved that we didn't have to walk the three or so miles to the field. My chest had tightened, and I was finding it difficult to breathe. I hadn't told them about my asthma, and they didn't want to know. I hid my face from Sarge so he couldn't see me trying to control my breathing.

We could see the DZ when the jeep juddered to a halt. It had run out of fuel. Sarge was brassed off, to say the least. He thrust the heavy kit bag containing the Eureka transponder at me and told me to get going to the field. The planes were due at 14.00 hours, and we needed to trigger the signal for them to find the DZ.

Bob and I saw a gorse bush about fifteen yards from the edge of the wood and crept down low behind it. After undoing the rope around the neck of the kitbag, we unwrapped the earphone and the aerial from their felt blankets and opened the wooden box containing the beacon. While Bob set up the tripod and extended the aerial, I pushed the plugs in, joining the two grey metal sets, covered in a mass of dials and switches, to fix them to the terminals on the batteries.

I listened through the earpiece to test it. Nothing. I turned the transmitter switch from B back to A, then back again to B, the prearranged signal. Still nothing. We dismantled it all and started again. This time, Bob re-attached the clips to the battery terminals and re-plugged the sets, hoping that starting from scratch would work. It didn't. The set was US.

Sarge crawled towards us and hissed a choice selection of swear words to describe our failure. I was impressed he could get so many into one sentence! He said he could do better, and he wished he'd never asked us to do it in the first stuffing place.

Watching, as Sarge was unsuccessful in his attempt to get it working, Bob rolled his eyes at me and I grinned, pleased that it wasn't us that had failed. Sarge saw us and raised his arm to hit out but stopped himself. He was furious and blamed us. It wasn't our fault that the flippin' thing didn't work.

He told us to blow it up, as it mustn't fall into Jerry's hands, even if it was US, and to get under cover quick as the fuse wasn't long. We waited until he got back to the trees, then Bob told me to get out of the way (he'd heard my laboured breathing) and said he'd arm the detonator. He placed the set beneath the aerial and fiddled with it, then ran like the clappers, diving to the ground as he reached the trees. It went up with a hell of a bang, scattering pieces of metal on the ground around the bush. Still no sign of Jerry. Perhaps we'd get away with it.

Sarge sent us out to mark out the field with white strips, but, as we moved out of cover, the shooting started the same time as we heard the buzz of the planes in the distance. Crawling on our stomachs, we set out some strips of the white signal ribbon, but the wind caught the end and one piece fluttered away. Again, he screamed at us to find some stones to weight it down. There weren't any, but we managed to bury the edges in the fine sand. Without the Eureka signal, the planes flew over our heads. The first was hit by the Germans sheltering behind the railway embankment. Although the pilot dropped as many canisters as he could before crashing in flames, the parachutes carried them away from us towards Jerry.

The second plane banked and dropped its load, but again the canisters floated towards the Germans, who cheered each one as it landed. Such a bitter sound. All our desperately needed supplies were gone. Sarge screamed at us to get back through the wood to the houses, and if he saw us again, he'd flay us alive and worse, and anyway he'd make sure all our mates knew it was our fault they were starving and running out of ammunition as we'd given their supplies to the Germans.

We trudged back to the houses where Lefty and Tug said they'd had a quiet day. When we explained where Jerry was, they knew why. When the lack of supplies sank in, they looked grief stricken for a moment but told us it wasn't our fault. None of the radios had worked, so why expect the Eureka to? And anyway, the Germans were waiting to shoot the planes down.

While we'd been gone, news had arrived from Arnhem. The Germans were taking control and rumours of over five thousand casualties were circulating. Trying to sleep with an empty belly and a raging thirst is tough, but I'm so exhausted it will come.

CHAPTER FIFTEEN

THE SILENCE after Zoe sat down was broken by Tom, who grabbed his two sticks, levered himself up and tottered towards the bar, followed by Judy carrying an armful of the glasses from their table. 'Don't know about you lot, but I need a drink after that.'

Laughter and 'Mine's a scotch', 'Are you buying then?', 'Aren't moths the only things in your wallet, Tom?' released the tension. The students held back and waited for the veterans to order their drinks, and some even acted as waiters carrying loaded trays to the tables.

As Steph brought Hale's beer and Caroline's wine to the table, she felt a hand on her back. It was Hendrik, who pulled up a chair from the next table to join them.

'Can I get you a drink, Henk?'she asked.

'Thanks, Steph. Same as Hale please.'

As she waited at the bar, sipping her wine so she wouldn't spill it, she saw Hendrik engaging Hale and Caroline in intense conversation, their heads huddled together. Across the room,

Zoe and her boyfriend were sitting with Ron and Alistair, also deep in conversation.

Someone opened the door to the deck and the distant barking of a dog was carried into the bar. A flash of emptiness hit her at the sound, and she wished Derek, her dog, was there with her. She was surprised at the depth of her reaction; she hadn't realised how important he had become in her life and how much she was looking forward to seeing him again. She vowed to text Fiona, the dog lady, to check that he was all right and enjoying his stay with the dog herd.

At last, she returned with the drinks and tuned into Hendrik. '...that's right, my boss said, as long as we obey those conditions, we can do it.'

Fascinating how the 'I' had become 'we', and Hale was frowning, as clearly he'd picked it up too.

Hendrik sounded excited, having got his plan approved. 'I'll stay on the boat with you, go on your trips and go back to the UK with you. You have space?'

'On the coach, yes, but we'll need to get you on the list and also a room in The Crown.' Caroline smiled her thanks to Steph as she reached for the wineglass.

'The Crown? What is The Crown?'

'The hotel in Oakwood, Suffolk, where we're spending two nights to finish our work on the book before going home. I'll see if I can book you in.'

'Thank you. I will get the voyage arranged. Proost!' Hendrik clinked his glass against theirs as they chorused, 'Proost.'

He downed his glass in three gulps and wiped his hand across his mouth to remove the foam from his top lip. 'I would like to meet some of your guests. You don't mind?'

Before anyone could answer, Hendrik bounced over to

Zoe's table, and within moments, was quickly involved in chatting with the group.

'He's making quite an impact.' They drank in silence, watching him laugh with the students. Caroline finished her drink. 'Another?'

'Please.' Hale and Steph held out their empty glasses to Caroline, who went to the bar.

'I'll have to contact our side and warn them he'll be coming back with us, as we appear to be involved in a new case.' Hale sighed.

'Couldn't it be good for you if it means we nail drug smugglers with his help?'

'Of course it would. Better have a word with my mate Potter in the Met and update them, too.' Hale sighed again.

'You sound fed up with it.'

'Do I? Sorry. Didn't mean to. All this stuff seems to have come from nowhere, and I'm pretty pissed off I didn't know about it.'

'You wouldn't, if the Suffolk link has only just happened, and he's been working with the Met.' Steph looked across at Hendrik as a burst of laughter erupted from their table.

'Yes, but if Ken's bringing drugs or even diamonds over to Suffolk and not only to the Met, it's very much our problem.'

The laughter had subsided, and Hendrik was deep in conversation with Zoe.

Caroline lowered her head as she placed the tray on the table and hissed, 'Don't look now, but guess who's come in!'

Trying not to make it obvious, Steph moved her head slightly. Hale's back was to the door.

'Who?'

'No, don't move. It's Jim Craddock!'

Caroline and Steph could see him as he paused inside the

door to check out the tables. At last, spotting his target, he joined Tom, who had been so aggressive in the question session the day before. Tom didn't look too thrilled when Jim joined him. He was hunched up, nursing his Guinness, ignoring his daughter Judy, who was smiling beside him.

Despite Steph's first impression of a miserable woman with a down-turned mouth, a chat over coffee in the lounge when she was by herself had revealed Judy to be a lively, interesting woman who was remarkably cheerful – quite the opposite to her father. Perhaps it was only when she was with Tom that she became subdued, but then spending any time with him would depress anyone.

Jim pulled his chair close up to Tom and appeared to be whispering in his ear. Judy was excluded from the conversation, and it was obvious she was irritated by the way the two men were whispering. Over the buzz and laughter in the lounge, the secret conversation looked odd, and it was apparent Hendrik had noticed too. Continuing his discussion with Zoe, eyes fixed on the whispering pair two tables away, he pushed back his chair as if he was going to get up but sat down again as Jim's voice fractured a sudden lull. 'Well, if that's your attitude, you know what you can do, don't you? Stuff it where the sun don't shine.'

Jim slapped the table hard, creating an enormous wave of Guinness that overflowed from the full glass and dripped off the edge of the table onto Tom's lap, who struggled to his feet and shoved Jim away. 'You bastard.'

As he displayed his wet trousers, Tom became aware that he was the centre of attention, He thrust the table aside, knocking over the glass so the rest of the beer sloshed onto the carpet, and swinging on his sticks, stormed out of the bar, shouldering Jim as he went.

Clearly, Judy wasn't sure whether to mop up the mess or to go out after Tom. After a slight hesitation, she ran out of the bar after her father, with an apologetic look on her face.

Jim sneered after Tom and followed him out. These elderly men may need to use sticks but they could certainly move when they needed to. Hale and Hendrick went after them, while Caroline stood and peered through the swinging doors. 'We should go, in case there's a fight.'

'I'll go. You stay and help those students clear up the mess.' As Steph dashed past Ron and Alistair she noticed they were agitated and pointing after Jim. Now what was wrong with them? She ran down the corridor where she knew Jim's room was, but all was silent. Where had they gone?

CHAPTER SIXTEEN

As SHE WALKED down the stairs, Steph soon found out where they'd gone from the row coming out of a room on the middle deck. She opened the door to find Hale and Hendrik holding back Jim, who was facing up to Tom with Judy in the middle – all three shouting.

'Will you stop it, NOW!'

Steph's high-pitched voice sliced through the shouts and they all stopped. 'That's better. Now, what is all this about?'

Scowling, Tom sat on one of the twin beds and Jim on the other, both men trying to avoid their knees touching. Judy plonked herself beside her father and stroked his arm – once again he shoved her hand away. Hale and Hendrik stood by the door and let Steph at the end of the beds take control. 'Look, this has to stop or you'll both make yourselves ill.' Her calm voice reduced the tension and the two men dropped their heads.

'He started it, not me,' Tom complained, his whiney voice appealing for her approval.

Steph had to stop herself giggling, as they sounded like naughty boys, not grown men. 'What did he start, Tom?'

'I didn't start nothing! He—'

'I asked Tom not you, Jim. Please, let's talk one at a time and listen to each other.'

'Humph!' Jim folded his arms. 'I bet you'll take his side.'

Deciding to ignore this potential cul-de-sac, Steph quickly fixed her gaze on Tom. 'Well?'

Tom shook his head. 'I don't know what he wanted.'

'Really?'

Tom raised his eyes to meet her laser stare, dropped his shoulders, and appeared to give in.

'Well, it wasn't important, anyway. Just wanted me to keep my mouth shut about the escape.'

'What about the escape?'

'That's it. I can't remember. No idea what he's going on about.'

Steph frowned and continued piercing Tom with her look. If either of them was going to give in, it would be Tom. 'I didn't come down with the last shower, you know—' She looked from one to the other then gave Tom a hard stare. 'Come on, Tom, you don't throw a perfectly good glass of Guinness away for something you don't remember. What was it?'

Jim interrupted. 'If he won't say, I will. We were in the same platoon and got out of that hellhole at the same time. There are some things you do in war that you're not so proud of – things that you wouldn't do in peacetime like, and I was reminding him it was a war, not a tea party.'

'What sort of things?' Steph was not going to let it go.

'Like leaving your mates wounded, to be picked up by the stretcher boys instead of staying with them – that sort of thing.' Jim waved his hand as if trying to dismiss the memory.

'And was there a specific incident that you both shared?' she ventured, almost dreading the answer.

'There was, but not to be talked about now.' Jim darted a glance at Tom, and it appeared an unspoken message to shut up passed between them.

Convinced that neither man was coming clean, she was about to speak when Jim turned on Judy. 'And as for you – you're no better than you should be. At your age, you should know better.'

Now what?

'I beg your pardon?' Judy appeared taken aback by Jim's aggressive accusation.

'Going after my Ken, at your age, disgusting – that's what I call it.'

'What's wrong with that? We've always been friends since school.'

'Friends? That's what you call it? Turning my house into a knocking shop, that's what's wrong with it.'

'Hey, watch what you're saying about my Jude!' Tom tried to get to his feet but couldn't get purchase on the springy bed, so bounced back down again. 'She's an adult and can do what she likes. Although why she does it with your flippin' son, God only knows.'

Steph leaned back slightly, letting this bizarre conversation continue.

'I don't care what she gets up to or who she throws herself at, but I think she had something to do with Ken's disappearance.' Jim's head went forward, bringing it close to Tom's.

'Really?' Steph could feel Hendrik about to intervene and moved to the side to block his potential route to Jim. 'What do you mean?'

'You think I've not seen you, don't you?' He poked a pointy

finger towards Judy. 'I may have been in my room, but that room has a window and I saw you and my Ken out there in that bar on the bank nattering. Tell me what you know about where he is!'

They turned as one to Judy, all waiting to hear whatever nugget she might give them. 'We were in that bar, chatting, you know, reliving old times, that's all, and I haven't seen him since yesterday when he went off after one of those students. I saw them together after he left me. Filthy old sod. Trying it on with a girl young enough to be his daughter.'

'And that was the last time you saw him?' Steph asked.

'Yes. I waited for him to come back, but he didn't. Only the girl did. Maybe you should ask her or the man who was following him.'

'What man?'

'The man he was talking to when I came into the bar down there. He scarpered when he saw me but followed Ken out.'

'What did he look like, this man?' Hendrik's voice boomed across the room.

'You know, just a man. About the same size as you two...' She waved her hand towards Hale and Hendrik. 'He was wearing dark clothes – didn't see his face, only his back. So, you see, I wasn't the last one to see him... and anyway, I'll thank you to keep your nose out of my business.' She stooped down and spat the last comment at Jim, who sat back as if she'd hit him. As she stormed out of the room, Hale and Hendrik stood aside to allow her to make her dramatic exit.

After she'd slammed the door, there was a moment of stunned silence, which Hale was the first to break.

'Right. Unless you have anything else to tell us, I suggest you return to your room, Jim. Would you like me to help you?'

Jim winced and hauled himself up. 'No, I bloody wouldn't.

That's Ken's job, and it's your job to find him. Why don't you flippin' get on with it and let me be?'

They stood aside to let him leave the room.

Steph bent down to Tom's eye level. 'Are you OK, Tom? Shall I get Judy?'

'No, leave her. I don't want no fuss.'

Hale raised his eyebrow at Steph, who nodded, and they left Tom's room to return to the bar.

'That was like a scene from your soap opera – East Enders?' As they climbed the stairs, Hendrik turned and grinned at Hale, who paused, then replied.

'You're right, it would fit in there very well.'

When they reached the top, Hale spoke. 'But now we know Ken met someone else as well as Zoe before he disappeared, and I'm sure Jim and Tom are not telling us anything like the truth. I wonder what they're hiding.'

CHAPTER SEVENTEEN

PANTING, Zoe stopped running and bent over, placing both hands on her thighs, trying to catch her breath. At last, Ollie, ahead of her, become aware she wasn't beside him, turned round and walked towards her.

'You OK?' He reached out his hand and touched her shoulder.

'Stitch.' She panted, then caught her breath. 'Let's sit there.'

Sitting at a metal table in front of the closed bar to get out of the sharp wind, they stared across the river and waited for their breathing to return to normal. They had run about a mile the opposite way to Arnhem Bridge and stopped to look at the river bank opposite, which was less manicured further away from the town. Then they had run back past the boat as far as the bar.

'I've got to get fitter' Ollie looked back at the boat. 'We can't have come that far, and already I'm puffed.'

'You're only saying that to make me feel better. You were

way ahead and could have gone on.' Zoe held her right side where the stitch had developed.

'It's good to be out here, isn't it?' Ollie kissed her cheek and held the hand that was on the table.

'Yes. Good to be away from them all.'

'You've done so well, you know. I don't think I could have stood up there in front of all those people and read all that and managed their questions.'

Zoe laughed and, leaning forward, stroked a large lock of Ollie's hair back in the right place. 'I didn't know I could, before I did.'

Ollie stood and extended each leg, then lunged to stretch his muscles. 'Right, let's get back – I need a shower and breakfast. That wind's freezing.'

'You go. I'll sit here a bit longer.'

'Are you sure?'

'Yeah, I'll be fine. Just want to sit here and think for a few minutes. See you at breakfast.'

Ollie bent down, gave her a kiss and jogged towards the boat. She watched him as he climbed the gangway and disappeared into the boat. She needed some space away from everyone to get her head straight and closed her eyes, breathing in and counting to seven, then out again. Opening her eyes, she concentrated on the waves slapping against the opposite bank until she felt her heart beat slow down.

Zoe didn't know how long she'd been sitting staring across the river, trying to get rid of the panic inside her. It was ridiculous getting in a state over something that happened seventy-four years ago. It wasn't as if she could do anything if she found out, but perhaps just finding out would change something.

Duncan's death had haunted her whole life, and she often wondered what would have happened if he'd returned to his classroom after the war. Perhaps she would have been part of a normal, boring family, not the dysfunctional one that she, her grandmother and mother had experienced.

And even now, it was having an impact on her. Ken was a vile man, and his threats, just being near him, scared her so much. She knew she couldn't escape him now he'd found her. But if he'd really disappeared as the gossip suggested – disappeared for ever – then maybe it would be over. It would, wouldn't it?

A scrape of metal made her open her eyes and gasp – someone sat down beside her. It was that Dutch police officer who had chatted to her in the bar the night before.

'Sorry, did I make you jump?' His deep voice was soothing and his broad smile re-assured her.

'I was miles away.'

'Really? Where?'

'Oh, I don't know. Back seventy-four years, probably.'

'It's important to you to find out what happened to him, isn't it?'

'Yes, it is.'

They sat side by side, as if in a car, facing the river, which made it easy to talk to him. She liked him and had found his jokes funny. Were all Dutch men so nice?

'And will you?'

'What?'

'Find out the end of his story.'

'I hope so.'

Another pause, as they became absorbed in watching a duck swimming and diving for food beside the edge of the other bank.

'Did Ken know anything to help you?'

The panic that she'd quelled rose up once again. Ken?

What did he know about her and Ken? She said nothing but continued to stare out. The duck had gone.

'You and he met before he disappeared, didn't you?'

She turned to face him and noticed his smile had vanished. He stared at her. 'Sorry?'

'Come on, Zoe – we have a film. It shows you and Ken sitting on a bench by the bridge speaking for about twenty minutes, before you return to the boat alone, and then you went with him here, to this bar.'

She said nothing, waiting for him to tell her what he knew first.

'We think you were the last person to see Ken before he disappeared. Had you met him before? In Suffolk perhaps?'

She remained silent and avoided looking at him.

'We can always go to my office and I can ask you there, but better here, isn't it?'

He smiled as he said this. Perhaps he was right. It would be better to talk now and get it over with rather than saying nothing and having to go to a strange police station. She'd done nothing wrong. Ken had been the threat, not her, so she had nothing to lose, had she?

'Right, I'll tell you.' She took a deep breath. 'I'd never met Ken before we came here.'

She looked at Hendrik to see if he believed her. His smile was re-assuring. 'I went for a walk and Ken came up and told me he had news about Duncan, and we sat on the bench together.'

'And what news was that?'

'He never said. I think it was a way of getting me to join him. He talked about knowing my mother.'

'What is she called?'

'Jo Miller, but I've never really lived with her. She left me when I was little, and I lived with her mother, Edith, Duncan's daughter.'

'How did Ken know your mother?'

She shivered. If only she'd not suggested the jog to Ollie or had gone back to the boat with him.

'Here – put this around your shoulders.'

Hendrik stood, pulled off his leather jacket and wrapped it around her. She let him. The blue silky lining was warm, and it smelt spicy. She snuggled down into it, feeling protected from the sharp wind, which was pushing up little waves along the river.

'Better?'

She nodded and returned his smile.

'I am on your side, you know. Ken was not a nice man to you, was he?'

She felt she should trust this man who appeared to understand.

'No, he wasn't. He told me dreadful things about my mother and threatened me.'

'Oh?'

'He told me they had lived together for a long time and that she – they took drugs and that my mother did... other things... you know... And he said unless I took a parcel home for him, he would tell all my friends and teachers and my gran about it.'

Hendrik moved a little towards her as she realised her voice had become weaker and the strong wind was blowing it away. The smell from him, the same as on his jacket, was stronger, and she rather liked it. 'I am sorry, Zoe. It must have been upsetting.'

'It was. A dreadful shock.'

Scanning his face, his warm eyes and his gentle smile, Zoe felt here was someone who could share her nightmare. 'He told me he could be my father...' She heard herself saying it, it had just come out.

'Oh?'

Pulling herself together, she closed up. 'He was talking rubbish, I'm sure, but I think he said it to get at me and persuade me to take the parcel.'

'And did you?'

'What?'

'Take a parcel from him?'

'Of course not.'

He frowned, and she felt herself blush.

'Really?'

'Well, not then I didn't, but I agreed to take one, but honestly, I only said it to get away from him – so he'd let me go. He scared me.'

Hendrik's gaze was steady, and he waited. What was he waiting for? For her to say something more? But she'd told him the truth – all of it.

'I've told you everything. He didn't give me any parcel and now he's disappeared, there won't be a parcel, will there?'

He continued to stare at her as if he didn't believe her. How could she convince him? 'You can have a look in my room if you don't believe me.'

He leaned in closer, and his voice was softer. 'Of course I believe you and I understand why you said you'd take it.'

He scraped his chair back a little, towards the metal shutters out of the wind. 'Did he say what was in the parcel he wanted you to carry?'

'No. But I think it would have been something illegal, wouldn't it?'

'Yes, it would. Did he mention anyone else when he was

talking to you, or did you see anyone while you were with him or after you left him?'

A picture of them on that bench and her trembling walk back to the boat forced its way into her head. She closed her eyes to try and see it clearer and to re-create the view along the river and down to the boat.

'No, I don't think he mentioned anyone, and there was no one there, just us. Then here, later, Steph came before he said anything.'

'Hello, you two.' As one, they both looked up at the path that ran above the bar to see Steph and Hale walk down the slope towards them. Zoe wondered how long they'd been standing above them.

Steph stood beside her. 'As we were leaving, we saw Ollie, and he said you were here. We thought we'd come out for a morning stroll before breakfast.'

Hendrik stood and spoke to Hale. 'A shame this cafe isn't open. Their coffee is excellent.'

Zoe slipped Hendrik's jacket off her shoulders and handed it back to him.

'No, you keep that on until we get back.'

'Yes, we don't want to miss breakfast, do we?' Hale grinned at her. Surely, he didn't think there had been something going on between the two of them?

Steph stepped back and appeared to be waiting for Zoe to join her, so she did, and they started walking back towards the boat. The leather jacket was a welcome buffer against the wind, which sliced through her bare legs. It had been so much warmer and brighter when she and Ollie left for their jog. The clouds zipped past, revealing some bright blue patches in the gaps. She became aware that Steph was waiting for an answer.

'Sorry?'

'I was wondering how you came to be with Hendrik.'

'He was taking a walk like you, and we chatted for a bit.'

Zoe was aware that Steph looked puzzled. 'Right.' Steph nodded at the jacket. 'Well, it looks as if it was a good thing you met him – you must be freezing.'

'Yes. I really need a warm shower.'

They chatted about the project as they walked back, and she could hear a gentle mumbling behind from Hale and Hendrik. She hoped Hendrik had got the information he needed, and she didn't have to go to his office. Surely Hendrik didn't suspect she was involved in Ken's disappearance, did he?

CHAPTER EIGHTEEN

Zoe sat beside Ron on the coach. Caroline had asked them to link up with one of the veterans so they could get details to include in their artwork or their writing. She explained that soldiers tended to talk to their comrades who understood their experiences and not those outside – even their families – but returning to the battlefield they may well share their memories with the students. She liked Ron and imagined that if he'd known Duncan, they'd have been good friends.

The coach took them around Arnhem, which some of the soldiers had seen in the battle, but many more of them had been stuck three miles to the west at Oosterbeek, as the German divisions sandwiched the British in the town, in a pincer movement from both the bridge side and inland. The original traditional houses around Arnhem Bridge had been demolished in the battle by German tanks, which drove right up to the house walls, blasting them to the ground to reveal the hidden British soldiers. Now modern buildings stood in their place.

Further out, there were examples of typical Dutch squares,

and little streets crammed with fascinating looking shops. They were shown the house where General Urquhart had been trapped for a day by a German tank parked outside its front door. Later, as they drove along the Rhine, the views of the river were stunning.

'Where were you, Ron?'

'We were dug in at Oosterbeek, like your Duncan. Poor beggars who made it this far to Arnhem faced death, dreadful injury or, in the end, if they were lucky, being taken prisoner.'

'Lucky to be POWs?'

'Strange word I know, but better than dying here, don't you think? At least there was a chance they'd get back home.'

'Suppose so.'

He stared out of the window at the passing streets, then turned to face Zoe. 'Do you know, the more you read, the more I feel as if I could have met him? Alistair and me, we were saying last night that account of his takes us right back.'

A drive out of Arnhem and about eight miles into the countryside brought them to the heathland, where the coach stopped.

'Ah! The landing ground. Now you can see what your Duncan was talking about. Look at it. A mass of heather and sand. Not easy to land anything on here, see?'

Caroline stood at the front of the coach with a microphone. 'We'll stop here for thirty minutes and you're welcome to walk around the site and into the woods, or you can stay on the coach.'

'Fancy a walk, Ron?'

'Certainly do, my dear.'

Zoe helped him down the steep coach steps, and with her arm through his, they tramped over the tussocky heath in the autumn sunshine. The weather had been spectacular. Zoe was aware of Ron tensing beside her and hesitating.

'Are you all right, Ron?'

He stopped, lifted his hand to shade his eyes from the sun and watched the slow crocodile of men and students heading away from the coach.

'I thought I saw Jim Craddock then, but I must have been mistaken.'

Zoe scanned the line. 'You're right – look, he's over there.' She pointed to his slight figure. 'Walking with Tom and his daughter – Judy?'

'Strange, he's not been with us on anything before. I wonder what's made him come here now.'

Zoe watched as Jim's group made slow progress over the tussocky field. She searched all the figures walking around the landing zone, panicking that Ken might have come back. Jim appeared to be determined to get to somewhere in the woods away from Tom and Judy, as he waved his hands at them to make them change direction while he carried on alone. Zoe couldn't see Ken anywhere and relaxed.

At a distance, but following, were Caroline's friend Hale and the Dutch man – Hendrik? He was easy to talk to, and she was sure it had been the right thing to do to confide in him. He'd also said lots of nice things in the bar in front of her friends about her reading and Duncan's account. As they watched, Jim disappeared into the shade of the trees and the other two followed him into the wood. What was going on?

Staring across the field until they were out of sight, Zoe turned back to Ron and took his arm again. 'You're right, this is so difficult to walk on, and the idea of gliders landing with heavy equipment appears impossible. Why did they choose it?'

'The largest space to land all the equipment safely, so they thought, but they'd underestimated the strength of the German Panzer divisions.'

'In the film, the man in charge refuses to believe the officer with reconnaissance photos showing German tanks and sends him home on sick leave. Was that true?'

'Something like that, but of course we didn't know at the time. That came out later.'

They strolled into the woods and arrived at a clearing, where Ron stopped. 'Do you know – I think this is it?'

'What?'

'Where we were held down in that trench by German fire for about five hours.'

Ron pointed to a little hollow in the ground ahead of them.

'What? In that dip? You can't call that a trench!' Zoe stepped forward and examined the slight depression in the ground. She found it difficult to believe anyone could lie in it and avoid being shot.

'Yes, I think that's it. It is!' Ron walked around it, examining it from various angles. 'All a bit overgrown now. It was probably a bit deeper than it appears now, but yes – that was the view through the trees to the Germans advancing and pinning us down. Three of us, there were.'

Ron pointed through the trees to the other side of the field. Amazed, Zoe tried to imagine three soldiers on their stomachs for hours in this small dip, defending themselves from German bombardment.

Ron grinned. 'We managed to fend them off, and when dusk came, we moved on our bellies back to the safety of our trenches.'

They were almost the last back on the coach. Caroline counted them on 'Good. Now, let's see.' She looked down at her list. 'Three more. Jim and... er Hale and er...' She mumbled something. She looked concerned as she scanned the empty field. Zoe looked out of the window towards the wood and saw Jim with his stick, doing his best to hurry towards the coach. 'Caroline, Jim's over there, coming out of the wood. Look!'

'Thanks, Zoe.' Caroline waited in the front seat and chatted to the driver. Zoe watched Jim stumble onto the coach. Behind him came Hale and Hendrik, but they emerged from the other side of the wood, not down Jim's path. As he passed her seat, she noticed a canvas bag slung across Jim's chest. Had he had it when he left the coach?

While they were driving the eight miles back to Arnhem, Ron asked how Zoe had ended up living with her gran. She felt confident talking to him and gave him an edited version of the latest news about her mother from Ken. It was a relief to talk about it, and somehow she knew she could trust Ron to keep his mouth shut. She didn't actually mention the package Ken wanted her to carry home, but from his expression, she suspected he knew there was more. She found him a good listener who sympathised with her.

As they parked beside the boat, he smiled at her. 'Your story's safe with me, Zoe. Will you try to contact her?'

Zoe sat still for a moment, watching the straggling line of adults and students climbing up the gangplank, then sighed. 'You know, Ron, now I think about it, I don't think I will. After all, she hasn't wanted to be my mum, has she?' Her voice became stronger. 'No... No, I won't.'

CHAPTER NINETEEN

ZOE WAS GETTING USED to the routine now and could eat the whole of her supper and even enjoy a Bitburger with it. Caroline frowned then smiled across at her – obviously checking her out — over eighteen, she passed. The fear she'd felt when she'd stood up that first night had gone. Her friends had all said they were fascinated by Duncan's journal, and she knew now it wasn't Ollie telling them to be nice to her.

She could see Jim sitting with Tom and Judy, but no Ken. Although she knew he'd disappeared, every time she walked into a room, she checked to see if he'd come back. He hadn't, and relieved, she relaxed.

It was strange that Jim should start coming to the sessions. This was the first day he'd joined them – first of all on the coach and now here in the bar. Oh, there had been the scene the night before, hadn't there? She'd forgotten about that.

Zoe shuddered to think that if Ken was right, and he was her father, that she and Jim could be related – he'd be her grandfather. Ugh! She wondered if Duncan and he had ever met. But then, she wondered that about many of the men sitting before her. No one had said anything, but several had commented that his story was so familiar to them.

She went towards the mic. Caroline smiled at her and gestured that she should calm her audience down. She now had the confidence to do it.

'Good evening, everyone.'

At once, the chattering and laughter stopped, and all faces turned towards her.

'Thank you. Tonight, I'm going to read the final instalment of Duncan's story – the last few days. You will notice these are shorter than the earlier entries, as he was no longer spending most of the day in the house but in a trench, which, as Ron showed me this afternoon, wasn't too comfortable.

A voice from the back shouted, 'You can say that again, love!'

'Add to that their lack of food and water and even ammunition, you will see what a tough time he and the other soldiers were having.'

She paused, and the fidgeting died down as she started to read.

Day 5. Thursday 21st September

Another disturbed night with little sleep thanks to Jerry. Don't they need sleep over there or are they taking it in shifts? The drizzle continues and the grey clouds are low and suit our grim mood. The saucepans we left outside gave us a few sips of water but not enough. It stopped some hungry rumbles, but it feels as if my belly is eating itself. Another day listening to the battle in the distance.

Those poor beggars, trying to hold that bridge. It must be hell on earth.

This afternoon, a few Germans used the cover of the tank to get further down our road. Three were killed, and the four taken prisoner were moved to HQ and held in the hotel tennis court, someone said. Not sure how he knew.

We now have a fourth in the house. Eric sought shelter from the gunfight and caught it in his leg. We bound it up as best we could, and it stopped bleeding, but the bullet is in there. We wanted him to go to the hospital, but he wouldn't. Said that would be the death of him for sure if they poked around to get it out. Said he'd wait until we got out of this mess. I asked him what it felt like and he said it was like a kick in the leg, like when you get fouled in football. The greatest danger is it gets septic. Not sure what I'd do in his place.

Day 6. Friday 22nd September

Only by looking at what I wrote yesterday do I know what today is. The days move into night, and I've had some rest, but not much. A tank came up behind the wrecked one, shoved it onto the pavement and started blasting away at the walls of the houses. Not sure how much longer we can stay here. The three houses between us and the crossroads are now rubble.

The anti-tank mine trick worked again, but not until the man doing it had been shot and his mate had to finish the job. His body lay blocking the gate, the back half of him under the hedge, the front part hanging over the pavement.

The road is now littered with bodies from us and Jerry. How many days ago did the first one shock me? Two more from 10th Para Div. arrived with Sarge, walking wounded from the hospital.

114

Able to fire a gun and wanting to return to the fray. At least that's what Sarge said. They didn't look convinced.

One of them (don't think I caught his name) had been talking to an NCO in the hospital about what had gone wrong with the op. He said we landed too far from the target; the LZ was too sandy, and we lost too much heavy equipment in the crashes, the radios didn't work and worst of all, they'd forgotten that the Germans might still be here. When listed like that, it sounds madness, but that's not how wars are won, is it? If it had worked as they planned, we would have been heroes by now.

This afternoon flame thrower tanks arrived and turned the street into an inferno. We escaped through the back gardens when we saw what was happening. At least we did, but the two men from the 10th weren't so lucky and bought it.

We are now in slit trenches in the grounds of HQ. It was tough work digging them with our entrenching tools when we have so little energy left. No food or water and ammunition is low. Not sure what will become of us. Only good news is that Lefty and Tug are with me.

Day 7

Stuck in the trench all night with continuous shelling. According to Sarge (who tours to check what we're up to) we are now being squeezed into a thumb or horseshoe shape, with Jerry coming closer each day. To think they thought he'd run back to Germany. From here, it sounds as if there are more joining them out there.

No food, no water, low on ammunition. We're sitting ducks. Our Denison smocks keep out the wind but aren't waterproof, so they get wet and heavy, and we never get dry. Sarge said we must keep them on.

Day is endless, tense, waiting for Jerry's arrival, and the night's not much better. Whining mortars keep us pinned down in our foxholes. More casualties. Pretty hopeless.

I close my eyes and eat Mary's steak and kidney pudding in my head, with mash and peas from the garden and rhubarb pie for afters. Helps a bit. This is hell on earth.

Day 8

A few Germans came with the dawn, and we got rid of them. Pleased I wasn't close enough. Fingers are numb with cold and not sure I'd have got them.

The crashes of the houses being demolished by the tanks reach us. Thought about the civilians in the cellar. Did they get out? Did the Germans let them go?

So tired can hardly think. So tired, feel drunk. Cheap way to do it. Breathing hard but trying to hide it.

Day 9

Exhausted. Would welcome Jerry if it meant getting in the warm. Inevitable they'll take us soon. Little chat. No jokes. My asthma is bad in this damp. Struggling to breathe.

Sarge comes round with the order to withdraw. At last! At 21.00 hours we're to wrap our boots with cloth, anything we can find, and leave off any metal that may clink. Then make our way north of the Hartenstein Hotel, through the wood to the Rhine, where boats will take us across to safety.

White ribbons from parachutes will be tied along the track to guide us and we're to hold on to them and the smock tail of the man in front of us. The rain will make it boggy, but the clouds should hide the moon. The 2nd Army will fire star shells to distract Jerry and help us see the direction of the river. Walking a path with Jerry a few yards on either side of us is a risk, but better than staying here. I can't wait to get somewhere warm and dry.

CHAPTER TWENTY

STEPH HELD HER BREATH, along with everyone else in the room, not wanting to disturb the tragic tension Duncan's writing had created. Zoe sat down, a tear trickling down her cheek. Everyone knew the final chapter to this story – that Duncan would die in the very near future. But how? Zoe, everyone knew, was on a quest to find out what had happened.

Apparently all Zoe knew was that an ex-pupil recognised Duncan's body and sent home his exercise book with one of his dog tags. Action so well intentioned, but, assuming the other dog tag had disappeared, his kindness meant Duncan hadn't been identified and buried with a named headstone – that is, if he was buried in the cemetery at all.

Caroline took over from Zoe, who looked as if she was just about holding it together. 'Wow, that was quite an ending. I'm sure we all picked up the difference in Duncan's writing when he was suffering cold and hunger in the trenches compared to the hours he spent in the house. Thank you, Zoe. Now I suggest we have a short break – please be back here in five minutes.'

The silence stretched. The usual hubbub and chatter at the end of a session was replaced by a subdued buzz. Ron and Alistair stared at nothing, clearly reflecting on what they had heard and the students, if they spoke at all, whispered to each other. Zoe's reading and Duncan's experience had created a powerful impression of what it was like to live those days in the battle.

Steph glanced at Hendrik, staring into the distance, apparently touched by Zoe's story. Now was her chance.

'An amazing young woman, isn't she?'

Hendrik lifted his head. 'Yes, she is.'

'And have you removed her from your list of suspects after your interrogation this morning?'

'Hey, wait a minute, Steph. Not interrogation, just a chat — for the background.'

'Not quite what she said.'

Hendrik frowned, clearly concerned at what Zoe had told her.

As he paused, Steph drove home her advantage. 'A bit of a coincidence you bumping into her like that.'

He grinned, his old confidence returned, and once again, she was pulled deep into his beguiling eyes. 'We both know Zoe was the student on the film, and rather than be formal, I found out what I needed to know the easy way.'

'And that is?'

'Ken knew her mother – sounds as if they dealt drugs in your town and he – what do you say – pimped her out? He blackmailed Zoe to take a parcel back to England for him. Could be the diamonds.'

'Did he give it to her?'

'She says not. I believe her. But we need to keep an eye on her, as one of his contacts may give her something.'

Hale was weaving his way through the tables with a tray of

drinks. She leaned in close to Hendrik and said in her 'don't mess with me' voice, 'One more thing, Henk. Please do not talk to one of our students like that again. I know this is your case and we are in your country, but they are our students and I insist on being there next time – if there is a next time.'

She sat back and fixed him with a hard stare. He appeared to be cowed. 'Understand?' she hissed as Hale plonked the tray down.

'Of course, Steph.'

Puzzled, Hale appeared to be about to intervene when Caroline stepped up to the mic. 'I'm sure you all agree that Zoe has done a wonderful job sharing Duncan's experience with us. I was fascinated by his description of the plans to escape. Now, did any of our veterans here make that audacious escape?'

Five or six men raised their hands or nodded, while others stared at the floor, also touched by the memories Zoe's reading had evoked, or simply wanting to avoid talking about it. A deep, rasping voice everyone recognised from his growly moans came from Tom, who holding onto the table, pulled himself up to his feet. 'I can tell you about that escape, ma'am.'

'Oh – Tom.' Caroline looked a little surprised, but quickly recovered. 'That would be great. Would you like me to bring the mic over to you or will you come up here?' Her broad smile made him blush. Perhaps they were about to see a new side to Tom.

Holding himself as upright as possible, with his row of medals glinting on his chest and his ever-present beret glued to his head, they waited while he made his way around the tables to the front. He even smiled at Zoe and appeared to think of patting her hand, but changed his mind and, settling himself on his sticks in front of the mic, started to speak.

His first words were lost, as apparently he'd fiddled with

the mic and turned it off. Caroline rushed up, flicked the switch, and his voice boomed out across the lounge.

'Now, can you hear me?'

'Yes, unfortunately!' came from the back accompanied by laughter.

'As I was saying before this damned technology stopped working, I was one of those in the white ribbon escape. Like Duncan, I was holed up for days, hungry and thirsty and out of ammo, waiting for the bloomin' idiots who were leading us to get us out of the mess they'd got us in.'

There were a few mumbles of agreement while others frowned, clearly expecting another rant on his 'lions led by donkeys' theme.

'Anyway, as Duncan said, we got ourselves ready – tied sacking on our feet, all clanking metal removed, and as it became dark, we were told to move towards the wood. We wore those Denison parachute smocks, so were pretty well camouflaged in the dark and they had them — what do you call it?' He moved his legs apart and indicated something at the top of them.

A wolf whistle, followed by 'Ooh, Sexy!' and 'If you don't know what it's called now, you never will!' Laughter across students and veterans was topped with Ron's voice. 'Do you mean a gusset?'

'Aye, that's the word. It was a sort of tail that went between your legs and did up at the front. Anyway, these gus-things hung down like and I grabbed the one of the man in front, while mine was held by the man behind and we walked one behind the other – a crocodile, they used to call it.'

'Like a conga!' a voice called out.

He ignored the heckle, reached for the glass of water Caroline had placed on the small table in front of him and took a gulp. Steph glanced around the room. Everyone was entranced by Tom, whose voice was getting softer and less grumpy the more he spoke.

Judy was looking puzzled, as if she was hearing the story for the first time. Perhaps she was. Steph had discovered that the men who served were like a secret society. It was OK to share something with your mates, but you didn't talk to those who hadn't been there with you.

'Like a conga, yes, but we didn't feel like dancing that night. Terrifying it was. Jerry a few yards on either side of our narrow path – the slightest noise would have given the game away. In front, the tracers from our guns on the other side of the river were like fireworks in the distance, trying to draw their fire. We were packing it, I can tell you.'

He moved his sticks as he talked, to show that the Germans were about an arm's length away, and pointed to the sky to indicate where the tracers had been. His audience was with him every step of the way.

'Then in the wood we found the white ribbons – you know, those long tapes that held us to the parachute canopies tied between the trees for us to hold on to in the pitch black. They shone sort of — guided us, you know. God knows how Jerry didn't see them, but without them I know I'd have been a goner. Got lost in the wood or stumbled into the guns a few yards away.'

Tom scanned the room, clearly checking that he was holding his audience, and winked at Judy, who returned a smile. Clearly, Judy was enjoying this positive, non-grumpy side of her father. It was obvious he was relishing telling his story. His voice lowered to suit his dramatic tale. 'Quiet as mice we were, creeping along in a line, knowing at any moment Jerry would rumble us and that would be that. It must have taken an hour or more to get through the wood and out to the riverbank. But we made it and joined the crowd of men waiting to be picked up by the canvas boats – Canadian they were.'

There was a murmur of appreciation and one man started clapping, only to receive a poisonous look from Tom. 'Oh no, I ain't finished yet! Not by a long chalk.'

'Sorry, Tom.'

'Should think so too.' He grinned at his colleague – Tom smiling? Now there was a first! 'Anyway, my mate Ted and me broke away from the mass for a bit. Thought we'd be safer hiding behind a bush, and we was exhausted, and believe it or not, we fell asleep. Dead to the world we was. All that noise of tracer fire and we slept through the lot.'

Another gulp of water, while he let this latest news sink in.

'Talk about stupid! We fell asleep. What a mistake that was! When we woke up, it was dawn and there was no more boats on the water. We could hear Jerry shouting upriver as they'd worked out what we'd done and were advancing along the bank to take prisoners who hadn't made it in time.'

He paused for dramatic effect.

'We had two choices, see? Give ourselves up or jump in the river. Well, that's what we did. We took off all our clothes—' This time several wolf whistles rang out. 'Never fear. We kept our pants on but left every other stitch of clothing behind the bush and sneaked into the river. My God, it was freezing! Amazed my todger didn't drop off, it was so cold.' He grinned and responded to some chuckles – he was obviously enjoying playing to the gallery. Judy shot him a 'take care' look; clearly, she must be concerned what else he was going to say.

'And that tide – it was that rough and strong. It dragged us further down river, well away from the Germans. We passed lots of floating bodies, too many – you know – those who weren't strong swimmers and didn't make it across or had been used as target practice by Jerry. To think they'd got that far and then bought it.'

Another gulp of water and a quick glance at Caroline, apparently to see if she was listening and happy for him to continue in his starring role. Her smile told him she was.

'Anyway, we got to the bank and clawed our way up the mud and nettles. They stung bits I wouldn't like to mention, I tell you, and we stood there dripping, freezing cold and not sure what to do next. Not a soul around. We thought we'd aim for a house, get some clothes and see if we could find our lot. We headed for a farmhouse, way away in the distance.' He lifted his stick and pointed far into the distance, high above the rapt audience.

'Anyway, we got to the house to find it unlocked – deserted, it was. Nothing inside it but one drawer in the bedroom full of ladies' petticoats – you know, those white dress things with straps that come down to your knees with fancy cotton bits on the edge with holes in it.' Tom mimed a shapely body with his hands and the wolf whistles applauded him.

'Broderie anglaise?' Caroline prompted.

'Yeah, that's the stuff. Well, it was Hobson's choice, weren't it? We put on the petticoats, found some welly boots in the shed that were a bit small, but better than bare feet, and limped our way across the fields towards where we hoped our boys were.'

Caroline moved as if to thank him, but he raised his hand to stop her – he wasn't finished yet.

'After a day's slog, we saw our men in the distance. You should have heard the catcalls and names when they cheered us in – the two of us in our petticoats. And guess what my nickname was 'til I was de-mobbed – Gloria!'

Rapturous applause and laughter greeted his last comment.

Caroline stood up to the mic. 'Thank you, Tom. Anyone else like to try to follow that?'

Ron and Alistair stood, and Ron spoke. 'Yes please, Caroline, we'd like Jim to tell us how he killed Duncan Shaw.'

CHAPTER TWENTY-ONE

EVERYONE FROZE; the silence was solid – drinks halfway to lips, mouths open, conversations cut. Zoe's scream became a sob, fracturing the silence, but all eyes were fixed on Ron and Alistair. They stood at the opposite side of the room to Jim.

Jim screwed his face into a frown, evidently aware that when everyone did move, they would move their heads to gauge his reaction. A strangled, 'What?' emerged from him.

Ron and Alistair appeared to stand taller, while Jim, holding onto the table, hauled himself up to face them across the room.

'You heard. We know how Zoe's Duncan died. You killed him, didn't you?'

'Fuck off. Stop talking rubbish.' Jim waved his hand, dismissing the accusation.

The heads of the hushed audience swivelled from one to the other, to catch who was going to say something next. Ron and Alistair, both calm and implacable, stared at Jim. They oozed confidence and strength and the conviction of being in the right. The silence stretched, making Jim bite his top lip and fiddle with one of the buttons on his blazer sleeve.

At last, he burst out, 'I'll get my solicitor onto you for this! I'm not staying here to listen to any more fucking rubbish from you two old men.'

He turned and took a step, but was held by Ron's now powerful voice. 'No, Jim. I think you should sit down and hear us out. Listen to what we've found out, then you can tell us we're wrong. Or are you afraid to hear what we know?'

'He's frit – look – he's frit!' Alistair mocked him.

A student asked. 'What's frit?'

A voice from one of the tables rang out in reply. 'Means he's frightened, son.'

Jim appeared to be weighing his options before slipping back into his seat, a scornful sneer aimed at his accusers.

'May I?' Ron pointed to the mic, which Caroline handed to him as he moved to join Zoe and Tom at the front.

'Since Zoe read us Duncan's story, we've been concerned that she never found out what happened to him. No one seemed to be able to tell her about Duncan's death. Not the army. Not the War Office. Not one of the organisations that hold records from the war, and she's certainly done her homework, has our Zoe.'

The audience appeared to be entranced by the slow but confident build up to the story Ron was telling. Jim held his head up, staring straight ahead, a sceptical look on his face. Steph felt both Hale and Hendrik tense – ready to move if anything kicked off.

'So, we've been asking around, as many of you can testify.' Ron swung his arm across the room to be met by murmurs of approval and nods from many of the veterans. The students were listening intently, fascinated by this unfolding drama.

Ron moved a step back and sat down in the chair behind him, next to Zoe. He had command of his audience and appeared to be settling in for a long story, and it looked as if it was going to be quite a tale.

'We know you were with Duncan in that escape line, and several of us saw you there.'

'Who's that then?' Jim called out as his eyes darted around the room.

'Quiet, Jim. Let's hear him out.' The voice belonged to Tom.

'That's later, Jim. First, we'll do the what, not the who. You've kept your head down while you've been here. Why was that, I wonder? Only when our comrades glimpsed you on the visit today did our questions prompt their memories.'

'Humph!' Jim shook his head in disgust.

Zoe stared at Ron, hardly blinking, clearly concentrating on each word.

'As I was saying, you and Duncan were in that line, and as Tom and Zoe told us, we all had to be silent, absolutely silent, or Jerry would get all of us. We now know Duncan suffered from asthma, which no one knew—'

'That's right, he said in his account he'd kept it a secret from the army doctors so he could join up,' Zoe burst in.

'Well, we now know he had an attack in that escape line when he was well into the wood. Maybe it was the damp or the stress, but whatever the reason, he started wheezing and wheezing loudly, so loudly that you intervened – didn't you, Jim?'

Ron's laser stare made Jim avert his eyes, and he looked around to see all eyes fixed on him. 'Can't remember. So much was going on.'

'Then I suggest you try harder. Alistair and I have found several witnesses who saw you with him.'

'Fucking rubbish. No one could see anything in that hellhole.'

'They may not have had light, but they had sound and they heard your voice all right. You told Duncan and the man on either side that you couldn't risk having the Germans hear him as they'd attack us all, and you'd take Duncan back down the line to the field and get help from one of the medics who'd stayed back there.' He paused, once again piercing Jim with his confident stare. 'Remember yet, Jim?'

Jim shook his head. 'Not sure, I may have helped him.'

'Yes, you behaved like a real hero. Saving all those men from being found by the Germans and volunteering to go back into danger to help Duncan. A true leader.'

Jim lifted his head, gauging the reaction of the men around the tables observing him.

'But you never got to the medic, did you, Jim? We know you came back to the line, told everyone Duncan – or Johnny, you called him – was safe and being looked after. Then you continued creeping out to the river where you were rescued. What happened, Jim?'

CHAPTER TWENTY-TWO

JIM FIDDLED with his cuff button once again, apparently realising he wasn't going to get away with claiming ignorance. 'You're right. I took him back like you said.'

'Ah, but you didn't, did you Jim? You took him to the end of the line, not to the hotel to a medic as you'd promised, but to the deserted field where you killed him—'

'That's not true. That's a fucking lie!' Jim screamed as loud as he could and tried to get to his feet but stumbled back into his seat. 'Not true! That's not right!'

'We know it's true and we know what happened. Duncan's asthma attack got worse, didn't it? And you left him there, at the edge of the field, instead of going back to the hotel and getting help as you promised. He died because you'd killed him!'

The room was in an uproar. Cries of 'Bastard!' and 'Murderer!' rose above the outraged blast of angry disapproval by the veterans. The students, clearly shocked by the story and the behaviour of the old men, sat open-mouthed.

Panicking, Jim desperately sought support as his eyes

darted from face to face. Tom sneered back at him and looked away in disgust. Others averted their eyes or stared him out until Jim looked away. It appeared Ron had finished, but everyone waited expectantly.

Zoe gripped the arms of her chair, her mouth slightly open, her face pale as the shock drained it of blood, apparently struggling to take all this in. Ollie, now kneeling by her side, was attempting to comfort her by stroking her hand.

Ron broke through the buzz, taunting Jim. 'If it's not true, then you tell us what happened and how Duncan Shaw died.'

A dramatic pause. Ron must have decided Jim wasn't going to answer. 'You never liked him, did you? You were the "sarge" he talks about in his diary. The sarge who was envious of his learning, of his dignity. You called him Johnny Come Lately and abused him for signing up late by putting him in danger, making him suffer, and in the end you killed him.'

A growing murmur among the veterans began to sound nasty as Duncan's death, hidden seventy-four years ago and only a few miles away, entered the room. On a table by the window, two veterans were getting to their feet as if they intended to take action, and Hale slid to the edge of his seat, ready to intervene.

Jim, who must have realized the potential danger, struggled to his feet and tried to speak, but his voice was drowned out by the angry mumbling. He waved at Caroline, who took the mic from Ron and held it out to him. Jim grabbed it and, adjusting his feet and positioning his stick to secure his balance, cleared his throat.

'All right! All right, pipe down! I'll tell you what happened. It was war, right? People get killed in war and we all did things we're not proud of now.' He turned his head to glance around the room. 'Well, we did, didn't we?'

A few nods and murmurs of agreement filled the space he left.

'It was a different world. A place of kill or be killed. Of watch your mate's back and he'd watch yours or you'd both be killed. None of us started out like the brutes that war made us into, did we?'

Again, a few supportive sounds appeared to give Jim confidence to continue, and he started to look cocky. Steph was surprised by his articulate ability to turn the crowd, but then he'd been promoted from the ranks, so he must have been good at persuading others.

'We don't talk about what happened to us in that hellhole, 'cos if you weren't there, you'd never understand. Oh yes, after a few jars we talk to each other, but even then, we never tell each other the full truth... do we?'

Lifting his beer mug, he took a swig and cleared his throat again.

'You're right, I didn't get on with Johnny – I mean Duncan. He'd got it all, educated, good job, lovely wife – I knew his Mary, by the way, and she was a good woman. He was a lucky man who'd got it all, then the silly beggar chucked it all away.'

He took another sip of beer.

'He joined us, to throw ourselves in front of those guns at the whim of some pompous, public school general or other. They had no flippin' idea, did they? Not really. How stupid could he be? Well, if he's come out here for a war, I thought, I'll give him a war. So I did. Then on that night, the secret he'd kept was about to kill the lot of us. He'd lied about his asthma; he shouldn't have been there—'

'You're saying it was his fault you murdered him, are you?' Ron shouted across to Jim and was joined by several angry voices shouting, 'Yeah, you are!', 'There's no excuse', 'You can't argue your way out of this one'.

'No, I'm not!' The amplified voice boomed across the room as Jim shouted into the mic. 'What I'm saying is that he lied and put us all at risk, and it was my job to get as many men as possible out of that mess and back home. If I hadn't taken him back, some of you wouldn't be sitting here now. You'd be dead and gone. I did what I did for everyone.'

In the pause, Steph could see doubt creep across the faces of some of the men who had shouted out in anger earlier.

Jim appealed directly to Zoe, his voice a pathetic whine. 'I'm sorry, my dear, but there was no choice, not really. He was weak, really weak. Could hardly stand. He wouldn't have made it as far as the river. He was holding us back, and when he started making that dreadful wheezing noise ... You must understand...'

Ron, however, was not to be swayed. 'But you could have taken him to the hotel, to the medics, and got him help and he might have survived, but you didn't. That was wrong.'

Looking abashed, Jim frowned and glanced towards the door. He picked up the mic from the table and sighed. 'You're right. But that's now, not then. Like you all, I wanted to get out of there alive and not get shot or taken prisoner. It would have taken another hour going back to the hotel and then coming back again.'

As what he'd done sank in, the faces of his comrades hardened. The hostility around Jim was increasing again and the whine in his voice became stronger. 'The state he was in, he wouldn't have made it as far as the hospital. I could of tried and risked both our lives by going back in the open. But I didn't. I protected the rest of you so I could get us out of there as quick as possible. It was an accident. An accident of war.'

CHAPTER TWENTY-THREE

AFTER THIRTY MINUTES of changing position, taking the duvet off, putting it back on, deep breathing and even counting the beats between the noisy on-off of the automatic air conditioning, Zoe gave up the effort of trying to sleep and got up.

Pulling the long window open, she dragged a chair to sit in the gap and took deep breaths. The air tasted salty, and the fried fish smell wafting from the bar on the wharf reminded her of fish and chip suppers with Gran on Southwold beach. They had always been a treat. As they sat side by side, staring out to sea, eating the searing hot chips with their fingers and the fish with the wooden prongs, they always recited the same script: 'Don't they always taste good eaten out here?'

How was she to tell her gran what she'd heard? Should she tell her at all? Both had been so excited for her to have the opportunity of stepping in Duncan's footprints, of seeing what he saw, of breathing the same air. She had wanted to come home with an answer, but now she wondered what the question was. They knew he'd died here, but they'd assumed he'd been fighting and died the honourable death of a soldier fighting in battle, not from an asthma attack.

Why did that make a difference? She tried to think it through, unsure why it felt as if he'd failed somehow. Duncan had lost his life because he'd hidden his weakness, hadn't told anyone, and shouldn't have been there. Should he have taken an inhaler, but didn't? Did they even have inhalers then?

All she had known until tonight was that he had joined up when he didn't need to and was a brave man, doubly brave, knowing he had asthma but still going to fight for his country. Now his death had been devalued by that contemptible man. Duncan had been sacrificed to save the lives of the others because he was making too much noise. If that was the truth, and she only had Jim's word for it. He struck her as someone who didn't always tell the truth.

Her gran had always blamed the war for taking away her father, then her mother, leaving her to the horror of her life in the orphanage. Gran believed if she'd had a stable family, then Zoe's mum wouldn't have gone off the rails and left when she did. Sometimes, when she was alone, she would play 'What if...'

What if Duncan hadn't died and Mary had survived? Edith would have been safe in her stable family. She wouldn't have married that awful man, who then took off, and her mother wouldn't have got into drugs and all the other stuff Ken said she had. All the 'what ifs' added up to Zoe having a completely different life from the one she'd had so far.

In English, they'd been studying a TS Eliot poem where he said something like they were all the paths they didn't take, as well as the ones they did. Her teacher had called it a Y-front model to help them see it. She yearned to have taken the path on the opposite side of the Y, to have a normal family, like

Ollie's. His family was like one of those in books where parents have time to play with their children, where they all sit around a table together for all their meals and where they all go to the seaside and museums together. If Duncan had come back, that could have been her family.

Instead, she had no idea who her father was. A picture of that bastard Ken pushed his way into her mind, claiming to be her father. His flash clothes and smelly teeth and threats made her shiver. He'd disappeared into the air and hadn't come back – yet. Good riddance. Now she was lumbered with his father. Did Jim know he might be her grandfather? The idea made her feel like she had when she saw that snake in the zoo.

What if Jim wasn't telling the truth? Ron said that some of the men could remember them going back down the line towards the hotel, but no one appeared to have seen what happened next or found Duncan's body until his ex-pupil had. Suppose Jim had actually killed him – murdered him.

Now she was sure Jim was the bully, the sadistic 'Sarge' in the diary, who was jealous of who Duncan was, so put him in danger. It was logical that, given the excuse of his asthma attack, Jim could get him alone and in Duncan's weak state kill him, simply because he could. The final act of his power and sadism.

She felt herself getting angry. A bubble worked its way up her through her body, making her want to hit out at something. Trying to get control, she took a deep breath, counted to seven, then exhaled and listened. The gentle slapping of the river against the side of the boat would have soothed her on another night; now it irritated her.

Laughter invaded her thoughts as a couple holding hands strolled, or rather staggered, past the boat, obviously having enjoyed quite a few drinks. Sitting back so they wouldn't see her watching them, she knew she had changed. No longer the girl who had sat in this cabin a few nights ago, scared to stand up in front of her friends. Now she had grown up. Jim's story had flipped a switch and made her angry and sad at the same time.

She wanted revenge. Revenge for what she believed Jim had done to Duncan, and what Ken had done to her mother. She was sure both had been innocent and exploited by father and son. To feel better, she needed to do something to put it right, to make amends for the years of misery her gran had endured. She owed her that, at least.

There would be an opportunity when they got to the hotel. She wasn't sure how she'd do it, but there was time to think. She'd have the two nights staying there to get her own back for what her family had gone through because of what he'd done. Maybe she could get Jim to tell her the real truth – all that rubbish about survival and sacrificing the one for the many – that was crap. No, she would get the truth out of him, then pay him back for what he'd done to Duncan.

CHAPTER TWENTY-FOUR

STEPH WOKE UP AND, after the tension of the previous night, felt relieved they'd be leaving the boat to spend two days at The Crown Hotel in Oakwood. She sighed as she realised it would be another two days before she could collect Derek. If only he could be with her in the hotel, but they only welcomed humans, so that was that. She'd just have to wait.

She was surprised how much she'd missed him in Holland. When she'd been invited to join the college party, she had explored the possibility of a dog passport but felt it was unfair to Caroline to bring him as he could be a massive distraction. But she wished Caroline had found a dog-friendly hotel back home.

'A penny for them.' Hale leaned across and kissed her passionately on her lips. His hands caressed her body, and he began to undo the buttons on her pyjama top. Glancing over his shoulder at the clock, she pulled back. 'Sorry, Hale. I would too, but we've only got thirty minutes to pack before breakfast and I promised Caroline I'd do a final check on the cabins, to make sure they've been cleared.

'So, you'd rather have a croissant than me?' Hale's low voice and provocative look were tempting... but no... she'd promised. And it was going to be a long journey before they got fed again.

'Sorry – duty calls.' She kissed him and climbed out of bed.

'Oh well, we do have a couple of days swanning about the hotel. Until later then.'

In the shower, odd lines from last night and Ron's revelation re-played in her mind. Ron had explained the motive behind Zoe's obsession with finding out what had happened to Duncan. Steph sighed; although Zoe had achieved her goal it probably wasn't the outcome she'd hoped for.

Zoe believed that her gran's life had been ruined when she became an orphan and blamed Duncan's death for that. Would Mary, his wife, have been ill and died anyway? Perhaps – but Zoe's gran, Edith, would have had a father. Zoe was convinced that their dysfunctional and fractured family life directly resulted from the war. Strange to think how something over seventy years earlier could have such an impact today.

After the shocking scenes of the previous evening, everyone had left the bar in near silence and gone to their cabins, not knowing what to say. It appeared that, after the awkward confrontation, no one wanted to stay in the bar drinking and chatting.

A tearful Zoe had been comforted by Ollie and Caroline last night. Now, as Steph arrived in the dining room, she could see Zoe playing with her food and pushing scrambled egg around her plate. Her eyes were swollen and red; clearly she hadn't slept much.

Although Zoe claimed she'd been on a mission to find out what happened, Steph was sure there was no way she could process the horror of what she'd heard. Saying it with her mouth was one thing, but accepting it was another. She must have thought that by finding the truth, the ghost would be exorcised, but clearly, it hadn't worked like that.

Caroline followed Steph's eyeline and nudged her. 'Not good, is she? I'll get the college counsellor to have a word when we get back.'

After the excitement of their arrival and the feeling of achievement as they worked on their project, it was a shame on this last morning in Holland that the group was subdued and appeared to be depressed by what had happened.

Glancing around the tables, Steph identified Ron and Alistair, who appeared acutely aware of Zoe's unhappiness. Did Ron regret what he'd done or the way he'd done it? He probably thought he was giving Zoe what she wanted, the answer to her question, but clearly from the concerned look on his face and his constant glances at her, he hadn't anticipated this outcome. Ollie appeared to be making polite conversation with Alistair and, from the sound of his voice, was trying to keep a positive tone to the conversation.

On the table by the door, Sam was having an intense conversation with Tom. She would never have predicted the strange bond that had formed between the two of them, after their aggressive set-to on the first night. Judy, clearly annoyed at being left out of the discussion, was glued to her phone, and Steph pictured her with the missing or dead Ken. Yes, she could see them as a couple, but wondered why Jim had been so angry about it.

No sign of Jim. As usual. Caroline had told the veterans they could order a tray to be brought to their room, but only Jim had requested it. It was difficult to feel sorry for him after what he'd done, but she was aware she was judging it from the security of peacetime, not from the horror of war.

Across the table, Hale and Hendrik were comparing cuts to their respective police forces. Both claimed that although technology had improved detection, the lack of human resources was creating an enormous barrier to their clear-up rates.

Hale had contacted his old colleague, Potter, to let him know he would come down with Hendrik in the next week or so, and he was looking forward to a curry at their favourite restaurant in Soho. Steph knew Hale was looking forward to showing Hendrik the ropes, as they moved onto his patch. There was a strong chance that working together, they could get the gang and put a stop to the line between Suffolk and London.

'What are you thinking about?' Caroline placed her knife and fork to the side of her plate and waved at the waiter to bring some more coffee.

'Like everyone else, I suspect, last night. It's really got under my skin.'

'Good. That's what this project was about. To give our kids a real experience of war. Not just the gun fights and heroism they see in movies but the appalling human cost of fighting – injury and death. They and their parents have been lucky, as we have, to have lived in peacetime, and they need to experience the horror of war.'

'They saw that all right.'

'Let's hope we can convey it in the book.' Caroline scanned the room and decided that it was time to move. Through the window, they could see their coaches lined up on the bank, waiting to drive them home to Suffolk.

Caroline pinged her spoon against her coffee cup. 'Ladies and gentlemen, thank you.' She waited for the clatter of knives and forks to stop. 'We have come to the end of the first part of our project, which I hope you have found stimulating.'

A general murmur of 'Yes' and mumbles of agreement swept the room. 'I would like you to join me in thanking the captain and his crew for their excellent hospitality and for giving us such a wonderful home for our stay in Holland.'

She started clapping and was joined by cheering, foot stamping and banging on the tables by students and adults. The captain and his crew appeared at the end of the dining room and smiled as everyone stood and the clapping and cheering got louder. For once the calm control of the captain dissolved, and he blushed, clearly touched by the sincere gratitude and warmth of the students and the veterans. He gestured to the chefs and the waiters to join him, and they received another monster cheer. At last, there was silence.

'Thank you. Now, students, I assume you've all packed. Please clear up any mess in your cabins and meet me by the coaches with your luggage at nine fifteen – that's in fifteen minutes' time. Any problems, see me before we leave. I look forward to seeing you at The Crown later today.'

At last, the boat was cleared. Steph was confident that the cabins had not been left in a dreadful state, and they climbed aboard the coaches for the journey back to Suffolk.

The excited anticipation evident on their way to Holland had disappeared. Both veterans and students chatted quietly, snoozed or stared out of the windows as they sped through the Dutch and French countryside. At last, they arrived in southern England, basking in the late afternoon sunshine, under a perfect white fluffy-cloud, picture-book sky, which stubbornly refused to give way to the dull days of autumn.

CHAPTER TWENTY-FIVE

THE OWNERS of The Crown in Oakwood had generously donated sufficient bedrooms and a conference room to the group for the two full days needed to pull the project together. The couple, who were well past retirement age but appeared to be energised by the group's arrival, greeted them with smiles and an extravagant tea, which everyone gratefully wolfed down. While the rest of the party was unpacking and settling into their rooms, Caroline, Steph, Hale and Mike Simpson gathered around a table in the lounge over another pot of coffee and planned how to manage the next two days.

Caroline suggested that the priority was to allow everyone to recover from the journey and to start work again the next morning. The others agreed this was the best strategy, and she thanked them and crossed her fingers. 'We can only hope the day's journey has diluted the dreadful atmosphere of last night and Jim will be more positive – or at least accepted.'

As Hale collected the coffee cups on the tray, it appeared he'd had a brainwave. 'Should I offer to take Jim home? He must be feeling awkward, and it would get rid of any further disruption.'

They stood for a moment, reflecting on his suggestion. Mike spoke first. 'I think that's a great idea, Hale, but coming from you, he might think it's formal.'

'Really?' Hale was surprised. 'Why?'

'He might think you'll get him away from the group, then arrest him for murder or something.'

'Even though he's got close to confessing he was involved in Duncan's death, I don't think we have anywhere near enough evidence to arrest him. But I take your point.' Hale looked at Caroline.

'Oh! Thanks!' She rolled her eyes. 'Sorry. Yes. It's a good suggestion and it might stop any more rows. I'll get it over with before I unpack. If I don't make it to dinner, come and rescue me!' Pulling her shoulders back, she marched towards the doors.

'I'll come with you and stand outside, just in case.' Hale headed after her.

Steph had hung up the last of her clothes and shoved her case under the bed when Caroline barged in with Hale.

'Not one of my best moments! Jim stormed out of his room before we left, and went next door to Tom and Judy, from where I heard some loud and vivid descriptions of me that I have no intention of repeating.' Caroline plonked herself on the bed, while Hale leaned against the door, looking morose.

'Caroline was brilliant and so diplomatic. Jim didn't appear to understand at first, then when he did, I thought he was going to hit her.' Hale shook his head. 'It's not as if he's been taking part in much, is it?'

Before anyone could answer, an explosive knock or kick on

the door was followed by a hard shove, which made Hale stumble forward as the door burst open. Steph was amazed to see Judy stepping into their room and surprised that she had the strength to shift Hale. A red-faced Jim sidled in after her and sat in one of the chairs with his arms folded, waiting for the show to begin.

Judy hadn't featured a great deal over in Holland, but she was certainly making an impact here, and it appeared she had become Jim's carer too. Her voice would be heard several doors down. 'How dare you treat Sergeant Craddock like this? He has every right to be here, and you want to get rid of him now we're back home.'

'No, it's not like that at all—' Caroline protested.

'Well, what is it like? Sounds to me as if you've judged him guilty without a trial. I thought in this country you are innocent until proved guilty. All Jim was doing was his job, protecting his men. Because Saint Ron trapped him into telling a story that should have stayed buried, you now want to ban him. He is devastated – no – distraught.'

They all turned to look at the distraught, devastated veteran who was observing the argument with a satisfied smile on his face.

Caroline knelt down so she was at eye level with Jim. 'I'm so sorry if what I suggested upset you, and I can see that you're distressed and angry. But we thought with Ken missing and what happened last night, you might want to get home. That was all. If you don't want to go, you don't have to. Of course, you're welcome to stay here.'

Judy, arms folded and head held high, apparently hadn't yet had her pound of flesh, as her voice grew louder. 'You should be ashamed of yourself making an old man suffer like that. A veteran of the war who was upset by doing his duty – and that couldn't have been pleasant – but no, you have to rub it in.'

Caroline, a good head taller, stood in front of Judy, her voice calm and steady. 'You may not have heard me, Judy, but I have just apologised to Jim for misjudging the situation and agreed that he should stay if that is his wish. Thank you for supporting his case so strongly, but I think we have resolved this to everyone's satisfaction, and we need to get changed for dinner.'

Judy tried to stand her ground, but Caroline's soothing yet assertive tone cut through her caterwauling. Clearly Judy couldn't think of a riposte and stared at Jim. 'Come along, Jim, we need to get dressed for dinner.' Tossing her head, she side-stepped Hale and left the room, not waiting for Jim.

Holding the arms of the chair, Jim levered himself up and out of the chair and followed her, making a sort of grumbling mumble as he passed Hale and Caroline. He slammed the door shut behind him.

The stunned silence was broken by Steph. 'Did you hear what he said?'

'Something about F-ing teachers.' Hale grinned at Caroline. 'Hey, not seen you in full frontal teacher mode before. I'd never dream of arguing with you.'

'Neither do the students.' She sighed. 'How ridiculous was that? Let's hope they keep their mouths shut. The last thing we need is another distraction at this stage of the project – we were doing so well. See you at dinner.'

Head held high, Caroline swept out, leaving Hale and Steph staring after her. Hale closed the door and sighed. 'Quite a performance.'

Steph shook the creases out of the navy dress she planned to wear for the evening. 'The question is, why did Jim want to stay so badly?'

CHAPTER TWENTY-SIX

Zoe walked through The Crown Hotel rose garden and counted along the fourteen French windows to number forty-three. It was bizarre that they started at thirty.

After a long day's journey from Arnhem, their coaches had arrived in Oakwood at four o'clock. Just in time for sumptuous sandwiches and cakes arranged on those plate pyramids she'd seen in posh films. She'd been excited by the prospect of staying in the swankiest hotel in Oakwood, but now she just wanted it over and to get back to normal life. However, there was something she had to do first.

Finding what she thought was the right room, she peered in through the French windows and, seeing Jim watching horse racing on the TV, knocked on the glass. Had he heard her? She waited for him to move.

The gleeful screams of some students playing with the metre-high chessmen on the enormous board in the garden made her turn to check no one could see her. She looked in the room once again. Jim didn't hear at first or ignored her, so she knocked again, this time longer and louder, and pushed herself closer to the shadows in front of the windows.

At last, he turned his head and scowled at her. It appeared he'd heard all right, but at last realised she wasn't going away.

He came up to the window and shouted, 'What do you want?'

'I want to come in to have a chat.'

He shook his head. 'Piss off – leave me alone.'

Zoe wobbled a little. She was losing her nerve faced with his stubborn resistance, but something drove her on and she knocked on the glass louder than ever. 'I'm not leaving until we've spoken.'

Jim turned away and returned to his seat in front of the TV. Rattling the door and smashing her fist on the glass, she shouted, 'If you don't let me in, I'll break the glass and let myself in.'

Nothing. She was shouting at his back. Inspiration struck. 'I need to tell you something about Ken.'

Amazed at the strength of her own voice and where her anger had come from, she glared in through the window as Jim shuffled towards the door. A little ashamed of using the same tactic Ken had used on her, she immediately justified it as fair play in the circumstances.

After a lot of fiddling about with the lock, at last Jim opened the door and stood back. 'Two minutes, that's all I'm giving you.' Leaving the door open, he sat and waved at her to sit on a brown leather armchair opposite the one he had been sitting in.

'What do you want?'

'The truth.'

'You've had the truth last night. Wasn't it good enough for you to see me humiliated in front of my men like that?'

The heat of his anger was palpable. Trying to get this vile man to break down and tell her the truth was going to be more difficult than she thought. But she was convinced that she hadn't heard the whole story. There had been something rehearsed about it, as if he'd predicted he might be asked and prepared the 'one sacrificed for the many' defence, just in case. Zoe stared at him, allowing him to become uncomfortable under her gaze.

She waited for him to speak. The pause stretched painfully between them. A grey horse thundered across the finishing line on the TV behind him to loud cheers of the crowd, and the camera panned to a jubilant jockey pushing his way through the admiring spectators slapping his back, saddle in hand, to the weighing room. Still Jim sat tight lipped and frowning.

Screams of laughter from outside highlighted the safe distance other students felt. To them, it was simply a project; to her it was a burning need to discover why her family had been torn apart, and she wasn't going to let the man who'd caused it off the hook that easily.

Jim looked away first. Instinctively, Zoe knew she held the power at that moment and wasn't going to back down. 'Well?'

'Well, what?' He spat out the words. 'Just who do you think you are?'

'The sad result of what you did to Duncan all those years ago. I want to know the truth this time, not that fairy story you told us last night. How did you murder Duncan and why did you do it?'

Glowering at her, he shouted. 'I told you. He had an asthma attack. It was an accident – an accident of war!'

Hearing those trite words made her so furious she wanted to hit him or shake him or spit in his face or do something to hurt him. It was obvious he didn't care less about what had happened. His only concern was that he should squirm out of it unhurt. Well, she wanted to make him suffer, as he'd made Duncan suffer.

'You had it in for him from the start. You were envious of him, and you admitted you couldn't stand him. You were out to get him killed from the start. How did you do it?' The venom in her voice made him wince.

'I told you, it was an accident.' He paused and appeared to be assessing how what he was saying was going down with her. She stared back, refusing to look away. Once again, she won.

'I told you. I had to get him out of the wood and take him back to save the rest of us.'

She sensed he was weakening a little. She took a step closer, her voice became a menacing whisper. 'I don't believe you. Tell me what happened when you got out of the woods, at the place where he died.'

'Then you'll leave me alone?' He squinted up at her, clearly trying to work out how he could get rid of her. 'I'm an old man who shouldn't be worried like this. All I want is a little peace.'

He patted his chest and shook his head, throwing her a pathetic look. His whiny voice nauseated her. 'My ticker – not good – you know.'

She sensed this was her moment and kept her voice level. 'Tell me and I'll leave you alone. And I won't tell anyone else, promise. I just want the truth for me and my gran. We want to know why her life has been so rubbish, that's all.'

He paused for a few moments. Frowning, he held out his hand. 'Here – show me your phone. I need to see you're not recording anything.'

Reaching into her jeans pocket, she was impressed that this foul old man was so tech savvy. 'I told you, I don't need to do anything with what you tell me – I just want to hear the truth.' Making a great show of turning off the phone, she placed it on the coffee table between them. They both stared at it. He took a deep breath.

'Your Duncan really got up my nose. Hoity-toity, he was. Always cheerful and positive about the shit we were in. Never complained, however hard I pushed him. The more I pushed him, the more he smiled and got on with it. I wanted to wipe that smile off his face, no trouble.'

He sneaked a look at her, his eyes narrow. 'And then there was Mary...'

'Mary?'

'Not sure what you youngsters call it, but we had a fling before she married your Duncan.'

The knot in Zoe's stomach tightened. She hoped she wouldn't need the loo – not now. Jim's voice was becoming gruffer, more aggressive, more common somehow, and she could feel her temper erupting. It was her gran's mother and father he was talking about. She couldn't believe Mary would have had anything to do with this horrid man, even when he was younger, but why would he say so if it wasn't true? And as for Duncan – he hadn't done anything to deserve what happened to him apart from joining up when he didn't need to. Biting the inside of her lips so she couldn't speak, she continued to stare him out.

He dropped his head and mumbled. 'All right. I'll tell you, but that's it – you'll let me alone if I tell you?'

Zoe nodded.

'We got to the end of the woods and to the open field. I was damned if I was going to risk my life for that waster. He had asthma and hadn't told anyone. He shouldn't have been there. I was angry. He stumbled over something on the ground and cried out as he fell. A loud cry it was – could have set Jerry on us – and I lost it with him and hit him over the head with my rifle butt. Not hard – honest. But he was so weak it knocked him out.'

Once again, he glanced at Zoe, testing her reaction. She said nothing and continued staring. 'When I left him lying on the grass, he was still breathing – or wheezing, honest. That's it. I went back into the woods.'

Furious, Zoe attempted to keep her voice calm. 'That's not the truth, is it? He wasn't alive when you left him, was he? He wasn't wheezing. He'd stopped breathing, hadn't he? You knew you'd beaten him to death.'

He grinned at her. 'No one will ever know now, will they?'

CHAPTER TWENTY-SEVEN

STEPH WAS PLEASED to see Caroline looking as positive and calm as usual when they joined her at their dinner table. When all the groups were seated, Caroline pinged a spoon against her wine glass, calling everyone to attention.

'Welcome back to Oakwood, everyone. As you know, this is the last part of our project, the important part where we pull together all our work and decide how we will present it in the book for the seventy-fifth anniversary. I've seen some superb drawings and photographs, and I know Mike has a file of your writing, which he says is outstanding, so we have masses to choose from. Tomorrow we have our final day to work on the book and then in the evening we have the trial, which will judge the success or failure of Market Garden. I suggest...'

Steph tuned out and scanned the room. Ron and Alistair sat together with Zoe and Ollie — all four appeared shattered after the day's journey. Tom was sitting at a table by himself with no Judy or Jim and, of course, no Ken. It was fascinating how no one had appeared to miss Ken or even ask if anyone had heard from him. He had melted into thin air, and no one cared. Even Jim didn't seem that worried.

Perhaps she should go to Jim's room and find him – he ought to eat something. It was strange Jim hadn't turned up at dinner despite his protestations that he wanted to stay, but then it fitted the pattern all the time they'd been on the boat. Should she organise a tray to be taken to his room? She whispered to Hale, 'I'll pop out and see where Judy and Jim have got to.'

'Shall I come with you?'

'No need.'

Trying to be as surreptitious as possible, Steph made her way through the double swing doors of the conference room. The cheerful chatter disappeared as the door closed and she walked along the thick navy carpeted corridor to the garden rooms.

She stopped to admire the ancient rose garden through a glass door halfway along the corridor. Her attention was grabbed by the perfect picture as the rays of the late evening sun lit the white roses still in bloom against the old terracotta bricks of the walled garden. Like LED lights, the roses glowed beneath the line of oak trees, their leaves turning a deep shade of ginger.

Reaching room number forty-three, she knocked on the door.

No answer.

She knocked again. 'Jim. It's Steph. Are you OK?'

She put her ear against the door, trying to detect any movement from within. Nothing.

'Jim.' Another knock. Still nothing.

Maybe he'd had a lie down and was asleep. They were all tired after the journey and he'd probably not set his alarm. She hoped that the recent drama hadn't made him ill, but he'd not looked that bothered by it earlier, had he? She knocked once more. No answer.

She walked back to the Reception desk where she found a bored-looking clerk who was playing Candy Crush on his phone and only became aware of her presence when she leaned over the shiny oak desk.

'Sorry, ma'am, may I help you?'

'Yes, please.' She peered at the silver name badge pinned to the lapel on his jacket, but he moved before she could read it. 'I'm concerned that the gentleman in room number forty-three may be ill. Please, will you bring the master key so I can check he's OK?'

The dark-haired clerk, who looked fourteen but must be in his early twenties, frowned as he searched for a master key in a drawer in front of him. 'Won't be a moment... It's here somewhere.' He scrabbled through the drawer and a blush swept up his face from his neck. The deep acne pock marks across his cheeks and neck were emphasised by his inflamed skin.

Impatient, Steph held in a sigh, unimpressed by his inefficient search. Surely, they needed to use the master key more often? His panic suggested it was a rare occurrence. Successful at last, he held up the key in triumph and appeared to expect her to congratulate him on a great find. She didn't.

Holding the key in front of him, he led her back down the corridor and also went through the ritual of knocking on the door and asking Mr Craddock to open it. Again, there was no answer, so at last he inserted the key and opened the door.

Steph peered over his shoulder and saw the French windows open, the right one swinging in the breeze. To the right of the windows, she saw a fully dressed Jim on the bed, his shoes placed neatly on the floor beside him. She was right. He'd needed a nap.

The last golden rays of the autumn sun, sieved by the oak tree outside his room, fluttered across his stomach. Jim looked so different asleep – so much younger. The grumpy frown lines that bisected his forehead above his nose had smoothed out and his downturned lips relaxed so he was almost smiling in his sleep.

As she stepped towards him and reached out to touch his arm, she stopped. Something was wrong. It was too quiet. Her stomach lurched. Jim wasn't breathing. He was dead.

CHAPTER TWENTY-EIGHT

'STAND BY THE DOOR, please, and wait there while I shut those. What's your name?'

'Dave.' He did as she ordered, walking backwards, his eyes fixed on the man on the bed. 'Is he all right? He's not... is he?'

'Don't worry, Dave. I'll take care of it.'

Steph shut the French windows, making sure she used the hem of her dress to pull on the edge of the handle while being careful not to wipe it. From the peaceful expression on his face, Jim looked as if he'd died in his sleep, and all this might be overkill, but better to make sure.

'Now you wait here, Dave, outside this door, while I get help.' Steph pointed to the spot where the shocked boy, as he'd now become, should stand. She was used to seeing dead bodies; she assumed he wasn't.

'Sh-sh-shouldn't we call the p-p-police or an ambulance?'

'They're already here. Don't worry. I'll sort it.'

He didn't look convinced, but did as she told him and stood, his back leaning against the door. Concerned he might faint, she dragged a chair from the bijou desk along the corridor and placed it in front of the door.'

'That's better. You sit there, Dave. I'll be back in a few moments with the police.'

She left him, white faced and looking terrified, his head in his hands.

Moments later, Hale and Hendrik followed her down the corridor, and she was pleased to see Dave had obeyed her. More likely, he couldn't have moved if he wanted to. 'Thanks, Dave, you can go back to Reception now. This is Chief Inspector Hale of the Suffolk police. He'll handle it. Don't worry.'

'If you're sure, ma'am?'

'Yes.' Steph smiled. 'Please don't tell anyone what has happened and could you leave that master key with me? We'll get it back to you as soon as possible.'

Dave handed it over with a shaking hand, then tried to stand but wobbled.

'Hendrik, will you see he gets back to Reception, please?'

Hendrik looked a little surprised at her request but put his hand under Dave's elbow and helped him to stand.

'And get yourself a drink – tea or coffee with lots of sugar in it. You must be shocked,' Steph called out after them.

Steph and Hale watched as the pair wobbled to the end of the corridor before opening Jim's door.

'And this is how you found him?' Hale stood on the threshold, looking around the room.

'Yes, the French window was open, so I shut it, using the hem of my dress to avoid touching it, but nothing else has been moved and Dave stood by the door. I don't think he actually stepped in.'

'Good.' Hale strode over to stand above Jim's body, taking

as few steps as possible. 'Looks as if he died in his sleep. I'll call it in.'

Steph was aware of a movement behind her as Hendrik leaned round her, his hand on the headboard, examining Jim's body. He raised his eyebrows, shook his head and strode over to the wardrobe door. Pulling out a beige canvas bag, he opened the flap, tipped it upside down and shook it. 'Nothing here. When we saw him collect it in Oosterbeek woods, it had something in it; it bulged.' Hendrik replaced it in the wardrobe.

'You're right. And I noticed he held onto it throughout the journey home. He didn't put it on the luggage rack but kept it on his knee.' Steph was pleased she could contribute some intelligence and felt good when she was rewarded with a smile from Hendrik, who was a bit like an enthusiastic Tigger at times.

Hendrik moved to the drawers of the walnut tallboy and pulled them out, the bottom ones first.

'All empty.' He looked all around the room, clearly puzzled. 'And where's his luggage?'

'We all took our bags off the coach when we came in. Caroline checked with the driver that the hold was empty. Jim had a soft hold-all – dark green material, I think.' Steph peeped inside the empty wardrobe.

'Could it be under the bed?' Hendrik bent down a little.

'I'll check.' Hale knelt down and peered under the bed. 'Nothing.'

'So, we've lost the bags we took from Ken's safe — the diamonds and the drugs?' Obviously frustrated, Hendrik kicked the bottom drawer shut.

All three scanned the room. There was nothing to be seen, apart from Jim's body on the bed with his shoes on the floor beside him.

Hale frowned, moved back to the body, and shone his phone torch over Jim's face. 'Right, stop, both of you. I've found some petechiae—'

'What?' Hendrik closed the top drawer of the tallboy.

'Petechiae –You know those little red marks around the eyes when someone has been strangled or smothered? He didn't die in his sleep. Someone killed him.'

CHAPTER TWENTY-NINE

HALE USHERED them into the corridor and shut the door.

'I'll call it in and get SOCOs out here. You'll need to give your prints and DNA, Hendrik, as will that Reception chap. Anyone else go in there, do you know?'

Steph shook her head. 'Don't think so. But we can check.' She pointed up to the ceiling at the end of the corridor. 'Look, there's a camera up there.'

'Well spotted.' Hale smiled at her. 'I suggest you ask your new best friend for the footage, while I find Caroline and see what she wants to do about telling the others.'

'And me?' Hendrik appeared a little over-awed by Hale's business-like tone, and stood almost to attention, waiting to receive orders.

'I suggest you guard this door until the troops get here. Shouldn't be long.'

Hendrik's face dropped and Steph felt sorry for him having such a menial role but knew it was best not to argue with Hale on his patch. Without a murmur, Hendrik sat in the chair outside the door while Hale strode along the corridor. As he opened the swing doors leading to the conference room, the gentle chatter of well-fed diners and cutlery on porcelain brought back a sense of the ordinary in the midst of this tragic death. Jim might have been an old man, but that didn't give someone the right to take away the time he had left or make it any less important to find his killer.

Steph returned to Reception, where a pale Dave stood up as they approached him.

'Have you had a hot drink, Dave?'

'Yes, but it made me feel sick. What will happen now?'

'Chief Inspector Hale will call in his team, who will check the room, and Mr Craddock's body will be taken away by the coroner's transport service. I expect they would like to use the garden entrance so the other guests don't see them. Is that the way into it – there on the right?'

Steph moved to a long window to the right of the Reception desk and pointed to a wide path that led towards the garden.

'Yes. It's where the laundry vans and kitchen deliveries go behind the hotel. There's a turn to the left, which will take them into the garden.'

'That's helpful, thank you. Now I noticed a camera on that corridor. May I see the film from the time we arrived, please? And do you have a camera on the garden side of the rooms?'

Dave flipped back the hatch at the side of the long Reception desk and indicated she should come through to join him. He pulled a chair over to face the screen in front of him. 'We don't have cameras there.'

'Really?'

'No, the doors to the garden only open from inside. No-one can get in from the outside. They have special security bars on them. We don't need cameras there.'

'Where do you have cameras?' Steph adopted a particularly soothing tone, trying not to panic the wobbly-looking Dave, who blushed so easily. Close to, she caught a pungent whiff of sweat. He needed calming down.

'Umm, all the public areas, the corridors, the bar, the dining room, the conference room and up there.' Dave pointed to the camera sited above the front door.

'That's helpful. Thanks, Dave. Now, could we go back through the footage from the time we arrived to now, please?'

Scrolling through the film, Steph saw their party arrive, being allocated their rooms and dispersing down the two corridors. She watched Judy carrying her bag and Tom's as they walked with Jim to his room. After helping him with his key to open the door and putting his bag in his room, Tom and Judy left to go to their room. At that stage, they could clearly see Jim had his bag in his room, and it was, as Steph had suggested, a canvas holdall.

Next, they watched as Caroline entered Jim's room, leaving Hale outside, then a furious Jim rushed next door to complain to Judy and Tom about his poor treatment. Judy, with Jim trailing behind, passed down the corridor to Hale and Steph's room, and then, after a pause, they emerged looking pleased with themselves, to return to their own rooms.

Later they saw Judy and Tom knock on Jim's door, wait and, clearly receiving no reply, go to the conference room. Over the next frame, the other occupants of the rooms along the corridor walked towards the conference room, leaving the corridor deserted.

It stayed like that until Steph knocked on Jim's door, then returned with Dave. She went in, came out, again shutting the door, and left him to sit outside until she came back with Hale and Hendrik.

Steph and Dave were scrolling through the conference room footage when Hale and Hendrik joined them. 'Caroline and I agreed nothing should be said to the whole group but that we would have a quiet word with Tom after dinner. I think the private ambulance and SOCO vans will have left by that time, but there'll be a police officer outside the room until they've finished – probably tomorrow. Luckily, Jim's room is towards the end of the corridor so it shouldn't attract too much notice. I have arranged for the kitchen to leave us some supper for later.'

'Well done. We've seen the corridor film, and no one goes into Jim's room after he shuts the door until I arrive. There are no cameras on the garden side, as they have security locks that can only be opened from the inside.'

'So, Jim knew his killer then? They must've got in from the garden.' Hale and Hendrik joined them behind the desk.

'And the doors to the garden were open when I arrived.' Steph shifted on her chair so he could share it. Hendrik peered over their shoulders at the screen.

Hendrik looked puzzled. 'But they were closed when we got there.'

'Yes, because I closed them after I found his body. Sorry, Dave, could you continue showing us the conference room, please?'

They saw the tables slowly fill up. Caroline stood to make her announcement, the waiters brought round the starters and Steph left through the double doors. Steph pointed to the screen. 'Go back a bit, please, Dave and press pause... Yes, there.'

They stared at the flickering image, and Steph pointed to a table on the top right of the screen. 'See, there's Tom alone with three empty chairs and no Judy or Jim.'

'Can you go back a bit further and see when Judy left?' Steph asked.

Dave nodded and pressed the replay button. They saw Judy and Tom enter and find their seats, and then Judy disappeared towards the top left of the screen.

'It looks as if she's gone to the bathroom, through that door.' Hendrik pointed to the door opposite the main entrance.

Hale grabbed a pen and wrote a line on the pad in front of Dave. 'Here's my email address, Dave. Will you send me all the footage from all the cameras from our arrival to now, please? And please keep the originals safe and don't wipe them or record over them. Can you do that?'

Dave appeared to have calmed down as they'd been looking through the film. 'Yes, I'll do it now.'

'Thanks.' Hale patted him on the shoulder. 'Oh, and no one is to go in Room forty-three and please ask your cleaners not to clean the corridor until I say so, understand? And I'd like you to give that message to all the staff through your manager.' Dave looked pleased with this responsibility.

All three went back down the corridor to see how close the team was to finishing their initial sweep of the room.

'I must talk with Zoe as soon as it is possible.' Evidently, Hendrik caught Hale's raised eyebrow as he continued, 'I mean, if that is OK with you?'

'And why is that?' Hale paused as he put the key in the lock and turned to face him.

'We know Ken blackmailed her, and she was one of the last people, probably the very last, to see Ken before he disappeared. Last night she heard Jim was responsible for Duncan's death. She had the motive and the opportunity for both deaths. She must be our chief suspect.'

CHAPTER THIRTY

From her seat in the corner of the conference room, Steph relished the excited chatter coming from each table as the students and veterans, heads down, worked on their part of the project. At regular intervals, the students left their tables for coffee re-fills, cans of soft drinks, biscuits or fruit, apparently enjoying the novelty of refreshments on tap.

Letting her mind wander, a picture of Derek kept pushing its way into her head. He had become a firm part of her life since moving to the Oakwood flat with a garden and it seemed strange to be in Suffolk without him. Only one more night to go and she'd pick him up from Fiona, the dog lady, where he would be having a whale of a time with the rest of Fiona's dogs and probably wouldn't be missing her in the least.

Caroline, in pale pink, floated from table to table encouraging, shaping and gently cajoling everyone to complete their work. Steph knew she was thrilled by the creative quality of their work, which would be an original contribution to the story of the Battle for Arnhem. Already she had received interest from a publisher specialising in war books, requesting a meeting to discuss a deal. She was planning to share the good news with students and veterans at the end of their stay.

Jim's disappearance had prompted little comment, as he'd hardly been a core member of the group and they were used to his absence. Over their nightcaps she, Caroline and Hale had decided not to announce his death but to mention it to a few of the veterans. Ron's reaction confirmed that was the best course of action, and Tom hadn't appeared particularly bothered when Caroline spoke to him.

Tom was a strange man who had surprised them all with his petticoat story after his general grumpiness. Over the other side of the room, he was deep in conversion with Sam, who grinned, then laughed out loud at something Tom said. He looked flattered that Sam appreciated his joke. Theirs was the only table of two. No Jim or Ken, of course – and where was Judy? Steph was sure she'd seen her earlier in the morning. All the other carers were helping, clearly fascinated by the artwork and writing being produced. Perhaps she'd gone outside for some air.

Steph left the room, wandered along the corridor, waved to Dave on duty behind the Reception desk and blinked as she opened the main doors and stepped into the bright sunshine in the garden. It was another one of those perfect days of autumn where everything was still, holding its breath until the east winds whooshed all the leaves off the trees.

They had been so lucky while they'd been away and now, again, here in Suffolk. The weather was bound to break soon, and they'd move into the solid grey steel skies of November. Although that month often gave the fieriest crimson skies at sunset, so there was always something positive to appreciate. But today it would be warm enough to sit outside if she found a sheltered spot.

The white roses in the beds outside the bedrooms gave way to deep purple and claret blooms across the lawn – the final fling of autumn. A variety of seats, from wooden loungers to elegant Lutyens benches, were scattered around the garden, facing the enormous chess board that had become a popular pastime with the students.

Hale had gone to the police station to work with the team investigating Jim's murder and Ken's disappearance. He was still waiting for the formal identification of the body to arrive from Holland. If it was Ken, then he'd have to liaise with the Dutch police, and he wanted to get as much background as possible prepared, so he didn't appear to be a Suffolk yokel.

Turning a corner away from the shelter of the trees towards a patch of sunshine, Steph saw Judy soaking up the sunshine – smoking a cigarette, her head back, eyes closed. Changing direction and walking around the box hedge, Steph approached her. It was time for peace talks.

'Do you mind if I join you?'

'Free country.' Judy shifted along to her left to make room for Steph, which wasn't necessary but presumably made the point that she didn't want to be contaminated by her.

'Lovely day, isn't it?' Steph could hardly believe that she had started with the weather. 'Would be a good day for hanging the washing out if I was at home.'

Judy stared ahead and hadn't acknowledged Steph at all after the initial scowl. This could have been a massive mistake, but Steph was here now so she might as well get on with it.

'Look, Judy, the last thing we wanted was to upset you or Jim last night. It was just after all that has happened, we thought he might prefer to be in his own home.'

'Bit late now, isn't it? He'll never go back home again, thanks to you.' Full of anger, her eyes drilled into Steph.

'Hey! That's unfair. I'm sure his death had nothing to do with us.'

Judy gave her another dirty look, and pulling out a packet of cigarettes from her pocket, she extracted one and held it to the butt end of the one she was smoking. It crackled as it lit, and she threw the butt on the gravel in front of her. They watched as it continued to smoulder, releasing an acrid smell as the filter burnt.

Judy took another drag. 'There'll be one of those coroners' thingies, won't there?'

'Coroner's Court, yes. All the evidence will be produced there.'

'No doubt your lot will cover it up, like you've covered up Ken's disappearance. He was my friend. Known each other since Primary. He was good to his father and good to me and now he's gone, thanks to you lot.'

'That's rubbish. We had nothing to do with it, and there's been no attempt to cover anything up. The Dutch police have been investigating it ever since he disappeared.'

'You would say that!' She paused to do up the buttons on her cardigan as the sun had moved behind a tree and the temperature had dropped. As she finished, Judy drew deeply on her cigarette and exhaled in the direction of Steph, who resisted the temptation of waving her hand in front of her face.

She was getting nowhere and had decided to give up when Judy moved a little closer and whispered, 'Does your inspector friend know you fancy that Dutch policeman?'

Steph was horrified. 'What? Whatever are you talking about?'

'You blush every time he comes near you, you know, and you put on your phone voice too – all posh. S'pect you think it sounds sexy.'

Feeling her temper starting to erupt, Steph stood up, facing Judy. 'You're talking absolute rubbish—'

'Listen, lady, you think you're above the likes of me, but just you watch out. Ken and Jim have friends, you know, really good friends who will want to get justice for what you lot have done to the both of them. Just watch out is all I'm going to say.'

As Steph took a step back, her phone rang. It was Hale.

'Hang on...' As Steph walked away towards the chess set and out of Judy's earshot, she felt the eyes of the woman boring into her back. 'Sorry. I'm by myself now.'

'Sounds interesting.'

'Not really, just Judy out here enjoying a smoke and stirring some poison.'

'Oh? Anyway, I phoned to tell you I've rushed the DNA through, and as well as mine, yours and Hendrik's, we have other unidentified results.'

Steph sat on a bench beyond the chess set. 'But loads of people would have been in that room—'

'But not touching Jim. You and I did, and I assume Hendrik must have before we realised he'd been smothered – but who else?'

'Hang on a moment.' Steph paused as Judy emerged from behind the hedge and headed for the hotel.

'See you at lunch.' Judy winked at Steph, who attempted to smile in return, then waited until she'd gone indoors before continuing.

'Sorry. Surely it could have been anyone on the coach who touched him?'

'Apparently not. The unknown samples were taken from his wrists and his face. At least we now have the DNA of whoever murdered him, but we haven't the faintest idea who they are.'

CHAPTER THIRTY-ONE

'Hmm, hmm.' Hale cleared his throat and found his notes, preparing to speak to the entire group, and Steph couldn't help but smile. He was used to briefing a room full of police officers, but she'd never seen him speak to this mixed group of students and veterans.

Caroline stood up first. 'Sorry to intrude on your work, which is going so well, but Chief Inspector Hale would like to ask for your help.' As she sat, she swept the air with her arm, indicating that the floor was his.

'Thank you, Caroline.' He paused and checked his notes before glancing around the room to make sure that everyone was listening. 'As you may know, Jim Craddock died last night, and I would like your help in finding out what may have happened to him, as we think his death wasn't natural.'

His announcement was greeted with little reaction across the room. It appeared the grapevine had been effective in communicating the news. Sam pushed his glasses further up his nose and put his hand up.

'Yes?'

'You're saying he was murdered?' Sam was voicing what everyone was thinking. Why was Hale being so careful? Why couldn't he say it himself instead of speaking in this awkward code?

'We have to wait for the formal conclusion of the post mortem, but yes, we are treating his death as suspicious.'

This time a murmur swept across the room. More fascination than shock. Jim hadn't been well liked and his death would not be mourned by many here.

'As far as we know, he came off the coach and went straight to his room carrying his holdall, which is now missing. If any of you had a conversation with Jim Craddock on the coach or saw him after he went to his room, or if you find that holdall, please come and see me. At this stage, any help you are able to give will be welcome. I shall be in room thirty-one.'

'Thank you.' Caroline stood and smiled at Hale. 'If you know anything that may help with Chief Inspector Hale's enquiries, please go to talk to him in room thirty-one.'

Hale whispered to Steph, 'Wasn't I clear or something? Why did she have to tell them the same thing again?'

'She's a teacher. That's what they do. Anyway, it's good for you to experience what mansplaining feels like!'

Sam raised his hand again. 'Please Hale, we know Jim's son Ken disappeared and could be dead in Arnhem and now Jim's been murdered. Is there a murderer on the loose or, even worse, could it be one of us?'

Hale raised his hand to quell the gasps and buzz of exclamations Sam's question had prompted, and when all was calm again, he looked around the room including all in his gaze. 'Thank you, Sam. You ask some very good questions, but we think both men were targeted. No, we believe you are not in any danger.'

173

Caroline stood up, clearly wanting to stop the growing panic. 'May I echo what Hale has said? We believe you are not in any danger so please don't worry. If you have any information, then please go and see Hale in room thirty-one.'

'Hmm!' Hale bent over to whisper again. 'Perhaps you should be there, too. Don't want to get tangled up in some safeguarding issue if I'm alone with a student – anyway, you're good at spotting things I miss.'

They left the buzz of conference room and went to their room to wait, hoping to receive some visitors. While Steph rushed around hanging up their clothes, tidying away their books and arranging two leather tub chairs around the low coffee table, Hale went to Reception and brought back two more chairs ready for the chats he hoped might throw some light on Jim's death.

They'd just finished arranging the room when the door opened to reveal Ron and Alistair. 'May we come in?'

'Please do and take a seat. Thank you for coming.'

Ron glanced across at Alistair, who nodded at him. After taking a deep breath, Ron spoke. 'We think you ought to know we had an altercation – a row with Jim after his confession in the bar that night. He came back to the bar and said he wanted to speak to me and would I go to his cabin as soon—'

'We decided we'd both go, as we didn't trust him one bit,' Alistair interrupted.

'Jim was surprised when Alistair turned up, too, and he was furious with what we'd forced him to say. Couldn't stop f-ing and blinding could he?' Ron turned to Alistair.

Alistair nodded his head in agreement. 'Never heard anything like it – so much swearing and cursing it was difficult to understand what he was saying.'

Ron took over. 'Jim threatened us. He told us Ken and his

mates would get us for humiliating him, so we'd better watch our backs. He said he'd get his solicitor to accuse us of slander – I was surprised he even knew the word.'

'Or had a solicitor! Ron was really calm and asked Jim why he'd admitted it – he could have denied it, couldn't he?' Alistair appeared to be eager to protect Ron.

'And what did he say to that?' Steph asked Ron. Hale had been making notes while they'd been talking.

Before Ron could answer, Alistair butted in. 'He said that Ron had trapped him in front of everyone and hadn't given him time to think—'

'Which was the idea. Jim said he was going to withdraw his confession and say he was forced to say it on the spur of the moment. I'm not sure how he could squirm out of it. Invent some medic who helped Duncan? That's all he could say isn't it?' Ron looked at Hale for his agreement.

'We found witnesses who saw him leave with Duncan,' said Alistair, 'but after that no one saw what happened, so he can claim Duncan was breathing when he'd left him and he'd died later, so it wasn't his fault.'

Having delivered their news, they sat waiting for Hale's reaction.

'Thank you.' Hale closed his book. 'That was really help-ful. And you didn't see him alone again after that discussion on the boat?'

Alistair answered for them both. 'He ignored us on the coach, and we didn't see him after that, did we, Ron?'

'Did you visit him in his room here?'

'Good heavens, no. Whatever would we do that for?' His hand on the door handle, Ron paused. 'Are you sure he was murdered? He was over ninety, you know.' Ron appeared to be puzzled that anyone over ninety could be murdered.

'Afraid that's what we think happened. Thank you both for your time, and if you think of anything else that may help, please let us know.'

Just as the two men were leaving, a serious-looking Hendrik walked in. 'Sorry, but I have some urgent news.'

CHAPTER THIRTY-TWO

'You should go and talk to Hale,' said Ollie, 'or if you don't want him, then see Steph. She'll understand and listen. I know she will.'

Zoe paced around the room and gulped water from the plastic bottle she was gripping.

Ollie took her hand and pulled her down on the side of the bed bedside him.

She sighed. 'He told me the truth – at least I think it's the truth. He did murder Duncan – it wasn't an accident of war and he didn't tell the truth on the boat, did he?'

Ollie stared at her as if he didn't recognise her. Did he believe her?

Her voice lowered as she tried to convince him. Or was she justifying the unjustifiable? 'But he was a murderer. And he didn't regret it much, did he? Or even want to tell the truth. I wanted to pay him back for what he did to us all.'

'But he was an old man who did something in the horrific context of the war. In wars, men die. You must accept that, Zoe.'

Ollie would never understand the full impact of Duncan's death on her life. Perhaps she should stop trying. 'I shouldn't have told you. It means you're implicated, too.'

'Don't talk rubbish. I'm not implicated. What you did was stupid and could be assault, but you didn't kill him... did you?'

Ollie looked deep into her eyes, and she felt herself blush.

'No, I didn't kill him. You know what I did. But what if that led to his death?'

Ollie sighed. 'How many more times do we have to go through this? I know what you did, and it was stupid, but now you need to go and talk to them about it. I'm sure it wouldn't have killed him.'

Her head dropped to her chest. She couldn't face him any longer. Why had she told him in the first place? They had been together for over a year, and she thought they shouldn't have secrets from each other, but there were great chunks of her life she hadn't told him about. Surely, if they were really, really in love, she would have, wouldn't she?

Ollie broke the silence. 'What I don't understand is what made you do it. I mean, it was almost seventy-five years ago and yet you've been behaving as if it was yesterday or your dad he killed. Not someone you've never even met.'

Zoe felt her temper rising inside her. Of all the people she'd expected to understand, it was Ollie. But he was a golden child. The perfect family – the family she should have had.

'I expected you to understand, but obviously you can't or don't want to.'

'What's that supposed to mean?'

She leaped off the bed and sat on the edge of the desk opposite so she could face him and was out of his reach.

'Come on, you've no idea what that man did to my family. It was because of him my gran became an orphan and

178

had a dreadful childhood. No one noticed she wasn't at school and her life was ruined. Then she had my mum and ended up as a single parent and then my Mum couldn't cope and she left me. All that comes from what that Craddock man did.'

Ollie stared her out. 'I think that is a real exaggeration, Zoe. All that could have happened anyway. Families are a mess.'

'Yours isn't.'

'I'm not sure what you think my family is like, but it's not the perfect family you seem to think it is.' Ollie's voice became louder, so she shut the French window in case anyone could hear them and stood with her back against the glass.

'Oh no? Well, tell me how you've suffered then – having two parents who still love each other, a beautiful house, no money worries, private school, expensive holidays.'

Clearly Ollie was getting cross. 'And that's what you see, is it? All you're talking about is money. Yes, I've been privileged, I admit it. But my father is never there, he's too busy making money, and my mother spends her life at the gym or the hairdresser. And they sent me away to school when I was six for other people to take care of.'

'What a deprived little boy you are! You sound like a spoilt brat. You've no idea about life, have you?'

And he didn't yet know anything about her mother's drug dealing and sex work and she certainly wasn't going to tell him. Had she blown it? Was he going to walk out on her?

Ollie stood, walked towards her and placed his hands on her shoulders so he could look her in the eyes. 'This isn't a competition – stop it now.' He shook her gently. His voice became softer. 'I know you've had a rough time and I'm sorry, but you've got to let it go. You're letting this whole project get all out of proportion. Now you know what happened, drop it.

It was wrong what he did. You got him to admit it and he's dead. Now, stop it.'

He leaned forward and kissed her forehead. 'You are a beautiful girl with a great future ahead of you. Looking at you standing up there on that boat, I was so proud of you. I'm sure I wouldn't have had the confidence you showed, but you did it. You achieved what you set out to. Now move on.'

Zoe ignored the tears that had overflowed and were running down her cheeks. Ollie wiped them away and she welcomed his gentle touch.

'Now, when you've calmed down, you need to talk to Hale or Steph,' he said. 'They'll find out you were in that room, and if you don't admit to it first, they'll be really suspicious and think you did kill him.'

'I don't know... No, you're right.'

'I'll come with you, but you must tell them the whole truth. Everything.'

CHAPTER THIRTY-THREE

RON AND ALISTAIR appeared relieved as they made space for Hendrik to come into the small room and left, closing the door behind them. Hendrik sat down heavily in the chair opposite Hale.

'I had a call from Arnhem, and they have identified the body in the river as Ken Craddock.'

'I see, and what will happen now?'

'I have been told to investigate from here. My boss will talk to yours.'

'Right.'

'I will also look for the missing drugs and diamonds that were taken by Jim Craddock's murderer.'

'Who shall I tell my boss to contact over there?'

'Commissaris van der Linden. My boss – she reports to him and he has been the formal liaison with the Met and your chief here in Suffolk. He is, as you put it, up to speed with all our news. Any more information here?'

Hale scanned the notes he'd taken during Ron and Alistair's chat. 'So far, we've heard that Jim threatened Ron, which

Alistair witnessed, and intended to take back the confession he made in the bar. After that, they say there was no further contact between them.'

'Do they have a motive to kill Jim?'

'Not a strong one. They appeared to believe his threat was nothing to worry about, or at least, that was the impression they gave.' Hale glanced at his notes again.

At that moment, the door opened and revealed Zoe with Ollie behind her. 'Is it a good time?' she asked.

'Absolutely fine, Zoe. Do come in, both of you, and take a seat.' Hale pointed to the chairs.

Hendrik appeared to dissolve from view as he sat behind them on the bed. Hale made eye contact with Steph, telling her to lead.

'Thank you for coming. You have some information for us?' Steph smiled.

Ollie nudged Zoe. 'Go on, tell them. You've done nothing wrong.'

Zoe squirmed uncomfortably in her chair. 'I went to see him after we arrived, and I was so angry and told him I wanted the truth and I wanted to hurt him so badly, but I didn't, honestly.'

Steph smiled. 'Now, go back to the beginning and tell us what happened, but slowly this time.'

Zoe swallowed, cleared her throat, and sat up straight.

'We got off the coach and I worked out which room he went to.'

Steph noticed she never said Jim's name. 'How did you do that?'

'I waited at the door from Reception along the corridor and counted the doors he passed and watched him go into his room.'

182

'Was he carrying his holdall when you saw him?'

Zoe frowned and closed her eyes. 'Yes, er – I think so – yes, he was.'

'What did you do next?'

'As his room was on the ground floor, I knew he'd have French windows, and as I didn't want to be seen, I went round the back through Reception and along the outside of the rooms.'

'And then?'

'I counted them until I saw him in his room watching TV. I knocked on the window and he let me in.'

Steph said nothing but maintained eye contact and waited for Zoe to continue.

'At first, he didn't want to talk to me, but I said I wouldn't leave until he'd told me the whole truth. He explained that Duncan had tripped up and cried out, and he'd hit Duncan with his rifle butt. He said he'd left him breathing, but I don't believe him.'

'Really?'

'No. He killed Duncan, all right.'

'That must have made you angry.'

Zoe's head dropped, but before she spoke, she lifted it and looked Steph in the eye. 'You have no idea. I was furious. He's the reason my family has suffered. All I wanted to do was to hurt him and make him suffer, too. So, I—'

Ollie reached out and grabbed Zoe's hand as she started to sob. 'Tell them what happened.'

Zoe rubbed her tears away with her sleeve and they waited while she controlled her breathing. 'I hit him. I slapped his face, but that was all, I swear. He was shocked, but he was fine. Honestly, he was. I wanted to hurt him really badly as he'd hurt Duncan. I wanted him to die, I admit it, but I didn't do it. You have to believe me.'

No one said anything as she looked in desperation from Steph to Hale for re-assurance and back to Steph again.

'I didn't kill him, honestly. He was breathing when I left him. He told me to fuck off out of it and leave him alone.'

'And did you go out through the garden or the corridor?'

'I went through the French doors.'

'Did you leave them open or closed? Can you remember?'

Once again, she closed her eyes, attempting to visualise what had happened.

'No, I left them open, I think. I can't remember. I didn't kill him. You have to believe me. You do believe me, don't you?'

CHAPTER THIRTY-FOUR

DEREK PEED against the wheel of Hale's car. A good job Hale wasn't there to see him. Steph had been greeted by Fiona, the dog lady, accompanied by her infectious grin and a herd of dogs barking excitedly as Steph waited at the five-bar wooden gate. Derek bounded through it, tail helicoptering, spotted the car, ran past her and marked it with his scent. Stowing Derek in the back, she drove off towards Oakwood.

Surprised at how much she missed Derek, she had decided not to stay the last night at The Crown but to miss supper and the trial and collect him. Concerned that if she told the truth about leaving early they would consider her barking mad, she mumbled something about needing to get back to her flat. From the grins that passed between Caroline and Hale, she suspected they had guessed the truth. Steph arranged to return the next morning to collect Hale and Hendrik and drop them off at the police station.

As she drove to Fiona's house in Wenhaston, Steph grinned to herself, feeling the excitement of the empty days before her. Although she worked in the college over half term holidays, she had the next two days off in lieu of the weekend she had given up going to Arnhem. She felt like a kid enjoying a couple of snow days off from school. A feeling of glorious freedom, totally unexpected, where time stretched out in front of her filled with endless opportunities.

Tomorrow, after delivering Hale and Hendrik to the station, she would take Derek for a long walk over the common before visiting the supermarket to find something to cook for their supper. They appeared to have adopted Hendrik, and he said he was looking forward to some English home cooking. Steak pie and mash would be a good choice, and she could always buy frozen pastry.

Vaughan Williams came on the radio – *The Lark Ascending*, or was it *Thomas Tallis*? She wasn't sure, and it didn't matter, but it made an appropriate accompaniment for her first drive back through the English countryside. In the dark she could make out the ribbons of mist swirling around the brightly lit Blythburgh Church, making it appear as if it was floating above the earth. Her few days in Holland had been lovely, but she was looking forward to being at home and back at college again.

The A12 was almost empty for once. Without thinking, instead of turning left towards Oakwood, she took the right turn and found herself on the road to Southwold. Should she turn around? No. Derek would love a walk and she could do with clearing her head. The beach it was then. Walking along the prom on a starlit night, the sea pounding the beach, would make her feel she was really home again.

Replaying the conversations with Ron and Zoe, she wasn't sure they were getting anywhere fast. Zoe had admitted to slapping Jim, so presumably it was her DNA on his face. But Ron hadn't been near Jim in the hotel – or had he? Hale had asked him if he had, but she was sure Ron had side-stepped the question. It would be a good idea to take their DNA for elimination to make sure. No way could she see Ron as a killer, and what was his motive? Ron, with Alistair in tow, and Zoe had been the only ones who had responded to Hale's appeal, so maybe they should start with them as potential suspects.

A discussion programme interrupted the romantic music, and as she changed station and raised her head, she was alarmed to find the glare of headlights reflected in her mirror and blinding her. The lights were higher up than a car, so it must be a van. It was getting closer to her boot.

She touched her brake as a warning that she was going to slow down, but the lights got even closer and brighter. The inside of her car was flooded with light. Again, she touched the brake a little to reduce speed – she knew she'd have to slow right down as she reached the sharp corner of the Z bend alongside the dyke.

Pressing on the brake harder as she took the corner, she was alarmed that whatever it was behind her hadn't appeared to slow at all. Just as she was convinced it was going to shunt her from the back, it swerved out and moved alongside her.

What a relief to lose the powerful beams of light from the mirror, but what madness to overtake on this corner! Could they be drunk? Relieved there was no traffic on the black road ahead, she slowed down further, allowing whatever it was to overtake her. But it didn't. It drew up beside her. She was right; it was a van. Although she couldn't see the driver, she saw a flash of yellow on its side as it matched her speed and they travelled side by side. What was it doing? Anything coming on the opposite side of the road would smash into it.

She pressed her foot harder on the brake so the van could move in front of her. Crunch! It drove into her door, forcing her to slew towards the edge of the road. Horrified, she hauled the car away from the dyke and pressed her brake foot to the floor so it could pass. But it didn't!

It crashed into her door again, this time maintaining its line. She struggled to hold her wheel to stay on the road. The van was the stronger. She felt herself going over the edge of the road and into the dyke, bonnet first. Derek's howls were louder than the squeal of metal on metal.

Steph screamed as she was thrown towards the windscreen. Her seat belt held her tight as the front of the car sank into the water, which invaded the foot well and slapped against her legs. The engine turned itself off. The lights, which had lit the murky water for a few seconds, went out. Despite her frantic pushing, the door wouldn't open, and the electric windows wouldn't work. She was trapped in a car filling with freezing cold water.

CHAPTER THIRTY-FIVE

STEPH STRUGGLED to pull her seat belt off. She peered in the driving mirror but could see nothing. The entire world around her was black. Derek must be trapped, lying against the bars between the boot and the back seats. The water had yet to reach him, but his whimpers told of his discomfort.

Thrown against the dashboard, she couldn't pull herself back into her seat, so leaned her forehead on the windscreen above the steering wheel. Thank goodness it hadn't smashed. The water had come up as far as her waist, then appeared to stop. Luckily, there hadn't been a massive amount of rain and the dyke was half full, so at least she wouldn't drown.

It hurt to breathe. She must have broken at least one rib when she'd smashed into the steering wheel. Taking a deep breath, she tested her lungs and squealed out loud. Shit! That hurt! She hoped neither lung was punctured. What did a punctured lung feel like? And what was that bone at the front of your chest? Maybe that was shattered? Why did it hurt so much – do bones have nerves?

The throbbing pain was getting worse, not helped by the

cold water, and it felt as if she'd done more damage than break a rib. Attempting to move her feet, she panicked when she realised they were jammed under the caved-in front of the car. Derek's desperate howls increased her pain.

'It's all right, boy, we'll get out of here. Don't worry.' Her words clearly soothed him, as he stopped whining and made a little whimpering sound. She tried to believe her own words. 'We'll be out soon.'

Although it was dark, she reached out and tilted the driving mirror in the hope she could see how Derek was doing. It didn't work – just solid black.

Her movement must have unbalanced the car, and, with a sickening lurch, the bonnet sank deeper into the muddy water. The freezing water crept up her body and increased the pain in her chest. Was it the pressure of the water on her broken ribs that was excruciating?

Derek, clearly sensing the shift in the car, began howling again. His screams tore her apart. She could cope, as she knew she'd be rescued, but he did not know what was happening. She would be rescued – wouldn't she? Taking a shallow breath and making an enormous effort, she tried calming him again. 'Someone will come and get us out soon, Derek.'

But would they? Hale wasn't expecting to see her until the morning, and this road at night was hardly busy. Anyway, what time was it? Trying to get rid of the awareness of the slowly rising water, now at mid-chest, she tried to work out the time. She'd left The Crown before eight, picked Derek up about nine-ish and would have reached here about nine thirty. How long had she been here? Was it ten or close to midnight?

Another sudden lurch and the water engulfed her shoulders. How much longer before it reached her mouth and nose? At least Derek was much higher and would be safe.

The car had moved, but she hadn't. Its weight must be forcing it down further into the mud. Her feet and legs were numb, but the pain in her chest was agony.

She had been in many threatening situations in her job – a man coming at her with a machete, a gun aimed at her, a knife thrown at her – she'd survived the lot only to have her breath stolen by sludgy, smelly water in a dyke. And to think of what chemicals or sewage might be in it – better not. They said your whole life swept before your eyes when you drowned. That hadn't happened yet, so surely there was hope – but did this count as drowning – this slow immersion in goodness knows what filth?

Steph relaxed her head on the windscreen while she could. She must save her energy for later when she'd have to hold her neck up above the vile smelling water to keep breathing. How much longer could she hold on? Did the car have any further to sink?

A howl from Derek made her lift her head, only to be blinded by a bright light coming towards her. Please, please let them see her down here. But could it be the van that had run her off the road? Her stomach lurched. Had the driver returned to finish her off? She was trapped – a sitting target.

The light moved and now appeared to be pointing at her. She squeezed her eyes shut. A knock on the window made her brace herself for the glass to be broken, and she waited for the smash and the shower of glass.

Instead of shattering glass, she heard shouting. 'Are you OK? Can you open the window?'

Aware of a dark head in her peripheral vision, she tried to turn her head – but ouch! It hurt! She shouted as loud as possible. 'Broken ribs – my legs are trapped. Electrics won't work.'

'We've sent for the fire brigade. They'll soon have you out. Don't worry!'

Don't worry? Why not? She was in pain, stuck in a dyke, and he was telling her not to worry? She almost smiled at the absurd comment. But she knew he was trying to keep her calm as she herself had done many times talking to those trapped in cars after accidents. Stop panicking. Someone would get her out of this now he was here, but would it be in time?

Taking as deep a breath as she dared, she shouted out as loud as she could, making sure she didn't move. 'Can you get my dog? In the boot.'

The shadow moved from the window. She could hear the boot opening and a whoosh of air come past her ears, but, as it did, the car moved forward and tipped. It forced her head further down the windscreen, and the steering wheel jammed painfully into her chest.

The car settled further in the mud, moving the water right up to her chin. She couldn't lift her head up any further. Keeping her lips tightly sealed, she breathed through her nose. Had she reached the bottom of the dyke? Was there further to go? The freezing water was getting even colder, and it was difficult to take even the tiniest breath through her nose.

The voice, now louder through the open boot, shouted. 'We've got your dog. He's safe. Hang on in there. They'll get you out.

She daren't reply in case she swallowed the filthy water. Where were they?

The voice through the boot continued to say something, but she couldn't hear what he was saying. Concentrating on keeping statue still, Steph forced her neck muscles to hold her head as high up the windscreen as possible above the edge of the water. But for how much longer?

The pain in her chest throbbed and was getting worse as the cold penetrated deeper into her body. She tried to stop shivering in case even that movement forced the car down further. Her chest screamed in pain, her neck ached, and she couldn't feel her legs or feet – she hoped they were still there – she must stay awake. They'd be here soon, and she could have a hot bath. The thought of sinking into the warm water made her relax. No longer able to fight the pain, she closed her eyes, and her world went black.

CHAPTER THIRTY-SIX

A PIERCING BRIGHT light forced Steph to squeeze her eyes tight, and an incessant beeping sliced through her pounding headache. Opening her eyes, she blinked against the searing beam of the doctor's torch.

'Welcome back. You're in hospital and you'll be fine.'

The James Paget hospital in Gorleston was at least a forty-five-minute drive from where she'd crashed. How had she got here? She remembered the car and the cold and drowning, but nothing else. She couldn't move her neck, or much of her body, and she was aware of tubes everywhere.

A smiling face filled her view. It belonged to a woman, with a kind face, about her age. 'I'm Dr Sykes. You've been in a car crash, Steph. So far, we've found three broken ribs and a minor fracture to your sternum, but no damage to your lungs, and, of course, you'll have massive bruising all over.'

Steph found it difficult to speak as the neck collar held her jaw up, so grunted something that sounded like thank you.

'We'll have that collar off you – you've not damaged your neck or spine and your legs should be fine once the bruising goes down. You're lucky.' She reached around Steph's neck and released the collar. Lucky wasn't the word Steph would use to describe the searing pain she felt all over. At least she was safe and dry. She tried to smile, but that hurt too.

'Where's Derek?'

Doctor Sykes turned her head and spoke to someone behind her. 'Right, Derek, you can have ten minutes, then she needs to sleep.' She replaced her stethoscope around her neck as she spoke to Steph. 'You need to rest, and we've given you powerful painkillers to help. See you later. Ten minutes, Derek.'

Hale's grinning face came into view. He leaned down and kissed her forehead. 'You had us worried for a while there. Thought you were never going to wake up.' He pulled up a chair, leaned across and held her hand. The one without all the tubes.

'Derek?'

'He's fine too. Back with Fiona, who sends her love, by the way.'

Relieved, Steph sighed.

'I'm sure you care more about that mutt than me.'

She squeezed his hand, not strong enough for a banter match.

'What were you doing, driving into the dyke? My car's a write off, by the way.'

She took a deep breath and winced – ouch – that hurt. 'Driving to the beach – suddenly full head lights – a van on my tail. I slowed, it got closer. On the straight it overtook – slammed into me, forced me off the road into the dyke.'

'Ah! That explains the battered driver's door. Did you see the number plate?'

'Get real, Hale.' She closed her eyes. 'It had a yellow logo or picture or something on the side. Saw it in my lights. All I remember. What happened?'

Hale told her about the efficient work of the firefighters who had pulled her and the car out of the dyke, thanks to the man who had stopped to help. She had been unconscious throughout.

'I bet the van driver was drunk and left the scene. No cameras on that stretch, but we may spot him turning off the A12 onto the A1095. There's one on that corner.'

'Not an accident. Deliberate. Had two attempts at shoving me off the road.'

Concerned, Hale frowned. 'Deliberate? Really?'

Finding it difficult to talk, Steph moistened her lips with her tongue. Hale held a bent straw poking out of a beaker of water to her mouth. 'Here, drink this, then I'll go and leave you to rest in peace.'

She swallowed the water gratefully and struggled to hold her drooping eyelids open. With a shudder, she recalled it almost had been resting in peace forever. The painkillers were doing their job, and she was drifting off.

A rustling made her open her eyes to see Hendrik appearing behind a gigantic bunch of flowers. 'Hi, Steph. Wow! You've been in the wars all right. Here, brought you some flowers.' He placed them on her stomach, making her feel even more like a dead body.

Hale swooped them off. 'I'll see if I can find a vase.' He turned to Hendrik. 'I thought I asked you to stay in the car.'

'Sorry. Got bored and thought you'd like these.' He grinned at Steph, who tried to smile back.

She murmured, 'Beautiful. Thanks.'

'Did you say it was deliberate? Someone did this to you?'

Her eyes closing against her will, all Steph could do was nod and grunt. Through the mist she heard Hale say, 'And it was my car, so whoever tried to kill Steph presumed it was me driving that car, not her.'

CHAPTER THIRTY-SEVEN

'ARE you sure you're up to this?'

'Yes, I just need to fix this cushion between my chest and the seat belt.'

Steph manoeuvred the softest of her feather cushions into place so her sore sternum and ribs wouldn't get jogged. Comfortable at last, she exhaled the pain away loudly, relaxing as it subsided.

'You don't need to come, you know.' Hale dropped into his seat, gently put his arm on hers and leaned across, looking concerned.

'It's driving me bonkers staring at four walls. The doctor said I could go out if I felt better and I do. Let's go.'

'If you're sure? I'll go steady.'

After her short stay in hospital, Steph had been relieved to be discharged on the understanding that she'd rest. It hurt like hell, but she found the boredom hurt more. Whizzing past the trees on the A12, she immersed herself in the rush of gold, with the occasional deep crimson splash of a dogwood or a maple squashed between the oaks and silver birches.

The colours appeared even more vibrant as she revelled in being alive and out in the world again. Only now she was safe did the idea of how close she'd come to drowning push its way into her head. An involuntary shudder attracted Hale's attention.

'Is this too much for you? We can always turn back.'

'No way. I'm fine.' She lied, trying to smile, but that hurt, too. 'Anyway, I want to hear what he has to say.'

At last, they reached the village of Snape where Hale parked her car outside a single-storey cottage. The sun glinted off the polished edges of the grey flint, which made it stand out alongside its red brick neighbours.

Gingerly, Steph removed the seat belt and the cushion and allowed Hale to help her out onto the side of the road. It was more painful than sitting in the flat, but it felt so good to be out. Taking the smallest breath, she savoured the taste of autumn bonfires and a peppery tang from one of the many cottage garden plants. Holding on to Hale's arm, she picked her way over the brittle leaves that covered the ancient flagstones leading to the front door.

The recent addition of a white painted wooden porch to the cottage offered protection from the powerful east wind, and, under its shelter, she turned to absorb the view of the marshes with their reeds swaying in the breeze. The front door, also recently painted, opened to reveal Ron.

'Amazing view, isn't it?'

'Yes, wonderful.' Steph stepped round to meet his eyes, which registered shock.

'Good heavens, what on earth have you been doing?'

She had been so concerned about her injured ribs and sternum she had forgotten the bruises on her face, having avoided the mirror.

'Oh, this? My car decided to see if it could drive through a dyke. It looks worse than it is.'

'Do come in, please.' Ron, who didn't look convinced by her explanation, shook his head but stood back. They entered the perfect cottage sitting room, complete with rocking chair, the walls filled with small watercolour landscapes and elegant displays of miniatures.

'Wow, Ron! That's quite a collection!' Steph peered as far as her chest would let her at the minuscule portraits of nineteenth century men and women.

'After Jane died, I had time to go to auctions and indulge my passion, which we'd both shared until she became ill. May I offer you coffee?'

'That would be lovely.'

'Why don't I take you out to the back? It's sheltered and it's a shame to miss such a lovely morning.'

Ron led them through an old pine door, with its distinctive black wrought iron Suffolk latch and long arrowhead hinges, into a spotless modern galley kitchen. They progressed through what appeared to be a lean-to extension with a pine table and four chairs, through an open stable door to a courtyard.

Surrounded on three sides by pitted russet bricks, they entered a perfect sun trap. The cushions on the wooden chairs were warm, and they relaxed in the soft sunlight as they listened to Ron making coffee in the kitchen.

They sat at a beautiful mosaic table with an enormous fish created in turquoise, grey and blue fragments of tile. Surrounded by terracotta pots lined up around the walls, Steph was impressed by the enormous collection of herbs, usually found in a specialist garden centre. Ron appeared to have some fascinating ways of spending his time and managing his life.

He arrived with a tray holding a cafetière and three mugs

and, after handing them out, settled in the chair opposite. Steph expected there would be the inevitable dancing around the handbags of small talk until they got to the message he'd summoned them to hear, so was shocked when, after the first gulp of coffee, Ron announced. 'I've asked you here as I'd like to confess to murdering Jim Craddock.'

CHAPTER THIRTY-EIGHT

STEPH WASN'T the only one to experience shock, as Hale's open mouth showed. Ron snatched a breath and was about to speak when Hale interrupted him.

'I'm not sure what you're about to say, Ron, but you do realise that I'm a police officer investigating a murder and what you say to us cannot be taken back but may be used in a court of law?'

'Yes. That's why I've asked you here. I'm fully aware of what I'm doing and about to say to you.'

Hale pulled out his phone, placed it on the table between them, and pressed record. 'In that case, I am recording what you say, and it must be done under caution, you understand?'

'Completely.'

Hale recited the caution, introduced all those present for the recording, and handed over to Ron, who appeared as calm as ever.

Ron sipped his coffee, took a deep breath, glanced at the phone then spoke. 'I would like to confess to the murder of Jim

Craddock. I killed him in his room at The Crown Hotel, Oakwood. I did so to avenge his years of lies and deception about the murder of Duncan Shaw he committed as we escaped from the battle for Arnhem.'

'Will you tell us how you did it?' Hale peered at his phone to check it was recording.

'When we got to the hotel, I noted which room he was in, and when everyone was unpacking and getting ready for dinner, I killed him.'

Hale frowned. 'Could you get into a little more detail, Ron? How did you get into his room?'

'I saw there were cameras in the corridor, so I went out of my French windows into the garden, walked along the path outside the bedrooms and knocked on his window. He was watching the TV – horse racing, I think it was – and told me to F-off. I continued to knock on the window, so he opened the door and I went into his room and killed him.'

'Just like that? You must have had a conversation or perhaps a struggle?'

'A brief conversation, yes. I told him he was a lying bastard and had ruined Zoe's family by taking away a life he had no right to do. He wasn't even sorry but defended himself with the spurious argument that he had taken one life to save many.'

'Well, he had a point, didn't he?'

'Did he? Don't believe a word of it. He made that up to excuse what he'd done. I've talked to some of the men who saw that incident, and although Duncan needed help, he wasn't making as much noise as Craddock claimed. Yes, he did the right thing taking him back for medical attention, but I'm now convinced he did it to get him away from the rest of the men so he could kill him.'

Ron finished his coffee and held up the cafetière towards them. They shook their heads. 'No thank you, Ron.' Steph said.

After topping up his mug and drinking a few mouthfuls, he placed it back precisely on its wet ring on the tail of the blue mosaic fish. Steph and Hale said nothing, waiting for him to continue his confession.

'He'd resented Duncan, he said so, and in his twisted mind, he'd decided Duncan was responsible somehow for the mess we were in, and he wanted to get rid of him. Maybe he'd hated Duncan ever since he married Mary. Craddock knew her too. He said so. Maybe he wanted to get his revenge on the man who stole her. We'll never know the truth now, will we?'

Clearly, Hale wanted him to return from the cul-de-sac he was exploring and return to The Crown. 'Let's get back to what happened in Jim's room. You accused him of lying, then what did you do?'

'I pushed him. He fell on the bed and that's when I did it.'

'What?'

'Smothered him with the pillow. It didn't last long – his struggling, I mean. Then he lay there as if he was asleep, and I left.'

Hale frowned. 'A few more details would be helpful, Ron. Did you see his luggage in the room?'

Apparently perplexed at this question, Ron frowned and closed his eyes, trying to visualise the room. 'Yes, I think so. I wasn't looking for it, but – yes –it was a mess, like Jim. You know, stuff pulled higgledy-piggledy out of his holdall.'

'The navy one, right?'

'Yes, that's right.'

'And was he wearing his shoes?'

Once again Ron frowned and appeared a little irritated. 'Yes. Why?'

Hale paused, checked the phone was recording, then said in a loud voice. 'Perhaps you can now tell us why you're hoping we'd believe this pack of lies.'

CHAPTER THIRTY-NINE

RON GASPED. His head drooped, but he said nothing.

They paused, giving him space.

'I could charge you with wasting police time, if that would make you feel any better.' At Hale's threatening tone, Ron raised his head, and they could see his eyes brimming with tears.

'How did you know?'

'Too many things that you didn't know. We're not the plods we're made out to be, you know.'

Looking sheepish, Ron blushed. 'I'm sorry. I didn't mean to offend you... but now I see how it could be taken that I did. Sorry.' He pulled a tissue from his trouser pocket and blew his nose.

'Well then, perhaps you'll tell us what made you confess.'

'Before I do, would you like another coffee?'

'Please, that would be great.' Steph accepted Ron's offer so he could have some time to regain his dignity.

It appeared as if all the blood in Ron's face had drained away, leaving him ashen. His breathing was laboured – he was almost gasping for breath – and his hand was shaking. It would have taken quite an effort to rehearse his story and cope with the stress of anticipating his arrest. Better to give him some time to calm down; they'd get nothing from him in this state.

The little vein to the right of Hale's forehead stood out, and she could see it pulsing. He was finding it difficult to remain calm and couldn't afford to lose time on a wild goose chase like this. Reaching across, she squeezed his hand, and he put his arm around her shoulders. 'Ouch! That hurt!'

'Sorry. Forgot.'

'Any movement kills me.'

'Perhaps I should move back to my flat and demote Hendrik to the sofa!'

'Don't think we need to go that far, do we?' She tried to hit his thigh, but the pain braked her halfway. Hale laughed but assumed a serious face as Ron returned with another pot of coffee, which he poured into their mugs, and handed round a plate of large chocolate chip cookies.

'This could be seen as bribing a police officer, you know.' Hale winked at Ron, who, for the first time, appeared to relax.

'Right.' Hale reached for his phone and stowed it away in his pocket. 'I'll delete the recording later. Now tell us what you're up to.'

Looking less terrified, Ron sat back in the sunshine and closed his eyes for a moment. 'I did it for Zoe.'

'Why?' Steph took a bite out of the enormous cookie.

'She came to see me before we both came to see you. She told me what she'd done and was scared it was her slapping him that caused his death, and she was terrified. I told her an old man like him would need more than her little tap to kill him, but she was convinced the shock of it could have contributed to his death.'

With a gentle swoosh, Steph removed the crumbs off her chest. 'If you were convinced she couldn't have killed Jim, even accidentally, what made you invent this confession?'

Once again, Ron looked embarrassed. 'Now don't take this the wrong way, Hale, but I was concerned that her admission might lead to the police hanging it on her.'

Now it was Hale's turn to redden up. 'For one thing, we gave up hanging people in the last century, and second, I can't believe you would think we would be so lazy as to grab her as the murderer and stop investigating.'

'Sorry. I panicked and thought if I confessed, then she would get off – free. I'm an old man at the end of my life. She's at the start of hers. I have a heart condition and high blood pressure – there was every chance I wouldn't even make it to a trial. She's a good kid, who's had a rough deal in life. I know it didn't all stem from the loss of Duncan and what that bastard did, but if he'd been helped by the medics in that field instead of dying, her family might have had a different story.'

Hale frowned. 'Ron, what you did was annoying and a waste of my time, but also a really generous gesture. Now it's time to come clean and tell us all you know.'

'I feel ashamed and stupid for trying it. Sorry, Hale. I shouldn't have underestimated you, but she's a good kid and deserves a bit of luck. I mean, finding out that reptile Ken could be her father is enough to give anyone a motive for murder.'

'And are you about to confess to making him disappear?' Hale sounded as if he was only half joking.

'Why? Is he dead then?' When Hale didn't reply, Ron continued. 'No, I wasn't involved there. But you might want to talk to that Judy – Tom's daughter. She spent a lot of time with Ken before he disappeared. I think they were – what do they say – an item? I also saw her having several chats with Jim Craddock in corners where they couldn't be overheard.'

'Thanks, Ron. We'll look into it. You have my number. If you can recall when you saw them together or anything else that might help, get in touch. Thanks for the coffee. We should be getting back.'

In the car, Hale let out an explosive sigh. 'Well, that was a complete waste of time!'

'But you can't help liking him. His heart's in the right place and it got me out into the sunshine. Suppose you'll be going back to work?'

'You suppose right.' About to pat her thigh, he remembered just in time and froze, his hand in mid-air.

'You know, I'm not convinced. There's something he's not telling us. Would he really risk facing a murder charge for what Zoe told us? There must be more.' Steph picked a stray crumb off her tee shirt.

'You're right. I think we need to see Zoe again, and those last comments of Ron's were interesting.'

'They could have been a distraction to get us off Zoe?' Steph moved the cushion to give more protection when they drove around corners.

'Could be – or there could be something in it. I think I'll get Johnson to visit Ron and see if he can be more precise about what he saw going on between Judy and the Craddocks.'

CHAPTER FORTY

'YOU DID WHAT?'

Zoe strained to hear Ron's voice through her phone, as he must be moving around while he was speaking to her and his voice kept disappearing. He sounded breathless and stressed.

'Why did you do it?'

Another long explanation with tiny, annoying gaps, but she got the gist of it. 'They haven't arrested you? That's good, but Ron, you shouldn't have done it... You're such a lovely man and I really appreciate what you tried to do for me, but I'll sort it. Please don't worry. I'll come over and see you next week, promise.'

Switching the phone off, Zoe threw herself into her usual armchair.

'Everything all right, love?' Her gran carried the ironing board and a pile of ironing she'd just unpegged from the line. 'Good day for getting the washing done – that wind dried these sheets in no time. I'll get them ironed before they get bone dry.'

Zoe grabbed the ironing board from her gran, slotted the legs into the brackets and upended it.

'Thanks, love. Now you must tell me all about Arnhem.'

'You sit down. I can do it.'

'What was that?'

'I said I'll do it – you sit down.'

Clearly Gran was relieved and collapsed into her armchair opposite. 'You're sure? There's only our bed linen, so it shouldn't take you long. And while you're doing it, you can tell me all about your trip to Arnhem.'

Zoe sighed. How many times had she told her over the last two days? Plugging the iron in, she rested it on the metal bars at the end of the ironing board, spread the first sheet over it and prepared to repeat her story once again – edited, of course. She didn't want her gran to be distressed by the full truth, although would she remember it even if Zoe told her?

Today was a bad day. Gran was convinced her mother, Mary, was living with them. Earlier, she believed a squirrel had moved into her wardrobe and she was scared to open it to get out her clothes. When Zoe had got back from The Crown, a trail of cups, full to the brim with cold tea, were littered all over the house. When Zoe collected them and put them in the dish-washer, she found the house keys in the cutlery basket.

Having been away for a few days, it hit Zoe for the first time how Gran's hearing had got worse and how forgetful she was. The excuse of 'senior moments' had covered most things when they were together. However, while she'd been away, there appeared to have been a change, or maybe she hadn't wanted to see what was happening before she left?

Was leaving Gran alone in the house becoming too much of a risk? Zoe hoped to go to college, and if this was the beginning of dementia or Alzheimer's, would she be able to go? Perhaps she should visit the GP and see if she could get some support – if Gran would accept someone with her in the house.

Every time Zoe hinted at her needing company, or help in the house, Gran had pooh-poohed the idea and told her she was fine.

When she'd finished repeating the sanitised version of Duncan's story, Gran wiped a tear from her eyes. 'Thank you, love. It's good to know he didn't suffer. He didn't, did he?'

Zoe swallowed the bile that had risen to her throat. 'No. He was so weak from days without food and water, as we know from his writing, then when the asthma attack came, he had no strength to fight it and he died quickly. That's what the man who was with him said.' She found lying to her gran so difficult.

'And who did you say was with him?'

Zoe placed the smooth sheet on the seat of her chair and pulled the duvet cover from the pile to iron next. 'A man called Jim Craddock.'

'Come again. Who did you say it was?'

'Jim Craddock.' Zoe almost shouted, making sure her gran could see her lips.

Gran frowned. 'No need to shout, dear. Jim Craddock? I know that name... Jim Craddock. Of course, Uncle Jim... Played hide and seek... And he had a little terrier dog he brought round... Now what was its name?' Zoe got on with the ironing while Gran closed her eyes to concentrate on recalling the name.

'Craddock, Craddock, that rings a bell... Ken, was it?'

'That's right. Ken's Jim Craddock's son.'

'Of course, Ken, that's it. He courted your mother and she was smitten all right. Dark curly hair, go to bed eyes and a grin that could charm the birds out of the trees. He did for her, he did. Swept her off her feet, and one day, she upped and left... Just like that... Let's forget about him. Tell me about Arnhem.'

Gran's voice wavered, and this time she drifted off, making

little grunting snores. Zoe finished the ironing and took the pile upstairs to the linen cupboard.

Despite tiptoeing, the crash as she folded the ironing board woke her gran. 'Charming, but a nasty piece of work, that Ken. I could see right through him and told Jo so, but would she listen? She changed when she was with him. Became a different person... not my Jo. Took no notice of you... Neglected you, she did ... No, we were better off without her in the long run.'

While Gran appeared alert and had her eyes open, Zoe sat on the arm of her chair, placing her arm around her shoulders, and asked the question to which she was dreading the answer. 'Tell me, Gran, was Ken Craddock my father?'

With difficulty Gran hauled herself out of the chair, checked her balance and headed towards the kitchen. 'What did you say, love? Look at the time.' She pointed to the old oak clock on the wall. 'Must get the dinner on. Can't sit here chatting all day.'

CHAPTER FORTY-ONE

STEPH JERKED AWAKE. Was it the doorbell or the noise from the train she was chasing? It rang again, this time longer, and Derek's barking convinced her it wasn't her dream. Wincing, she struggled off the sofa and, trying only to move her legs, shuffled to the door.

She had been surprised how exhausted she felt after the short trip to Ron's. The pain from her ribs was intense and the normal dose of co-codamol hadn't touched it. Checking the instructions on the box, she had taken a further half dose and was at last able to breathe without a shooting pain. Hale had spent the rest of the day working with the team and left her in the flat to rest. At last, she'd found a comfortable position on the sofa, wrapped in a blanket, with Derek curled up at her feet, and had fallen asleep over her book.

Opening the door of the flat, Derek barked at a small, dark shape through the stained glass of the house front door and jumped up, scratching the oak varnish.

'Down, Derek!' He stood alert, head wedged against the

door, tail wagging, so he would be first through the moment she opened it. As soon as the gap was wide enough, he squeezed through. Steph's attempt to catch his collar made her gasp out loud, but she managed to haul him back from jumping up at Zoe.

'Hi, Steph, I didn't know you had a dog.' Bending down to stroke Derek, she smiled up at Steph. 'Whatever have you done to your face? Have you had an accident?'

'Yes. I drove into a dyke, but I'll be fine,' she lied.

'Sorry to come round like this, but could I have a word with you, please?'

For a moment, Steph considered the procedure she should follow. Although she was a Civilian Investigator and was helping the police on the case, she couldn't make an arrest and, in theory, she should stop the conversation now and get Zoe to talk to Hale at the station. But then, she didn't know what Zoe had come round for, and perhaps she would tell her more here than she would in the police station. She stood back from the door.

'Sure, come through. Don't worry, Derek will follow you. Can I get you a drink or anything?'

Zoe followed her into the flat. 'No, I'm fine, thanks. What a lovely room!' She stood on the threshold and scanned the room. 'I love your art déco lamps. The copper goes so well in here, doesn't it?'

Slightly taken aback by Zoe's high-level social skills – Steph was sure she had been nowhere near as confident when she was her age – she indicated one of the fireside seats, and carefully lowered herself into the one opposite.

'How did you find out where I live?'

'Everyone knows everything in Oakwood!' Zoe laughed. 'I thought you knew that!'

Feeling a little put in her place, Steph wriggled around until it stopped hurting.

'Now, how can I help you?'

'I had a phone call from Ron earlier. He told me what he tried to do, and I want to explain to you what happened.'

The knot in Steph's stomach tightened. Should she be doing this? 'Look, Zoe, you may not know but I was a police officer in a former life, and I now help the police as a Civilian Investigator. I need to warn you that if what you say has anything to do with Jim Craddock's death, you will need to make a statement to the police, and I can't promise to keep anything you say confidential.'

'That's fine. I'd like to talk to you first anyway – I have nothing to hide.'

Steph settled herself back in the chair and held the cushion to her front. 'Broken ribs – feel better with this.'

'First of all, I didn't kill Jim – or didn't mean to. I mean, he may have died after I left, but I didn't hit him hard. I did push him and he fell back on the bed, but he was breathing when I left, I swear.'

'Perhaps you'd better tell me all the stuff you left out, Zoe, because you didn't tell us the whole truth, did you?'

'I couldn't with Ollie there. I don't want him to find out what I found out at Arnhem.'

Zoe's pale face and anxious expression made her look like a small child, and Steph had the urge to hug her and re-assure her, but that would hurt too much. 'And you're now going to tell me the truth?'

'Yes. I told Ron. He's such a lovely man, and he's the only one who knows it all. Now I need to tell you.'

Steph sat mesmerised, saying nothing as Zoe recounted her meeting with Ken and his revelations about his relationship with her mother based on her drug use and sexual exploitation. She told Steph how scared she was when he blackmailed her into carrying a parcel home – which she insisted she hadn't done – and how he claimed to be her father. She repeated the story Jim had told her about how he'd killed Duncan. Then she stopped.

'You must have been so upset with Jim and Ken. If you told Ron all this, you can see why he assumed you could have killed Jim – you have such a strong motive.'

'Yes. I know. I really regret going to Arnhem at all. I can't even tell the truth about Duncan to my gran, as she's... losing her memory... and if she did understand, I can't tell her that Duncan was killed by that snake.'

Tears flowed unnoticed down Zoe's cheeks and dripped off her chin. Steph couldn't bear to get up, so waved at the box of tissues beside her on the table. Zoe got up, pulled one out, blew her nose, and wiped her face.

'But you haven't told us the whole truth about what happened in that hotel room, have you?'

'Not quite. I couldn't with Ollie there. After he told me about Duncan's murder, he went on to my family. That's the bit I can't let Ollie know. He told me he'd had what sounded like an affair with Duncan's wife, Mary. I can't confirm it with Gran. She was too little, but she remembers "Uncle Jim" coming to the house.'

'I see. That must have been painful.'

'It was. He kills Duncan, then makes a move on his wife when she was so vulnerable. He was a total shit. Then there was Ken.'

'Ken?'

'He confirmed what Ken had told me. It was disgusting. He said that Ken was a real man who could attract any woman he wanted. My mother fell for him and did drugs and dealt for him. He said she was a good fuck and why did she want to be saddled with a stupid kid like me when she could be fucked all day by his Ken? That's when I lost it.' Zoe burst into tears. Steph waited for her to calm down.

'And?'

'And then I slapped his face to shut him up, and I pushed him – not hard – honestly, it wasn't hard – and he fell back on the bed. He didn't hit his head on the wall or anything, I promise. He fell on the bed and lay there across it.' She shut her eyes. 'His head was on the edge of the pillow, I'm sure. And then I left through the doors into the garden, like I said earlier.'

At last, Zoe stopped, and Steph watched her blow her nose and blot her face once again. Her eyes were swollen, an angry red, and stood out against her pale face. She sounded convincing, but it was suspicious that she'd revealed her story in instalments – each part forced out only when she had to explain it.

'And the package? Did Ken give you anything?'

'No. I didn't see him again after you came to the café. What was in it? Drugs?'

'We're not sure. What did your gran say about Ken being your father?'

'She avoided the question. The idea of being linked to that family makes me sick.'

'Don't you have a birth certificate?'

'Yes, but it has a gap where my father's name is.' She paused and looked at Steph from below her eyelids, as if weighing her up. 'Can I ask you a favour?'

'It depends what it is.'

'You've taken my DNA, as I was in Jim's room. Is there any way you can check to see if I'm related to him?'

'It must be part of the investigation... so I'll see what I can do to help. Now, have you really told me everything? Is there anything else to do with Ken or Jim Craddock that you haven't told me?'

'No, nothing else, that's the truth. I mean—'

The door opened and Hale stepped in, pushing down an excited Derek, who must have been hoping for a walk. 'Hello, Zoe. Good to see you. You were next on my list.'

CHAPTER FORTY-TWO

STEPH WAS WOKEN by the sound of the key turning in the lock. She must have drifted off again.

'Hi, come and give me a kiss.' She wiped some dribble from her chin – not a good look.

'Pleased you've missed me.' A grinning Hendrik appeared.

'Hendrik! You've got a key?'

'Here.' He held up a key ring and jangled it in front of her. 'It is with the keys to Hale's flat.'

Hale had let Hendrik use his flat while he was in Suffolk. Clearly, he was puzzled by her reaction. 'Sorry. Should I not have used it?'

'No. Sorry. Side effects of these painkillers. I was asleep, and you made me jump.'

Hendrik came closer and bent down to examine her face. 'Oh, Steph, how you have been battered. It looks worse today.'

'Thanks, Henk. That's made me feel so much better!'

'Hale thinks they were after him or me.'

'So I shouldn't take it personally? Anyway, please sit down. Can I get you a drink while we wait for Hale?'

Hendrik frowned. 'Don't move. I can get it if you tell me how.'

She nodded towards the kitchen area in the open plan room. 'Fridge under the island, glasses in the cupboard above the taps.'

'Anything for you?'

She shook her head. Hendrik found the fridge and returned with a bottle of lager, plonking himself down in the chair opposite. He took a large gulp from the bottle.

'Umm! Good! Now, where is Hale and your hound?'

'He's walking Zoe back home.'

'Ah! Our beautiful young suspect, Zoe.'

Steph tried to sit up straight to make her point and gasped – it hurt. 'She's not really a suspect, is she? More of a victim.'

'Perhaps you are right.'

The door flew open and Derek bounced on her legs. 'Ouch! Derek! Get down.'

Hale breezed in. 'Ah, Henk, you're here. I'm glad I ordered enough for the three of us. Come to the table while it's hot. Steph, I'll sort it – you concentrate on making yourself comfortable.'

Soon the table was crowded with the foil containers from the local Chinese restaurant, which had a great reputation for its crispy duck, and the three munched happily on their supper. As they finished, Hale got up to refresh Hendrik's beer and to grab another for himself.

'Right, Hendrik. What have you been up to in the wilds of Ipswich?'

They listened while Hendrik told them of the complex dealing lines he'd tracked from Holland to Suffolk and to London via Ipswich. 'With your man Johnson's help, we have found four – you might say major players, with many young people below them working to move the drugs on.'

'Four? Are they local?' Hale started clearing away their plates.

'I think so. They get the drugs from Holland, divide them up and pass them to their people who run the lines to Ipswich and Norwich and the places between. I need a map to show you the places they go to. It is a strong operation.'

'And how long do you think it's been going on?'

'More than a year, and I'm convinced Ken was the boss.'

'But until a week ago, there was no record of him visiting Holland.'

'None. He was the boss here. Now we have lost him and his father, we need to trace the other names.'

'And have you made progress on the diamonds?'

'We have the name of a dealer in – what is it called? – your jewellery area – something garden, and your Met watches his shop.'

Steph felt more alive after her supper and assumed the effect of the drugs was wearing off. 'Hatton Garden?'

'Yes – Hatton Garden.'

'Have you traced the drugs and diamonds Jim carried home?'

'No. I found the tracker dumped in his empty bag. It was in a bin in the park beside the hotel. Nothing in it.' Hendrik took another swig from his bottle.

Hale frowned, and Steph realised this was news to him. 'I didn't know about the tracker.'

'I'm sure I told you.' Hendrik looked puzzled. 'On the coach when we talked about the plan.'

Hale shrugged his shoulders. 'So, now we have four people

we know are involved with the drugs. That's good progress. Did Johnson know them?'

'No. But Johnson said he would help me.' He darted a glance at Hale and must have seen his deep frown. 'If that is OK with you?'

'So, you've got on well with Johnson, then?'

'A good man, I think. He knows all the people here, so could help find the group. It was through him I got the names.'

'Right. I'll talk to him tomorrow and ask him to continue working with you.'

'Any closer to finding the killer yet?'

Hale piled up the empty cartons and took them over to the bin. 'No. A slight distraction earlier today, but no real progress.'

'But you have Zoe, the main suspect?'

Hale rinsed the plates and stacked them in the dishwasher. 'I walked her home after she spoke with Steph.' He turned to Steph. 'What did you make of her story?' He stopped and waited for her to respond.

'I was convinced she was telling the truth, and she didn't kill Jim. I know her story has come out in instalments, but I understand why – I'm convinced she didn't kill him.' Steph passed her water glass to Hale for a re-fill.

'But Zoe was the last person to see Ken before he disappeared,' said Hendrik, 'and the last one to see Jim. That makes her a main suspect, no? We have evidence of no other person, do we?'

'Not yet, but we will.' Hale resumed his seat at the table. 'Now tell me the names of the four locals you've got – see if I recognise any of them.'

Hendrik rooted in his jacket pocket and pulled out a small notebook, which he opened and passed to Hale, who read them out loud. 'Hartfield, Brown, Vickers and Ridgeon – no – none of them rings a bell.'

CHAPTER FORTY-THREE

ONCE AGAIN, a ringing intruded on her dream. Steph shook herself awake and grabbed the phone before it rang off. She had to stop taking these pain killers. It was like living a half-life, permanently drowsy and dropping off to sleep.

'Hello.'

'Sorry, did I wake you?' Hale sounded concerned.

'No – yes, but it doesn't matter. Getting so bored, feeling like this.'

'I've got news. We've spotted the white van that hit you. I'm coming to get you so you can see. That is, if you're up to it?'

'Please. Take me away from these four walls. Derek and I are going spare.'

'Right. I'll be there in twenty minutes.'

Struggling out of her dressing gown, Steph stood under the shower, relaxing as the warm water flowed over her body and eased her pain. The bruises that spanned her back and right round her chest were now starting to turn yellow. At least the blue swellings around her eyes and cheek were fading, and the shape of her face was returning to normal, so she no longer resembled a hamster.

She was able, just, to raise her arms to wash her hair, which was limp and greasy, but she wasn't sure if she could manage to lift the hairdryer long enough to dry it. Oh well, she'd have to let it dry naturally.

Hale appeared as she was almost ready. 'Well done. You're getting there.' He appeared excited and energetic, as he always did when he was making progress.

He held out her jacket, eased it over her shoulders, then fixed the lead to a jumping Derek. 'Come on, mutt. We may even take you for a walk by the harbour.'

It was great to be out in the air and breathe in the crisp air of another bright autumn day. They had been so lucky with this weather. This was the driest spot in England and, although the farmers needed the rain, it was wonderful to feel the warmth of the sun and look up at the empty blue skies. Once again, the cushion helped her cope with the pain during the drive through Oakwood, and they were soon in a relatively quiet police station.

Although it was Sunday, three members of Hale's team were working on tracing the dealers Hendrik and Johnson had uncovered. Their heads were down at a row of computers arranged in front of a large board on the wall, where a complicated family tree traced the links from Holland to Suffolk. As yet, there were no photos alongside the names.

Hale led Derek into his office, where he fished a treat for him out of his bottom drawer, and Steph sat in the chair he'd pulled out for her. He found the section on the CCTV he was looking for and pointed to what looked like his Renault driving away from the direction of the dog lady's house. It was difficult to make it out in the darkness, but the shape was right.

As it cleared one of the cameras on the A12, they could see the number plate and a blurred shadow at the wheel. Soon a white van came into view and appeared to be following Steph, keeping about three cars behind.

The Renault turned onto the A1095, followed by the van. As it turned the corner, it was clear the van was now close, very close, behind the car, its full beams lighting the back of the Renault. Then both disappeared out of the camera's range and that was that. Steph shuddered. Seeing it shocked her, and once again she realised how close she had come to drowning.

'Can we see that part again when he turns the corner, and the camera catches the front of the car – but slow?' Hendrik's voice made her jump. She had not seen him enter Hale's office. Hale rewound the pictures.

'Should we also watch to see him come back again?' Hendrik knelt down beside her to get a better look at the screen.

Hale fiddled around with the buttons. 'No, he doesn't come back.'

'But you said Southwold was at the end of the road.'

'It is, but there are at least three left turns that would let him get away through Wangford or Wrentham to the A12. We can try to pick him up there and see where he goes. Anyway, how are you getting on, Henk?'

Hendrik stood up, his hand on his hip, and rubbed his back. Surely his back wasn't stiff at his age.

'Not too good. The names we have don't fit anyone on your records and even your main list—'

'The Electoral Roll?'

Hendrik flexed his back and stretched up to the ceiling. 'Yes, that's what Johnson called it. Can't find them anywhere. Perhaps we need to go to the Met. Ah! Again – you have it.'

They all leaned in close to the monitor to watch the start of the van's chase.

'Stop! There!' Hendrik pointed to the screen.

He moved it back a few frames and the picture on the screen was frozen showing the side of the van.

'Not in colour – but the logo looks like B–something... Carpets... L...Lowestoft, I think that says.' Hale moved his hand towards Steph's shoulder but changed his mind and let it rest on the back of the chair. 'Do you think that could be the logo you saw?'

Steph shook her head. 'Honestly, Hale, there was no way I could read it as it flashed past. I thought it was yellow as it moved beside me. That's all.'

'At least now we have a lead to follow.' Hale's excitement was palpable.

They watched the freeze frames jump from one to the next, until Steph shouted, 'Stop!'

'What is it?' Hale followed her finger, now pointing at the screen.

'The driver! Look! That's Ken!'

CHAPTER FORTY-FOUR

'KEN? BUT HE'S DEAD!' Hendrik voiced what they were all thinking.

'Print it off and let's see if there's a better angle. It's blurred, but you must agree it does look like him.' Steph pointed to the screen.

Hale flipped through a few more screens; he found two more side angles and one more from the front and printed them. He laid them out on his desk in a line, where they scrutinised them closely.

'I have never met your Ken, but the man there does look like my photo.' Hendrik held the photo on his phone over the print-offs. Hale and Steph compared them.

'It's dark, so the quality isn't great, and it's blurred, but I agree it looks like him.' Hale stood back and took the phone from Hendrik to check from his angle.

'But in Holland you thought the body might be Ken.' Steph turned to see Hendrik frowning.

'I thought at the time the body found by the fisherman looked like the photo I had, and they must have investigated him since I left. The face had been changed by the water, so it might have been another man of the same age.'

'But the other night in the hotel, you said it was Ken who had died.'

'That is what they told me.'

'They haven't asked for a DNA sample to compare Jim with him as far as I know.' Hale turned the screen off.

Hendrik looked suddenly embarrassed. 'I think they had the identity and did not look further. Ken had disappeared by the river, and they had a body. Case closed. Like you, we have the efficiencies to make, and DNA tests are expensive.'

Hale frowned. 'Well, now we have Jim's body and have taken a DNA sample, we can send it to your people, and they can check. It looks as if they need to.'

'I agree. You are right, Hale. Now, what do we do about this van? It could have been you or me the van was trying to kill, not poor Steph.'

'I suggest we go to the carpet shop or warehouse, wherever it is, and see for ourselves.' Hale had already started looking on Google and had come up with an address. 'It's on the industrial estate on the way to Lowestoft. About twenty minutes' drive. Are you up for it?' Hale looked at Hendrik.

'Up?'

'Sorry, would you like to come with us?'

Hendrik nodded.

'And Steph, would you like to come, or should I drop you back at the flat?'

'I'm coming. I'm fine,' lied Steph, swallowing her pain. This was so much better than sitting around at home. The pain was going to be there wherever she was, and at least this would be a distraction.

'I must explain to Johnson and ask him to continue

searching for those names – if that is OK with you?' Hendrik added, catching Hale's eye.

'Good idea.'

'Will we use one of your police cars?'

'No, we'll go in Steph's car, so we don't attract attention. If we need back-up, we can always call it in.'

With Derek stowed in the boot, the three of them drove north up the A12 until they reached the Asda and Homebase roundabout at the entrance to the industrial estate. They cruised around, looking for the distinctive yellow logo they had found on Google – a cartoon of a flat-capped man carrying a carpet over his shoulder.

'There! To the right, down that road – ouch!' Steph pointed, but realised too late she shouldn't have moved.

The notice at the end of the road listed Bickers Carpets Lowestoft, with a diagram showing a left turn at the bottom of the road. Hale slowed as they approached the turn and drove towards a line of warehouses. Right at the end, they spotted a metal shuttered door with the cartoon logo on the wall above it. Parking the car in the first space in the row, away from the camera, they climbed out and looked around.

As it was Sunday, it was quiet. A brass bed company was open, and they could see people inside walking around and lying on the beds, trying them out. Next door to it, the trade paint company was closed. The carpet warehouse looked empty too until they got closer and saw a light coming from the office to the right of the shutters.

As Hale rang the bell by the glass door, they could see a man sitting at a desk working at a computer. He waved and shouted at them. 'We're shut. It's Sunday.'

Hale held his warrant card up to the glass door. 'May we have a word, please?'

With a surprised expression, the man swept some papers into a drawer and unlocked the door.

'I think you want the paint shop next door, where the burglary was.'

Hale smiled. 'No, it's your company we're interested in. May we come in?'

With what appeared to be a reluctant grunt, the man pulled the door wide open. He showed them into a reception area where three wood-framed armchairs were arranged around a coffee table strewn with some dog-eared magazines. 'Please.' He indicated they should sit and wheeled his desk chair over to join them. 'Now, how can I help you?'

'And you are?'

'Graham Bickers, the owner. I'm here going through the accounts. During the week it's frantic, so I come here on a Sunday sometimes to sort out the accounts, while it's quiet.'

Hale pulled out the print of the side of the van with its logo. 'Mr Bickers, is this one of your vans?'

The man reached for the photo, peered at it, and nodded. 'Call me Graham. Yes, why?'

'It was involved in a serious accident about nine thirty last Wednesday evening.'

Graham sat back, frowning. 'Are you sure?'

'Positive. It was driven by this man. Do you recognise him?'

After a cursory glance at the photo, Graham shook his head. 'Not one of our drivers. Never seen him before.'

Hale moved it closer to him. 'Please, look again. This man was driving a van with your logo on it and hit another car.' Hale pushed it at Graham's hands, so he was forced to take it. He held it and stared at it. Producing a picture of the car deep in the dyke, Hale held it up so Graham could see that too. 'And this was the accident.'

Steph had not seen the photo, and faced with it, she felt faint.

Graham's eyes grew behind his glasses. 'Bloody hell! That looks serious. Were they all right?'

'Luckily, the driver escaped with minor injuries but almost drowned.'

'No one has reported anything like this.'

'Can we check your vans, please?'

Graham rose, went to his desk, opened a drawer and picked up a bunch of keys. 'Sure, follow me.'

From his tone of voice, Steph was convinced he knew nothing about the accident, but she wasn't convinced he was telling the truth about not knowing the driver.

He led them past his desk, where they could see piles of receipts and some printed accounts, through a door into the showroom. The walls were filled floor to ceiling with vast rolls of carpets on long wooden rods, in complementary shades, different styles and depths of pile. In the centre, light wood stands held sample books, and little pieces of carpets hung in strips from hooks around the edges. In the closed room, the glue smell was overpowering, and she tried not to breathe it in.

They crossed the floor to another door at the far end, which Graham unlocked. They walked into a garage with a row of white vans, parked neatly, their front bumpers in a perfect line.

Hale and Hendrik started walking along the sides to check if any of them had scratches or dents. Graham, standing beside Steph, put up his hand as if to stop them. 'It's no good looking there. There's one missing!'

CHAPTER FORTY-FIVE

At Graham's horrified voice, Steph turned too quickly and winced as the electric pain shot through her side. She bit her lip to stop herself from crying out. Hale and Hendrik rushed over to join them.

'How many should there be?' Hale came up close to him.

'Six. There are only five. See that space there?'

They all swivelled to stare at the gap at the end of the line. Graham had gone pale and his voice had risen by several notes. 'I had no idea. It isn't here. Where is it?'

Evidently sensing his panic, Hale put his arm on Graham's arm. 'Don't worry. We'll find it. Shall we go back into your office? Looks like you could do with a sit down.'

They trooped back through the showroom and returned to their chairs, but Hale insisted Graham should sit in an armchair while he stood. 'You sit here. I'll get you a glass of water. Through there?' Hale waved at a door behind the desk. Graham nodded. Steph was concerned he might faint, as he had his head in his hands and kept mumbling. 'I had no idea. How?'

'We'll find out, don't worry.'

Glass of water in hand, Hale returned and handed it to Graham, who sipped it. At last his breathing appeared to have slowed down. Hale waited and wheeled the desk chair over beside Graham. Hendrik was about to get up to look at something he'd noticed on the desk, but Hale shook his head and Hendrik sat back down. Steph tried to peer around to see what he'd been looking at, but moving her head hurt too much, so she faced forward again.

'Now it would appear your missing van was involved in the accident. When did you last see it in your garage?'

'You don't understand. I'm the owner and there's a manager who sorts out the orders, the deliveries and the fitters. I own an accountancy firm and do the accounts, so don't come in on a day-to-day basis.' The panic in his voice had not receded.

'Do you have a list of drivers and their jobs – say, from last Tuesday?' Hale spoke slowly, trying to calm the man, who was now shaking. If Graham didn't know anything, this was an overreaction, or was he really nervous?

It appeared that Graham's brain wasn't working well, as he paused and scrunched his face in deep thought. 'I'm being so stupid. Sorry. Yes, there's a list on the computer. Let me get it for you.'

They watched as he went behind his desk, woke up his computer and searched for the right page, then they heard the whirring of the printer. He returned to stand beside Hale, the paper between them.

'See, this shows the number of the van – the missing one is number six. You can see it went to Pakefield on Tuesday to deliver a carpet with the fitter. They were there all day. On Wednesday, it went to Harwich to pick up a delivery—'

'From the Hook of Holland?' Hendrik could hardly hide his excitement.

'That's right, we import a lot of our carpets from the continent, as it gives us a niche market the other shops around here don't have.'

'And Thursday?'

Graham turned over the page. 'Nothing. Look.'

Graham held out the paper and they could see the final two columns hadn't been filled in – they were blank. 'It looks as if someone stole the van after it picked up the delivery at the port and went off with it.'

'Wouldn't anyone have noticed? It's Sunday now.' Hale held out his hand for the paper, which Graham gave him. He moved his finger down the columns while he waited for Graham to reply.

Graham appeared to be flustered and gabbled. 'Well, yes, of course they should have – will have – noticed – I mean – should have told me or you or – the manager – or someone. But there's nothing – nothing on this schedule, is there? Oh dear! It looks as if whoever stole the van was involved in the accident, doesn't it?'

For a moment the panic oozing from Graham dissipated, as he realised it might not be his problem after all. 'It couldn't have been one of our drivers, could it?'

'Why not?' Hale smiled as he asked the question.

'Well, if the van was stolen in Harwich, it wouldn't have our driver driving it, would it?' For a moment, Graham sounded almost cocky.

Steph could see Hale had also picked that up, as he paused before his next question. 'And what do you think happened to your driver?'

Nonplussed, Graham stammered. 'I don't know – I mean,

it can't have been one of ours or he would have brought the van back, wouldn't he? I'm sure he would – all our drivers are good men.'

Hale smiled at him. 'May we have a list of your drivers, especially the one who went to Harwich, as according to you we could now be dealing with a missing person?'

CHAPTER FORTY-SIX

ZOE WAS SURPRISED to hear the doorbell ringing on a Sunday evening. She assumed it was a delivery – so late? But then, they worked all hours. Gran watched shopping channels most of the day and was always buying stuff she fancied, and Zoe was constantly making trips to the post office to return the parcels. Presumably it was something else they didn't need, like an air fryer or a pasta maker.

She opened the door. It flew open and hit her in the face, making her fall backwards. Hands seized her, turned her over, grabbed her hands and fixed them together with something tight and sharp. It hurt. She was terrified – was she going to be raped?

Flipped over again, she felt herself being dragged by her shoulders into the front room and pulled up onto a wooden dining chair. Her hands were fixed to the back of it – she tried to pull her arms free, but she couldn't move. At last, she could see who it was as he came round to face her – Ken Craddock.

'But you're dead!'

'Obviously not. Alive and kicking. Aren't you pleased to

see me?' He came in close, and she was forced to inhale his cigarette breath. 'Now, girlie, are you going to do what I say or are you going to force me to have a word with your gran in there?'

Zoe became aware of the sound of the TV. The volume was turned up as far as it would go, blaring out a show of audience laughter and cheering. Gran loved talent shows and Zoe was relieved Ken appeared to want to leave her alone – at least for the moment, but the threat made her shudder.

'What do you want?'

'The package.'

Her stomach somersaulted. 'What package?'

He took out his knife and started cleaning his nails with it.

'You know what package.'

'I haven't got any package. You disappeared before you gave it to me. I've never had a package!' She was terrified. If she had it, she would hand it over. He had that knife.

Ken prowled around the edge of the room, his eyes darting and exploring each surface, as if he'd find the parcel there. He picked up a porcelain vase from the mantelpiece and turned it upside down to inspect the mark on its base like an experienced antique dealer. Holding it away from his body, he opened his fingers and let it drop to the tiled hearth, where it shattered into tiny shards, the pink cabbage roses no longer visible.

'Oops. Butter fingers!'

He moved towards its partner and repeated his deliberate destruction. Gran's vases probably didn't cost much, but they mattered to her, and now all that was left was a pile of splinters on the hearth. No way could they be repaired.

'Please, stop!'

Being unable to do anything but watch his slow prowl

239

around the room gave her the creeps. And what would he do when he was finished finding stuff to break?

'I will when you tell me where it is.'

He picked up a framed photo of her in a pram, looked at it, grinned, then dropped it and ground the glass into splinters with his heel. With a swift movement of his left hand, he swept all the tiny glass animals she'd collected as a child to the tiles, where they lay in a chaotic heap, most of them broken.

The noise hadn't alerted Gran to what was happening. Would it be better if it did? It might give her the chance to escape. No, the noise of the talent show, with a song from *Les Miserables*, came through loud and strong. Whatever happened to her, she must protect Gran.

As he walked behind her, she froze, waiting for the knife on her neck.

A crash made her jump. It sounded like a drawer being pulled out of the sideboard and its contents trashed. Cutlery jangled to the floor – at least it wasn't broken. Another followed. This time something was smashed, but she couldn't remember what was in that drawer. This was a nightmare.

Cupboard doors slammed, and she winced at the sound of broken crockery. Not Gran's best Wedgwood tea service? She'd be so upset. The audience screamed in appreciation at the end of the song and Zoe was relieved Gran hadn't been disturbed.

She must find a way of getting out of the chair. Despite pulling as hard as she could on her restraints, she felt the plastic cutting tighter into her wrists and stopped. What would he do when he'd finished trashing the room? She couldn't move an inch.

Once again, Ken appeared in her peripheral vision, grabbing papers from an old bureau and throwing them onto the floor. Another drawer seized and emptied; his foot sorted through its contents.

'Are you going to tell me where it is? Or do I have to search the house?' His face came close to hers; their noses touched. She closed her eyes. His whisper made her flesh creep. 'And have a little talk with your gran?'

She was desperate. How could she convince him she was telling the truth?

'If I had a parcel, I'd give it to you. Honestly. I haven't got it. I wouldn't want anything to do with it. If I had it, I'd give it to you, but I haven't got it! Why won't you believe me?'

The knife came up to her neck. 'Why would I keep it, when I don't know what's in it?' Her voice had become a squeak.

'Oh, I think you know what's in it. A bright girl like you.' He stepped back, stared at her, then lunged, grabbed a handful of her hair and cut a lump off. He dangled the large strand in front of her face and let it drift down to the floor.

'That didn't hurt you, did it? But next time, it will...' Again, the whispering voice was horrific and she could do nothing.

Not caring who could hear her, she shouted as loud as she could. 'But I told you! You never gave me anything, and neither has anyone else!' Her shouts became screams.

His snake-slow move towards her, the knife creeping closer to her face, made her pull back as far as possible from the sharp tip. He stopped millimetres away from her neck. She didn't see him move, but felt the tip pierce her skin.

'I know I didn't give you anything. But you took it, didn't you? A little bird told me you took it when you visited my dad and killed him.'

Horrified, as the point of the knife went in further, she

cried out in pain. He moved back. How could she convince Ken she hadn't killed his father or taken anything from him?

'Look, I did go into this room and shouted at him for murdering Duncan, but I didn't take anything and I didn't kill him.'

The point pricked her skin again. This time, he pushed it further in. She gasped. Was the jugular vein around there? Was she going to die?

'Now, we're getting closer to the truth.'

He appeared to relax, stood back, and the sting of the knife receded.

'I would tell you if I knew anything. Honestly.'

He grinned at her.

'Honestly.' He imitated her desperate plea, making it sound whiney and pathetic.

The knife came close again. 'You killed your own grandfather – then you stole from him.'

'I didn't kill him and didn't take anything. Why won't you believe me? Someone else must have – it wasn't me!'

His cold expression as he looked her in the eyes convinced her he'd had enough. Now she was sure he'd kill her. If she screamed loud enough, at least Gran could call for help if she heard. Zoe had to get out of this. Her voice was at full volume and desperate. 'It wasn't me – I haven't got anything. There's nothing here—'

The doorbell rang.

Out of nowhere, he hit her. She felt her head jolt sideways, a sharp pain followed by yellow lights, then nothing but black.

CHAPTER FORTY-SEVEN

'WELCOME BACK.' Steph smiled down at Zoe, who squinted as she opened her eyes and scanned the group around her hospital bed.

'You've got ten minutes, that's it. She needs to rest.' The nurse pulled the curtain back, so they had more room.

Zoe spotted Ollie and reached out her hand, which he took. Her face was porcelain white; a wide plaster covered a cut on the side of her neck and a black bruise was developing around her left eye.

'What happened?' She croaked and licked her dry lips. Ollie handed her a beaker of water with a bendy straw, which she sipped.

Steph smiled at Ollie, prompting him to tell the story. 'I came round, rang the bell, saw that the door wasn't shut properly, pushed it open and found you lying on the floor tied to a chair. You were unconscious, so I called the police and an ambulance—'

'Gran? Is she all right?'

'She was watching TV and didn't know anything about it,

but your front room was trashed! She's fine. I left her looking at some shopping channel to find some vases to replace the ones he broke.'

Zoe rolled her eyes.

Steph leaned in slightly. 'Did you recognise who attacked you?'

'Ken Craddock.'

'Are you sure?'

'Absolutely. He wanted a package – he said I'd taken it from Jim Craddock's room. I didn't, honestly.' Clearly, something had shaken her again and tears dripped down her cheeks.

The nurse must have been keeping an eye on them and bustled over. 'That's enough now. Off you go, all of you. Zoe needs to sleep.'

Ollie gave Zoe a kiss on the unbruised side of her face, and they all moved away from the bed.

'Can we give you a lift back to Oakwood, Ollie?' Steph walked beside him, their steps echoing down the empty corridor.

'Thanks, Steph. That would be great.'

'It was a good job you arrived when you did.'

'Pure chance. Zoe wasn't answering her phone, which is not like her, so I drove round to see if she was OK.' He sighed. 'Good job I did, wasn't it?'

'Certainly was.'

They had reached the car park and followed Hale to one of the few cars parked there so late on a Sunday night.

'Did you see anyone else leaving as you arrived?'

'Hale asked me that while we were waiting for Zoe to wake up. No. Her gran was watching TV in the back room and hadn't heard anything. When I went through to the kitchen, I found the back door wide open. He must have escaped through the gardens – they back onto the lane that leads to the common.'

Hale got to the car first and waited for them. 'Ollie, could you come down to the station tomorrow morning to make a statement and give us your fingerprints and DNA? We need it to eliminate you and provide evidence that Ken was in the house.'

'If it means you get that bastard, of course. You will, won't you?'

Hale looked serious. 'We'll get him, have no doubt about that.'

They dropped Ollie off outside Zoe's house and watched him get into his car and drive away.

'Amazing piece of luck, him arriving.' Wincing, Steph re-adjusted the cushion.

'Painful?'

'Getting better. Think what he could have done to her or her gran if Ollie hadn't arrived.'

'Nasty piece of work.' Hale drove down the deserted High Street, past the dark shops, until he reached Steph's flat. As soon as they put the key in the lock, Derek announced himself. Throwing him a treat from his pocket, Hale dropped into his armchair while Steph remained standing by the bar. It was too much effort to find a comfortable sitting position, only to get up a few minutes later for bed.

'I wonder where he's staying?' She poured herself a glass of water for the night-time painkillers.

'While you were chatting with Ollie, I got a patrol car to go past Jim Craddock's house and see if there was any sign of Ken. No news yet, so I suppose they haven't found him there. We're not sure if he's driving a car—'

'—or a van?'

'Amazing how he disappeared off the radar in Holland, and I must say I'm not impressed with the way the Dutch pathologist and police identified that body erroneously as Ken's.' Hale leaned forward to stroke the top of Derek's head.

'I suppose you can understand how it happened. A man disappears by the Rhine and a body of a man about his age turns up in the river where he was last seen. They probably thought it was Christmas!'

'But that's exactly my point. No such thing as coincidences. Surely it was worth a DNA test to confirm it?' He found a dog treat in his pocket, which Derek inhaled.

'Well, they'll have to now. Ken's racking up quite a list of charges—'

'—attempted murder for you, GBH for Zoe, and that's without kidnapping or doing goodness knows what with the van driver.'

Steph moved towards the bedroom, hoping Hale would take the hint. She was exhausted. 'Unless he was the driver? Maybe he worked for the carpet company regularly, picking up the Dutch delivery at Harwich. It would be easy enough for him to smuggle drugs in those rolls of carpets, and the glue smell would put the sniffer dogs off.'

'You're right. I think I'll make another visit to Mr Bickers' showroom.' At last, Hale stood, stretched, and yawned.

CHAPTER FORTY-EIGHT

DESPITE HALE'S PROTESTS, Steph insisted he drop her off at college for the start of the week. She promised she would take care – the pain was easing, and anyway, she'd be climbing up the walls if she stayed in the flat much longer.

When they'd dropped Derek off that morning, Fiona, the dog lady, had agreed to bring Derek to college with her at the end of the day as Hale was driving Steph's car to London that afternoon. They'd agreed to look for a replacement for his car at the weekend, hoping they'd get the insurance money through quickly. They certainly couldn't cope with only one car, and she hoped these complex arrangements wouldn't last longer than a week, by which time she was sure she could drive again.

Students from the group who had been on the Arnhem trip came to visit her during the day to chat and check how she was getting on and admire her bruises. Having shared their time together on the project, it seemed a strong bond had been formed and they wanted to remain tightly bound.

Caroline was also a frequent visitor – although she was also after the detail on Zoe's adventure and the latest news about Ken. She had invited Steph, Hale and Hendrik to supper later in the week, as she wanted to introduce her partner, Margaret, to Hendrik. Margaret was one of Hale's greatest fans and always rose to his defence when Caroline or Steph gave him a hard time. Steph was looking forward to an exquisite supper, as Caroline was a superb cook. After her accident, Steph was getting bored with takeaways or SOT – something on toast.

Peter, the principal, was sympathetic and said he was impressed by Steph's fortitude by coming into work when she could have claimed sick leave. He insisted she had a bar-height chair, ideal for the Reception desk, and ordered her not to move around, unless absolutely necessary.

As she had almost finished collating the piles of papers for the board of governors' meeting, her mobile phone rang. It was Hale, who sounded energetic and happy.

'Well done, you.'

'What?'

'Guess what we found in the rolls of carpet picked up from Holland? Traces of coke and heroin. Not sure where the diamonds went. But there's firm evidence this is the way they've been smuggling drugs from the Hook of Holland to Harwich, then to the warehouse. Just need to crack their distribution network.'

'That's great news.'

'And guess who was employed as a driver? None other than our very own Ken Craddock! We haven't got a missing driver – he was it and it was his van he used to force you off the road.'

'Great job.'

'He is nowhere to be found, unfortunately, but we've arrested the manager, who looked as guilty as sin, and they've gone off to bring Bickers in. Although I'm not convinced he was involved, but we'll see.'

'Fantastic! Drive safe. See you tomorrow.'

She smiled as she hung up and replaced her phone in her bag. A great result. All they had to do was arrest Ken and find sufficient evidence for it to go to court. Hypothesis proved, but it was finding the hard evidence and tying it all together that got a conviction.

Ken Craddock was a snake and deserved everything coming to him. Even if they couldn't get him for the drugs and diamond smuggling, his violent attacks on her and Zoe would ensure he would be put away – and for a very long time.

Just as Steph resumed her counting of papers for the governors' packs, her mobile rang – Hale again.

'And that photo we saw Henk noticing – it was Bickers' wife, Judy – you know, petticoat Tom's daughter.'

'Even you have to admit that is a coincidence!'

'See you—'

'Hang on, Hale – Hale? Are you still there?'

'Yes.'

'I wonder if the Vickers person – you know one of the four names given to Johnson and Henk – is actually Bickers? They misheard, or it was mistyped? That would make sense, wouldn't it? Judy Bickers, Tom's daughter. I bet she's involved, too.'

'Well done. I'll get cars out to Tom's and her house to see if we can find Ken and bring Judy in for questioning. Enjoy your date!'

The phone went dead. What a result! At last, everything appeared to be falling into place. But that final comment? What on earth was wrong with him?

CHAPTER FORTY-NINE

AT LAST, Steph was finding it easier to walk, and each step no longer sent pain darting through her body. The soft light gave everything a gentle glow. The leaves that clung stubbornly to the trees filtered the flickering light, which made the walk across the common magical.

Watching Derek smash through the crisp leaves, she smiled. And as she went past the pond, she paused to enjoy the deep claret leaves on a group of Japanese acers planted to create a perfect reflection on the mirror surface of the water. All the colours of autumn had seemed so much sharper since her accident, and it felt good to be alive.

Derek appeared to know she was fragile and didn't pull on his lead, but trotted bedside her, the epitome of a well-behaved dog. He even passed a German Shepherd and a sausage dog without dashing off to sniff their backsides.

Hale's flat was about a mile beyond Oakwood Common, the opposite side of town to Steph's. He had left Oakwood that afternoon for an update with the Met team working on the drugs ring and he couldn't wait to tell them about the progress they'd made in Suffolk. When she'd left the Met for Suffolk, she had to field masses of jokes about carrot crunchers and tractor boys and jokes about an early retirement. Hale, who no doubt had experienced the same digs, was looking forward to making the report on their excellent progress.

Hendrik declined the invitation, as he had to join the weekly Skype meeting with his Dutch team, and he, too, was looking forward to sharing their success. She checked her watch – five thirty; he should have finished his meeting by now.

She planned to take Hendrik for supper at The Leg of Mutton and Cauliflower. They offered a typical English pub menu of fish and chips, cottage pie or pie of the day and welcomed well-behaved dogs. The penny dropped. That's what Hale meant by his comment about a date. Surely, he wasn't jealous – was he?

At last, she reached Hale's garden flat, in an imposing Edwardian house. She sometimes wondered if they'd be better off living there with its walled garden, large rooms with high ceilings, wine cellar, and masses of storage in the two bedrooms. So much bigger than cramming everything into her one-bedroom, open plan flat. But as Hale didn't appear to want to discuss it, she left the subject well alone. Anyway, she didn't want to live in his ex-wife's world with her choice of froufrou blinds and fussy furniture.

Reprimanding herself for being catty, she climbed the three steps up to the front door, turned the key, opened the door and called out, 'Hi Henk, it's me, Steph.'

There was no answer to her call, but she paused as she heard what sounded like an argument in the front room between a man and a woman. She recognised Hendrik and – yes, she'd heard that voice before – it was Judy.

What was she doing there? Had Hendrik brought her here

for questioning? Had Hale left them here while he got back-up? She moved closer to the door and was about to push it open when she heard Hendrik's voice.

'Tell me your side, if I've got it wrong.'

'Not wrong exactly, just different.' Peeping through the crack in the door, she could see Judy running her fingers through her hair. She was putting on a good show, but Steph detected a lack of confidence in her voice.

'And how is that? Please tell me.'

Hendrik was standing beside the hearth, looming over the petite Judy, who stood facing him, her back to the bay window. Rather an unconventional way to carry out an interrogation.

'I am waiting.' Hendrik's voice had a menacing edge to it.

'Look, I do as Ken says.'

'As Ken says!' He slapped his hand down hard on the mantelpiece as he shouted at her.

Judy flinched, then leaned towards him, pulling herself up to fight back. 'Henk, you may be a big shot in Holland, but here it's Ken and me running the lines. You need us here. You wouldn't know where to start.'

'You have had enough out of me, do you hear? Enough!' Hendrik went towards Judy, threatening her. He must have been well over a foot taller, and as he moved in, Judy winced and stepped back out of his reach.

'You do as I say. I will deal with Ken. You hear?' His voice was loud, intimidating – so different from the charming man she thought she knew.

Judy took another step back, but Hendrik matched her until she was up against the wall beside the window. His voice got louder as he jabbed the air in front of her face with his finger. 'Without me, you are nothing. You cannot survive. You and Ken are greedy. Without me, you are finished!'

Another jab. This time into her chest. Her confidence dissolved. Judy looked petrified.

'Do you want to continue, or shall I cut you out – for good?' Whispered, his last two words were terrifying.

Hypnotised, Judy stared up at him.

'If you want out, I can arrange it for you and Ken. A final way out – final – understand?'

She stared up at him. Scared stiff, she said nothing.

'I need an answer now. You hear?'

He stepped back, and a horrified Judy looked down at his hand, which held a gun. A gun? This was getting serious. Steph had to get back-up.

Pulling Derek towards the front door, Steph crept back to the top of the steps and was just about to close the door behind her when Derek barked at a white fluffy Pomeranian strutting on the pavement below. Her stomach lurched. Maybe Hendrik hadn't heard her. Her feet left the ground as she was pulled back into the hall and thrown against a wall. She screamed in agony. She hadn't been quick enough.

CHAPTER FIFTY

HENDRIK GLARED DOWN AT HER, then smiled – it didn't reach his eyes.

'Steph, good to see you. Hale – he is with you?'

'In the car.'

He dragged her by her hair further inside the hall and threw her to the floor, pressing her down with his foot on her back while he scanned the road. Her ribs screamed out, but she tried not to. Slamming the front door, he dragged her to her feet and once again threw her against the wall. The shooting pain was excruciating, but she did her best to keep her face straight and not let him see her agony.

'Good try.' He moved the gun up to her throat and rammed the barrel in hard, so she could feel the cold metal.

'And for how long did you spy on us?'

Taking a deep breath, she tried to sound as normal as possible with a gun stuck in her throat. 'Only just arrived.'

'But you heard enough, right?' Almost a seductive whisper. He smiled, his eyebrow raised, inviting her confidence. She now found him repulsive.

The best idea was to say nothing. Over his shoulder, she could see the hallway, which was empty. Where was Derek? He must have run off when Hendrik grabbed her off the top step. Was that a blessing? At least he wouldn't get shot, but would he get run over on the road? Oh no, not Derek! And where was Judy? Had Hendrik shot her?

'Sorry, Steph.'

The gun came closer. He swivelled his hand sideways, ready to take the shot. She closed her eyes, waiting for it. It was no good fighting him. Her ribs were killing her, and she hadn't the strength, had she?

Rubbish! With a massive effort despite the vicious pain, she kicked him on his calf and kneed him in the groin – hard. Every movement was agony, but the gun fell from his hands. She couldn't bend to pick it up. He kicked it out of her reach, knocked her over, then lost his balance and fell on top of her.

She screamed in pain and tried to stretch for the gun, but his reach was longer and he got to it, while she was hampered by the pain that shot through her with every move.

'You have courage, I give you that.' His voice, breathless, in her ear.

With an athletic bounce to the side, he was up on his feet and he dragged her up beside him. He pushed the gun deep into her shattered ribs, and she screamed. He drove her to the door at the end of the hall.

'Open it.'

She did. It was the cellar.

'Sorry, Steph.'

His hand at her back, he shoved her hard. She tumbled down the concrete steps and lay in a heap at the bottom. The door slammed and she heard the key turn in the lock. She screamed. The pain was excruciating – she passed out.

When she opened her eyes, it was pitch black. No light anywhere. Not even a glimmer or pin prick of light. Had she lost her sight when she hit her head? How long had she been out of it?

Blinking hard, she scrunched her eyes shut and then opened them again, but the blackout was total. She heard herself sobbing but stopped, as each breath hurt so much. Trying to take the smallest breaths possible, she lay still on the cold floor until the acute discomfort receded a little.

The damp smell of drains edged up her nose and she listened hard – would there be rats down here? Think positive. Maybe, when her sight accommodated, she might find a way out, and there had to be a light switch somewhere. Scrap that idea – she visualised the light switch outside the door in the hall.

Lying flat on her back, she gingerly stretched her legs and arms – they felt battered, but in slow motion she lifted each in turn so didn't think she'd broken them. Her ribs were another matter. They hurt like hell. She hadn't got her bag, so no pain killers or phone, and, closing her eyes, she could see it where it had fallen on the floor in the hallway. She took slow breaths, trying to breathe through the pain. Moving was hell. And where had she got to move to?

Hale had brought her down here once, and closing her eyes, she tried to recall the layout. There were five steps down – thank goodness there hadn't been more – then a long line of wine racks along the wall to the left. On the opposite wall were shelves storing sports stuff, Christmas decorations and other rubbish. At the far end was a coal chute covered by a wooden hatch, just inside the back gate to the garden. If she could reach the hatch, perhaps she could force it open, if the wooden latch that held it in place would give way. Only one way to find out.

Using the bottom of the steps, she hauled herself up to her feet – shuddering and catching her breath as the pain cut through her. Whatever healing had taken place since the accident must have been undone by her fight with Hendrik and her fall.

Holding onto the wall, she steadied herself with the protruding edge of a brick. Maybe she should try shouting and screaming, but from memory the walls were thick, and the hatch was in the garden. Who would hear her?

Eyes closed – why keep them open? With her toes against the bottom step, she shuffled sideways until she found the opposite wall and felt her way along the rough bricks. She was feeling pleased with her progress, but once again crashed to the floor as she fell over the edge of the wine rack.

Luckily, it was screwed to the wall, so it didn't fall on her. From memory, Hale hadn't many bottles stored in it, so at least she didn't get bombarded by falling glass.

Was it really worth dragging herself up only to fall over again? Maybe she should crawl to the hatch. No, she'd shuffle her feet along the floor, so this time she'd be aware of any obstacles.

After using the side of the wine rack to haul herself up, she continued on her step-by-step journey across the cellar, until she walked into a wall. Where did that come from?

Moving along it, she felt a draught of air on her face – could it be the hatch? She tipped her face up, hoping for a chink of light, but could see nothing – it would probably be dark outside too. Lifting her hands above her head towards what she hoped was the hatch, she screamed. Something wrapped itself around her hands. Lowering them, she scraped them – ugh! Cobwebs. Please don't let there be spiders too.

Taking a deep breath, she knew she had to do it, so she

raised her hands again to what she hoped would be wooden slats. Yes! They were there. For a moment Steph felt a surge of hope and she was thrilled she was right – but so what? She could only just about touch them with her fingertips, which wouldn't allow her to push up with any power. Anyway, holding her arms above her head shot flashes of pain everywhere. Moving across to the opposite wall, she groped for a box or something solid to stand on. As she reached out, she once again found herself flat on the floor as she tripped over a pile of material. At least this landing was soft.

Lying back on what felt like some old velvet curtains, she started to cry. Tears of frustration and pain and hopelessness. How long would she have to stay down here before anyone found her? Hale would arrive – eventually. He wasn't due to be back until tomorrow afternoon and then he'd go to the station and wouldn't miss her until the evening when he turned up at the flat – late as usual. And she had to warn him about Hendrik.

Hendrik. He wouldn't leave her here, would he, to reveal all? He'd be coming back to shut her up. How could they have been so stupid not to see his treachery? But Hale had checked him out, and they knew he'd worked with the Met before they met him.

All the time he'd been the one smuggling drugs and diamonds out via the Bickers carpet deliveries. He was the one working with Judy and Ken, who ran the lines across Suffolk and probably Norfolk. Had he said that the diamonds went to a man in Hatton Garden? What a bastard he was, and how they'd all been taken in by his charm.

If only she'd been a bit later arriving at the house. Hendrik could have continued with his pretence and she wouldn't be down here in the coal hole dreading his return.

A picture of Derek, squashed on the main road by a car, forced its way into her head, and she shoved it out again before she started howling her eyes out. She'd only owned him for three years, but he'd become a vital part of her life. Derek seemed to understand exactly what she was doing: when she was getting ready to take him for a walk, or when she told him 'sorry' when he had to stay at home, or when it was time to claim his good night treat. She sighed and clung to the desperate hope that he was safe somewhere.

It was no good sitting here. She had to get up and try to get out... but she was so tired, exhausted living with the pain and now stuck forever in this dark hole or until Hendrik came to get her. Perhaps she should lie, huddled up on the smelly nest of curtains, and after a sleep, try again. After all, there was nothing else she could do. Exhausted, she closed her eyes and allowed herself to relax into the damp velvet.

How long had she slept? No idea. At last, she could see tiny slits of grey light between the wooden slats of the hatch. Would Caroline contact Hale to find out where she was when she didn't turn up at college? And if she did, how long would it take for him to drive back from London and how would he know where to look when he found her flat empty?

Maybe after realising how much Steph had heard, Hendrik could have made a run for it, but where would he go? Also, who would know? Only her. If he got rid of her, he could claim that he didn't know where she was and continue working with the police.

What would he do? She knew only too well that murdering someone was difficult, but it was more difficult getting rid of the body. He didn't have a car. But Judy did. Would she want to get involved in a murder? Having seen her fear yesterday, she'd probably do as Hendrik told her.

Was there anything she could do? There were the wine bottles, but he'd overpower her in a fight and her ribs prevented her hitting anything with any strength, and then there was his gun. No, she was stuck down here until he came to get her.

She coughed as the dust penetrated her throat, which was parched. Desperate for a drink – should she crawl to the wine rack and try to find some wine? Feeling hopeless and despondent, she lay back on the musty velvet, aware there was nothing she could do but wait. Once again, she drifted off, escaping into sleep.

A sudden blaze of light shocked her awake. She squeezed her eyes shut as the cellar was lit up by the bright fluorescent tubes that ran across its ceiling. Hendrik – coming to finish her off. Pulling the curtains over her, she hid deep in the dusty folds and dragged herself further back into the alcove beneath the hatch. She heard the key turn in the lock and the door scrape open.

CHAPTER FIFTY-ONE

THE ATTACK when it came was unexpected. She felt paws digging her out of the curtains and a tongue licking her face.

'Derek! You found me!' Her voice was hoarse, and she cleared her throat to get it back to normal. Derek ran round in circles, prancing on his hind legs, making little squeaks then dropping down to lick her face.

Squinting up into the light, she held up her hand to shield her eyes and made out a shadow standing over her. Hale smiled down, offering his hand to pull her up. As she emerged from the pile of faded red velvet curtains, Hale laughed.

'What's funny?' How could he laugh at what she'd been through?

'You look as if you've been trekking through a jungle. Your face is filthy.'

Now on her feet, ignoring his comment, she fell into Hale's arms and held onto him as hard as her ribs would let her. Derek stood on his hind legs, joining them in the team hug.

'What a grim time you've had. I'm so sorry. Are you really OK?'

'What day is it?'

'Tuesday.'

'Time?'

'Just gone four o'clock.'

'I've been here almost twenty-four hours.'

'Sorry. I got here as soon as I could. You seem to be in one piece, thank goodness. Let's get out of here and you can tell me what happened.'

With great care, Hale helped her to climb the concrete steps, each one purgatory and taking an enormous effort. At last, they arrived in the kitchen, where, holding her breath, she sank into one of the chairs. He handed her a glass of water, which she gulped, washing the layer of dust and damp away.

'You tell me first. How did you find Derek?'

'Caroline phoned me this morning when you didn't arrive at college. When I got back here and found your flat empty, I phoned Hendrik to see what happened last night after your pub meal.'

'And what did the bastard say?'

He gave a slight smile, clearly amused at the strength of her venom.

'Nothing. No answer. Anyway, when I found no sign of you or Derek at the flat, I drove along the route you'd have taken from college and found him barking by the back gate. When he saw me, he started howling and scrabbling at the wood.'

Steph leaned down as far as she could to pat him – his tail helicoptered.

Hale reached for her empty glass and re-filled it. 'He must have stayed there all night. The neighbours must have loved it!'

She sipped the water gratefully. Crouched down in front of her, he gently massaged her thigh. 'If he'd been left much longer, he'd have scratched his way through the wood and rescued you single-handed. As soon as I let him into the garden, he made for the coal hatch and stood there looking at me as if I was a prize idiot. It took a lot of pulling to get him to come with me through the front door, I can tell you.'

Derek manoeuvred his head under her hand so she could stroke him again. 'I'm so sorry you've been down there for so long. I drove back as soon as I could.'

Hale kissed her on the forehead and stood up. 'What a dreadful time you've had! I would never have heard you from that cellar, even if you'd had the strength to shout. If it hadn't been for Derek, I dread to think when I'd have found you.'

'I'd just about given up. Good boy, Derek.'

Once again, Hale handed water to her. 'Apart from the dust and grime smeared across your face, you really are in one piece? Honestly?'

'I think my ribs have gone back to square one and I must have added a few more bruises to the collection.'

She took another sip of water. 'When I got here, I found Hendrik and Judy in the front room arguing about payment for running the drugs line. He was so nasty to her. He threatened her with a gun, and as I tried to escape, he trapped me. We struggled for the gun, but he got it, then threw me down the cellar steps.'

Steph coughed, trying to clear the dust out of her throat. 'All the time he's been the one smuggling drugs and diamonds through Bickers' carpet deliveries, while Judy Bickers and Ken Craddock have been running the lines.'

'We know.'

'How?'

'I've just heard they've arrested Judy at her father's. She's cooperated and confessed to it all. We have an alert out on all ports and airports to pick up Hendrick and Ken, who seems to have disappeared again.'

'How could he? How didn't we know? I mean, neither of us is stupid, but we had no idea Hendrik was bent.'

'He's a very clever man and I've no doubt an outstanding police officer. Maybe that was the problem. He was too clever and worked out a way of policing himself, so he was never caught. They say to be a good cop you have to think like a criminal – he certainly did.'

'But he was so—'

'Sexy?'

Steph felt herself blush. 'Well... He was rather good looking – charming perhaps... but not as sexy as you!'

Hale leaned forward and was giving her a passionate kiss when they heard the creak of the kitchen door.

CHAPTER FIFTY-TWO

'STEPH! YOU'RE HERE AND OK!' They both jumped as they recognised Hendrik's voice.

At once, Hale moved behind him in front of the closed door to prevent him from leaving the kitchen. Instead of attempting to escape, Hendrik knelt by Steph's feet, reached for her hands and, holding them gently, looked up at her.

'I am so sorry, Steph. I never wanted to hurt you, but you must see it was necessary.'

'Necessary? Throwing me down five concrete steps with broken ribs? How was that necessary?'

Hale moved forward and put his hand on Hendrik's shoulder. 'Hendrik Bakker, I am arresting you on suspicion of—'

Hendrik leaped to his feet. 'No! You don't understand! I'm on your team! It's Judy, Ken and their gang you need to arrest, not me.'

'But I heard you arguing with Judy about her cut.' Steph was determined she would not be conned for a second time.

Hendrik dragged a kitchen chair from under the table and

sat down, facing her, while Hale moved to his side to stop him from escaping. 'Look, Hale, I've no intention of running, so why not sit down and I'll explain it all? It's not what you think.'

Reluctantly, Hale pulled out the chair nearest the door and lowered himself into it, sitting on its edge so he could take action. 'It had better be good.'

Steph and Hale fixed Hendrik with hard stares as he cleared his throat. 'As you know, I'm a Dutch police officer, an inspector—'

'Are you really? You must have thought we were a pushover.'

Hendrik paused. 'Here is my badge. You saw it when first we met.' He held it out for them to see. 'You discussed how I would work here with you in the UK with Commissaris van der Linden, didn't you? And your colleagues in the Met – they knew and worked with me before I even met you in Holland.'

Hale thought back to the detailed phone call to Holland, and Hendrik was right. They had discussed his role in the UK, and he had worked with the Met before their visit to Arnhem. 'That doesn't mean anything. You could still be a bent cop.'

'Oh, yes. I am bent, as you say. Not bent to the police but bent to the gang. I'm under cover.'

'Under cover?' Hale frowned. Clearly, from the tone of his voice, he was not convinced.

Steph reached for her glass and took another sip of water. 'Let's go through this slowly. What you're saying is that you're under cover in plain sight?'

Hendrik nodded and smiled at her. 'Right, Steph.'

'Ken and his gang thought they'd got a bent police officer working for them on their side, but all the time you were investigating them from the inside for the Dutch police?'

He smiled at Steph. 'You got it, Steph. They think I am a cop who wants to make money and use my position to run a smuggling gang.'

'But why lock me up and – even worse – throw me down those steps?'

'I had to look convincing to Judy. She was scared when she saw the gun and I had to keep her that way. She and Ken were getting greedy and planning to set up their own lines to get rid of me. If that happens, we have no way of busting them.' He reached out and took her hand, looking deep into her eyes. 'I am sorry if I scared you or hurt you. But you came too early.'

Hale cleared his throat. 'And about the gun? Where is it now?'

'Here.' Hendrik pulled it out. Instinctively, they both sat back as he placed it on the table. 'It is important that I have it to convince them.'

'How did you get it over here?'

'Easy. Hid it on the coach.' Hendrik grinned, apparently thinking himself very clever. 'Now, may I make you both a pot of your excellent coffee, as we have a long night ahead of us?'

While Hendrik busied himself making the coffee, Hale reached for the gun, checked it, locked it in a drawer and raised a questioning eyebrow at Steph, who acknowledged it with a shrug of her shoulders. He moved beside Hendrik, who, aware of his presence, stopped making coffee and met Hale's gaze.

'You won't mind if I check this out with your boss, will you?' said Hale.

'You want my phone?'

'No thanks. I have van der Linden's number.'

'Good. You take your coffee with no milk Steph?'

Steph nodded as Hale made the call. As soon as he was

connected, he moved out into the hallway, keeping the door open to make sure he could still see Steph and Hendrick. Steph could hear his voice and some long pauses.

Hendrick appeared cool about Hale checking up on him, and passing Steph's chair to put her coffee on the table, he touched her gently on her arm. She winced.

'You must be starving. Let me see what is in the fridge. Hale was kind with the food he left for me.' He returned from the fridge with a chunk of cheddar, butter, and a bread roll. 'OK?'

Steph nodded. Anything would taste good after her starvation diet in the cellar. She was right. It was the best cheese she had ever eaten.

Hendrik watched her devouring the food. 'And Steph, I owe you that meal in the Cauliflower pub. We'll go after all this is over?'

Steph was too busy munching her cheese roll to accept his offer. Anyway, she hadn't forgiven him for throwing her down those steps so viciously. She knew only too well that in the situation he described he had to be authentic to be convincing, and that shove was certainly convincing.

'I haven't forgiven you yet for pushing me down those steps. You knew I had broken ribs; you could have made it look good without being so vicious.'

'I'm sorry, Steph, but this case means all to me. I had to show her I am the one in charge and you were in the way. I am sorry I hurt you.'

Before she could vent her anger further, Hale returned.

'My boss is well?'

'He sends his regards and confirmed your story.' Hale joined them at the table, drank his coffee and gave Hendrik a penetrating stare. 'Before we go any further, can we get a few things straight?'

'Of course, I will do my best to answer your questions.'

Hale took out his phone, pressed the record button and placed it on the table in front of him. Hendrik saw it and nodded. 'That's fine.'

'Whose body was it in the Rhine? Was there even a body?'

'Yes, there was a body found by a fisherman, like I told you. We discovered he was a man from Antwerp, Finn Jensen. He worked for a diamond dealer – we suspected he was at the top of our chain, but he got greedy, and he started working on his own. The information got to Ken.'

'And Ken killed him?' Steph wanted to hear him say the words.

'Let's say Ken was there when he fell into the Rhine.'

In the pause, Hendrik appeared to realise why Steph was waiting. She raised her eyebrow, giving him a silent prompt.

He nodded. 'Yes, we believe Ken killed him.'

Hale shifted in his seat, clearly uncomfortable with what was being said.

'You may have been under cover, but surely you are bound by the law?'

A puzzled look flashed across Hendrik's face. 'Oh, I see. I did not get what you're saying. I did nothing. It was Ken who killed him.'

'But you gave him the information?'

'Authorised.'

'So, you knew all the time who it was then?'

'Yes, but we decided not to give his identity out until it suited us, so Ken could disappear.'

'And what was Ken doing?'

'Setting up new contacts, who we have tracked and who we are watching. As you know,' he nodded at Steph, 'Ken and Judy are thinking of cutting me out and going alone. We know he has been setting up a new network away from my control.'

Steph rubbed her ribs and squirmed a little, as they hurt if she stayed in one place. 'So, Ken was after you when he forced me off the road?'

'Yes. And Hale was to be – what do the Americans call it in their wars? – collateral damage. Judy must have phoned him when Hale's car drove away from the hotel. It was dark and Ken didn't know it was you driving– he thought he had got rid of me.'

'And Jim? Who killed him and took the bags?' said Hale.

Hendrik got himself a top-up and held out the pot to them both. When he sat down again, he looked straight at Hale. 'After Zoe left, Judy went to Jim's room. He tried to blackmail her – threatened to tell you, unless they cut him in. She didn't want to take the risk, so...' He shrugged his shoulders.

'But you kept blaming Zoe for it all.' Steph coughed and reached for the glass. Her throat was still dry and dusty.

'At that stage, I didn't know who had done it, and Zoe was the obvious suspect. Only that afternoon before you came did Judy tell me what happened.'

Hale checked his phone was still recording. 'So, you knew about the carpet imports?'

'We weren't sure. We suspected Ken used the Hook to Harwich route but not the details. I had to leave it to them to arrange the journey for me to appear authentic.'

'It was the photo, wasn't it?' Steph smiled, as the memory of Hendrik scrutinising Bickers' desk came back to her.

'Well done, Steph. Johnson and I had been told Vickers, so

it didn't register until I saw Judy's photo on her husband's desk. I knew it must have been Bickers.'

Hendrik paused and looked from Hale to Steph and back to Hale again. 'Is there anything else you want to test me on? We need to go soon if we are to have a chance to grab them all.'

CHAPTER FIFTY-THREE

THE BITTERLY COLD wind cut through their down coats as they crouched behind the weather boarded fishermen's huts on Blackshore, the Southwold Harbour side of the River Blyth. Driving there in Steph's car, they'd arrived about an hour after sunset and now hid in pitch black.

Judy had told Hendrik that Ken had organised a consignment to arrive in a small boat some time before midnight at Blackshore Harbour between Southwold and Walberswick. The source of diamonds appeared to have dried up, but she didn't know why.

Earlier, from the kitchen, Hale had phoned Johnson, who was with Judy at Oakwood Police station, and she confirmed it all. Hendrik was pleased she had provided further solid evidence of his story and proved he was on their side.

Hendrik slid from his hut to join Hale and Steph behind theirs. 'Which way will they come?'

Looking to the right, Hale indicated the string of lights glinting outside the Harbour Inn, swinging precariously in the wind. 'That way, they'd avoid most of the town, and the other way,' he nodded to the left, 'they'd have to drive through town but there are fewer potholes. Could be either way but I'd put my money that way.' Hale nodded right, towards the Harbour Inn

'But, Henk, you do understand that we'll not intercept them here, but observe them and report back? Border Force will pick up the boat at sea and an armed patrol will follow the van and arrest them at their destination.'

'Yes, Hale. We would do the same.'

'We must keep out of sight – OK?'

Returning to his hut, Hendrik was swallowed up by the night. The shape of the boats and the row of huts emerged, as the moon floated out from behind the heavy rain clouds. The tiny waves on the river glittered in the pathway of its reflection.

Steph hoped they'd miss the rain forecast for after midnight. It was bad enough being exposed to the cutting wind from the North Sea, which found the smallest gap in her coat, but to stand unsheltered in pouring rain would be really grim. Hale had attempted to drop her at the flat, but she had protested, and as they were only observing, he gave in.

The wind was getting stronger. It howled around the huts and jangled the lines and metal bits on the masts of the boats moored along the harbour. The sound of the wind made it difficult to hear a van or even a boat coming into the harbour, and her eyes ached staring into the darkness.

The biting cold, and keeping as still as possible behind the hut, was becoming more painful every minute. She was desperate to lie under the warm duvet in her bed and she was so tired her eyes felt as if they were filled with sand, but no way was she going to miss this.

A rustle under the hut by her feet made her freeze. Rats. Must be. Fishermen's bait and pieces of food dropped by the visitors to the fish and chip hut along the row to their left would keep a herd of rats well fed. Hale must have felt her tense, and he put his arm around her. She leaned into his body, seizing the chance to share his warmth. He whispered in her ear. 'Not much longer. You're amazing coping with this after all you've been through.' For a moment, his words made her glow, but they failed to reduce the pain. Maybe it hadn't been such a good idea to spend hours standing in the bitter wind.

Above the sea, the solid clouds showed streaks of silver as they caught the reflection of the moon. Keeping well back behind the hut, Steph squinted up the river for any sign of a boat arriving. The moon lit Hendrik doing the same but stepping out a little from the shadows.

She waved at him and hissed, 'Oy! Henk! I can see you, get back!' At once he stepped back into the black. How stupid was that? There was no one else to hear them – apart from the rats.

The slapping of the ripples against the bank got louder as the incoming tide rushed past from the sea to fill up the river. It nudged the boats against one another, making the masts jangle and hum. As the moon went behind a cloud, a few pin-prick lights in the houses on the opposite bank became visible and defined the edge of Walberswick, giving the solid black some perspective. The damp smell of rotten fish invaded her nose, and despite turning up-wind, she couldn't get rid of the taste of it.

Then they heard it. As Hale had predicted, it came from the right. As the van turned left round the corner past the Harbour Inn, the dipped headlights cut through the night, weaving around the potholes, past the sailing club and the chandlery. It slowed to a crawl and stopped alongside the first hut.

Hale and Steph edged further back into the hedge behind

their hut, keeping well out of the headlights. As the van crept past them, full beams on, it lit up the ferry landing stage, pulled up beside the rickety wooden pier and turned off its engine. Almost within touching distance, it faced the sea and the entrance to the harbour. All was still once again as they waited.

Hoping the howling wind, along with the solid slapping of the water against the bank, covered any small sounds they might make, they held themselves rigid. Steph's ribs hurt like hell, and she had to take shallow breaths to keep her lungs away from them.

She was desperate to sit down, and the bruises from the accident and the fall down the cellar steps ached in the cold. The picture of her duvet was banished as soon as it appeared. At last, her night vision came back, and helped by the faint moonlight, she could just make out the shadow that was Hendrik crouching down behind his hut. They would be seen by whoever was in the van if they got out and walked around to the back of it.

A frantic Hale waved his hand at Hendrik, who stuck his thumb up and leaned back further into the cover of the hedge. Not daring to move in case they attracted attention, they froze. How much longer would they have to wait? The pins and needles in her foot had moved up her leg, and she flexed it, pressing her foot hard into the ground to get the feeling back. If only she could stamp it, but she daren't.

Once again, an engine shattered the silence – this time from the sea. The throbbing came closer and the tiny light at the top of the mast became visible as the boat chugged up the river towards them. Anyone watching would assume it was returning early after a useless night's fishing.

What a brilliant spot to choose for a night's smuggling. After loading the van, they had several ways to escape. It would take them about ten minutes to reach the A12 and then off to Norwich, Ipswich or London. Hale had arranged for all the possible routes to be covered so they would be picked up by armed officers and followed. Who would suspect a small van making an overnight delivery along with the other heavy traffic making the most of the empty roads at night?

The boat's engine slowed, stuttered and stopped as it reached the landing stage. They saw the doors at the front of the van open. The driver came around to fix back the double doors, ready to receive the cargo. He joined his partner, now standing at the end of the thin wooden landing stage, waiting for the boat to tie up at the end.

Having manoeuvred itself into the right position, the splash that echoed along the river told them the boat had dropped anchor. The sudden silence that followed was dramatic. Only the twittering of some disturbed birds punctuated the black night.

Hale had told them to do nothing but observe the men unloading the drugs from the boat, as well as those waiting to receive them. The sound of footsteps reached them as two dark shapes, carrying armfuls of packages, trudged along the shaky wooden platform towards the van. They were met by the other two men, who helped them stow the drugs in the back of the van. It appeared to be an efficient operation, with not a word spoken.

Clang! A sudden metallic crash from where Hendrik was hiding tore through the silence. He must have kicked over a metal oil drum. How clumsy was that? He'd been standing there for ages. Why hadn't he noticed it before?

Immediately the shapes froze, listened for a moment, then shouted to abort the operation. Hale yelled into his phone, shoved it in his pocket and ran towards the van, shouting,

'Police! Freeze!' A bright search light appeared from the lifeboat station and Steph shielded her eyes from the beam.

From behind the large hut and the fish and chip hut to the right of it, four police officers sprinted towards the group by the landing stage. A fight broke out as one of the van men made a run for it, only to be grabbed by two of the officers, while the other two captured one of the sailors.

Steph tried to keep up with Hale as he ran towards the men. But her body was screaming out, and she trailed behind a dithering Hendrik, while Hale had thrown himself on another sailor and was handcuffing him. The harsh light illuminated him perfectly, and he wasn't being too gentle.

Steph stopped at the edge of the landing stage, holding her side as the insistent pain forced her to stand still. At the end of the pier, she saw a shadow leap aboard the boat, and as he did so, he yelled out, 'Henk! Henk!' Then something in Dutch.

Someone brushed past her, running on the shaky wooden slats towards the boat. It was Hendrik aiming for the boat. As the engine fired up, she shouted over the noise to Hale, a few feet away. 'Hale – the boat – Henk!'

Racing past her, Hale chased Hendrik, who, hearing their steps on the wooden planks, sped towards the boat. In pain, she managed a slow jog behind him.

The pier wobbled under their weight and the force of the incoming tide, but Hale was gaining on him. As Hendrik was about to jump aboard, Hale executed a perfect rugby tackle, hitting him at chest height.

Losing his balance, Hendrik toppled into the river. The splash halted all action. Steph reached Hale and they stared into the black water, rough now as the rip tide rushed in, waiting for Hendrik to emerge, but he didn't.

CHAPTER FIFTY-FOUR

Caroline always gave brilliant parties, and this one was up there with the best. Two months after the drugs' bust, the college hall had been transformed. Bunches of helium balloons hovered above each table, anchored to stones covered in silver foil. The walls were filled with enormous photos from their trip to Arnhem.

A supper of fish and chips, a well-stocked bar and some great music encouraged the students, carers and veterans to celebrate their reunion. Zoe and her gran were on a front table with Ollie, Ron and Alistair, and from the raucous laughter coming from their direction, they were having a great time.

Zoe had been relieved to learn that her DNA wasn't a match for Jim's, so Ken wasn't her father, after all. However, it appeared she'd adopted a new grandad in Ron, who apparently was now a frequent visitor to see her and her gran.

Steph moved across to their table and sat beside Zoe. 'How are you?'

Zoe smiled back. 'I'm fine now, thanks. Have you heard

we're giving Duncan's exercise book to the Imperial War Museum to help with research projects into the Battle of Arnhem?'

'Really? You and your gran are happy to let it go?'

'Now we know what really happened, we can get on with our future and we can always see it in London.'

'I'm sure Duncan would have approved.' Steph was about to leave when Zoe stopped her.

'Have you seen it in the proofs of the book? Caroline has got some really sharp photocopies of it, so we'll always have it as part of the project.'

'Yes, it looks brilliant, doesn't it?'

'And have you recovered?'

'Yes, getting there, thanks. I'd better get back. Caroline is waving at me.'

Steph walked back to her table, through the chatter and laughter, to join a worried Caroline. Her ribs still hurt like crazy and taking part in the operation at the harbour hadn't helped.

'Hale has just disappeared with his phone. What is wrong with that man? Can't he stay still for one evening?' Caroline sounded nervous, which was unusual for her.

Steph patted her arm. 'That's the job, I'm afraid. Always on duty. Another?'

Caroline nodded, and Steph wandered up to the bar, Derek at her heels. He had been invited too. Through the glass doors she caught sight of Hale, phone glued to his ear, gesticulating as he talked. He had spent the past two months ploughing through the piles of admin, tying up the case, made more complicated as it involved the Met and the Dutch police.

Hendrik had been arrested by the Border Force waiting

beyond the harbour as they stopped the dinghy he had managed to swim to and steal. It was rather optimistic of him to think he could make it across to Holland in such a small boat with only an outboard motor, but he'd been desperate. The driver of the Dutch boat had been alerted when Hendrick had kicked over the oil drum and had managed to evade capture. Hendrick would have too, if Hale hadn't rugby tackled him.

Hendrik would face a long sentence in the UK for smuggling, dealing drugs, GBH and possession of a prohibited weapon and that was before the Dutch police got hold of him. Apparently, he had told them the truth in Hale's kitchen. He had worked as a double agent on behalf of the Dutch police, but then had flipped again to become a fully bent cop. The Dutch police, hearing Hale's story when he phoned them from his hallway, shared their suspicions with him and were grateful to him for providing evidence of Hendrik's treachery.

When they questioned Hendrik, he'd been as pragmatic and charming as ever. He'd expressed surprise and wanted to know how Hale had got his police officers to the harbour for the raid, when the three of them had been together all the time. Hale reminded him of the slight delay when Hendrik and Steph were settling Derek in the car, and he had gone back to check he'd locked the back door. Hendrik had the cheek to congratulate Hale on running an excellent operation!

Ken, Judy and three members of the gang, arrested at the harbour, were now in custody, awaiting trial. Judy had admitted going into Jim's room, smothering him and taking his bag containing the drugs and diamonds, which were found in her father's spare room. As far as the police were concerned, Tom was innocent and didn't know about the crimes his daughter had committed.

Waiting at the bar for the glasses of wine, Steph glanced

around the room and smiled at the laughter and the firm friend-ships that had been formed across the group. Caroline grinned, left their table, picking up the glass of wine Steph handed to her, and took her place at the mic.

The room became silent. 'Thank you all for coming to this final celebration of our Arnhem project. I'm sure you will be thrilled with our book. If you haven't already seen it, there is a proof copy over there on the table at the back.'

Several heads swivelled round to see where she was point-ing. 'The publishers are excited with the excellent quality of your work and predict it will be a best seller for the seventy-fifth anniversary of the Battle of Arnhem.'

A ripple of applause became deafening when the whoops and cheers were joined by the stamping of feet. Caroline held up her hand. 'We have enough money left over for those of you who would like to return to Arnhem for those celebrations. I've been told that Prince Charles will attend, and he has already requested a copy of our book.'

More cheers and foot stamping. 'Now a toast – please raise your glasses to all you brave men who fought in that battle and who are here tonight and to all those whom we salute in their absence. To the brave soldiers at Arnhem.'

The scraping of chairs as all stood and raised their glasses led to a moment of silence as they reflected on the reason for their being together. Many heads were bowed across the hall. Ron's eyes were filled with tears and Zoe held her gran's hand.

'What's going on?' Hale's arm crept around Steph's waist, and he pulled her towards him for a cuddle, which was no longer quite so excruciating.

'Shh!' She handed him his glass of wine so he could make the toast.

'What was she saying?'

'That we're going over in September for the seventy-fifth anniversary celebration.'

'Are you sure that's a good idea? You promised me a holiday last time and all I've had is weeks of work.'

'You know you'll love it – won't he, Derek?'

Derek wagged his tail – clearly, he agreed with every word.

ACKNOWLEDGMENTS

I was inspired to write this novel after I visited the Hartenstein Museum at Oosterbeek and found their booklets 'White Ribbon Mile' by Jan Vierdag and 'The Battle for Arnhem' invaluable.

When the Fighting is Over by John Lawrence and Robert Lawrence (Bloomsbury, 1988) gives a vivid description of fighting on the front line in the Falklands war and the struggle to live with the wounds back home, both metal and physical.

The Cauldron by Zeno (Macmillan,1966) is a brilliant fictional account that transported me to 1944 to experience the battle.

The well-known film 'A Bridge Too Far' (1977) crammed with brilliant actors, was supported by DVDs: 'Last Words' (2015, Simply Media); 'Arnhem – A Bridge too Far – The True Story' (2001, DD Video); 'Arnhem: The Battle for the Bridges' (2012, Pen & Sword Digital).

Thank you

Rebecca Collins and Adrian Hobart – the talented, tireless power-couple behind Hobeck publishing, for their excellent feedback, inspiration, and encouragement.

Sue Davison, for an outstanding edit and spotting details I missed.

Jayne Mapp, for a creative, evocative, and sensational cover design.

Graham Bartlett, for his advice on police procedure and suggesting great solutions to the problems I'd created. Any remaining mistakes are mine.

Mark Wenham for giving me a personal insight into the challenges of active service in the army and advice on making Duncan's diary authentic.

Rene Moor, originally from Holland who now lives and works in Suffolk, for his detailed suggestions on making Henk's dialogue convincing.

Brian Price for helping me to get the details right.

Jo Barry, for her constant encouragement and for asking the right questions.

Gerry Wakelin for his patience and finding the holes I needed to fill.

Debby Hurst, Mary Luke, Freda and Bob Noble, Julie Mursaleen, Elaine and Alan Lyons – my first readers for their enthusiasm, critical appreciation and helpful suggestions.

And finally, the lovely man who, on my visit to Arnhem, told the true story of his father's escape with the help of the white ribbons and a petticoat!

ABOUT THE AUTHOR

Lin Le Versha has drawn on her experience in London and Surrey schools and colleges as the inspiration for the Steph Grant crime series which now includes four books and a novella.

Lin has written over twenty plays exploring issues faced by secondary school and sixth form students. Commissioned to work with Anne Fine on *The Granny Project*, she created English and drama lesson activities for students aged 11 to 14.

While at a sixth form college, she became the major author for *Teaching at Post 16*, a handbook for trainee and newly qualified teachers. In her role as a Local Authority Consultant, she became a School Improvement Partner, working alongside secondary headteachers, work she continued after moving to the Suffolk coast. She is the Director of the Southwold Arts Festival, comprising over thirty events in an eight-day celebration of the Arts.

Creative writing courses at the Arvon Foundation and *Ways with Words* in Italy, encouraged her to enrol at the UEA MA in Creative Writing and her debut novel was submitted as the final assessment for this excellent course. The first book in this series, *Blood Notes*, was based on her final assessment piece.

Lin is now working on the fifth title in the series.

X

THE STEPH GRANT MURDER MYSTERIES

Blood Notes

'A wonderful, witty, colourful, debut 'Whodunnit',
with a gripping modern twist set in the dark
shadows of a Suffolk town.' EMMA FREUD

Edmund Fitzgerald is different.

Sheltered by an over-protective mother, he's a musical prodigy.

Now, against his mother's wishes, he's about to enter formal education for the first time aged sixteen.

Everything is alien to Edmund: teenage style, language and relationships are impossible to understand.

Then there's the searing jealousy his talent inspires, especially when the sixth form college's Head of Music, turns her back on her other students and begins to teach Edmund exclusively.

Observing events is Steph, a former police detective who is rebuilding her life following a bereavement as the college's receptionist. When a student is found dead in the music block, Steph's sleuthing skills help to unravel the dark events engulfing the college community.

Blood Lines

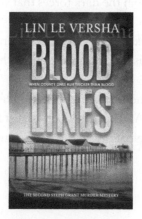

'**This wonderfully fresh take on a crime fighting duo, expertly explores dark, contemporary themes brought to life by a fabulous cast of characters who will stay with you long after the last page.' GRAHAM BARTLETT**

Eighteen year-old Darcy Woodard appears to have it all – intelligence, good looks and artistic gifts. His teachers adore him, as does former policewoman Steph Grant, who is now the receptionist at Darcy's college.

But beneath the surface – all is not as it seems.

Darcy is convinced he doesn't fit in with his peers and tries to ignore their online taunts.

There's Darcy's dysfunctional mother Esther who is trapped in a literary time warp.

289

Then there's his sister Marianne, who Darcy desperately wants to protect from the dark forces that surround her.

Then tragedy rocks Darcy's life when a drugs gang forces its way into his life and all the people he cares for.

What can Steph and her former boss DI Hale do to protect the local community? And can they really trust Darcy to help them defeat the county lines gang?

Blood Ties

'Lin Le Versha and Team Hobeck have done it again!' MONIKA ARMET

Hector Percy appears to have it all. He shares his magnificent home, Glebe Hall, with his beloved wife Esme and son Jack, alongside their two closest friends and their daughter. But beneath the veneer of entitlement, Hector lives in fear of those who might snatch away his inheritance. Esme suspects he's right; they'd created the perfect existence but now the arrangement is crumbling. If that happens their blissful life at Glebe Hall would be over.

Then tragedy strikes, forcing Hector and Esme to confront their future far sooner than they expected. One moment tearing the two families apart. Is this the end of their dreams?

Former detective Steph Grant finds herself embroiled in the family dynamics as she, along with partner and former boss, DI

Hale, are pulled into the investigation. Delving into the history of the two families and the Hall, Steph and Hale unearth buried secrets – secrets that shake the very foundations of Glebe Hall, secrets that will change the future forever.

HOBECK BOOKS – THE HOME OF GREAT STORIES

We hope you've enjoyed reading this book by Lin Le Versha. Lin has written a short story prequel to this novel, *A Defining Moment*.

Hobeck Books offers a number of short stories and novellas, including *A Defining Moment* by Lin Le Versha, free for subscribers in the compilation *Crime Bites*.

- *Echo Rock* by Robert Daws
- *Old Dogs, Old Tricks* by AB Morgan
- *The Silence of the Rabbit* by Wendy Turbin
- *Never Mind the Baubles: An Anthology of Twisted Winter Tales* by the Hobeck Team (including many of the Hobeck authors and Hobeck's two publishers)
- *The Clarice Cliff Vase* by Linda Huber
- *Here She Lies* by Kerena Swan
- *The Macnab Principle* by R.D. Nixon
- *Fatal Beginnings* by Brian Price
- *A Defining Moment* by Lin Le Versha
- *Saviour* by Jennie Ensor
- *You Can't Trust Anyone These Days* by Maureen Myant

Also please visit the Hobeck Books website for details of our other superb authors and their books, and if you would like to get in touch, we would love to hear from you.

Hobeck Books also presents a weekly podcast, the Hobcast, where founders Adrian Hobart and Rebecca Collins discuss all things book related, key issues from each week, including the ups and downs of running a creative business. Each episode includes an interview with one of the people who make Hobeck possible: the editors, the authors, the cover designers. These are the people who help Hobeck bring great stories to life. Without them, Hobeck wouldn't exist. The Hobcast can be listened to from all the usual platforms but it can also be found on the Hobeck website: **www.hobeck.net/hobcast**.

Other Hobeck Books to Explore

Silenced

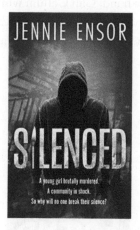

A teenage girl is murdered on her way home from school, stabbed through the heart. Her North London community is shocked, but no-one has the courage to help the police, not even her mother. DI Callum Waverley, in his first job as senior investigating officer, tries to break through the code of silence that shrouds the case.

This is a world where the notorious Skull Crew rules through fear. Everyone knows you keep your mouth shut or you'll be silenced – permanently.

This is Luke's world. Reeling from the loss of his mother to cancer, his step-father distant at best, violent at worst, he slides into the Skull Crew's grip.

This is Jez's world too. Her alcoholic mother neither knows nor cares that her 16-year-old daughter is being exploited by V, all-powerful leader of the gang.

Luke and Jez form a bond. Can Callum win their trust, or will his own demons sabotage his investigation? And can anyone stop the Skull Crew ensuring all witnesses are silenced?

Her Deadly Friend

The Suspect
Bullied by Steph Lewis at school, then betrayed by her lover, Amy Ashby still seethes with fury. Despite the decades-old resentment, she's on the hunt for a new man and a fresh start. This time for keeps.

The Stalker
When both women are stalked by a figure from their shared past, danger threatens.

The Detective
Now Detective Inspector, Steph follows a tip-off to her old rival. After quarrels exploded and changed lives forever, she vowed never to see Amy again. But that was then.

The Deaths
Murder rocks the city. The body count reaches five, and all Steph's leads point to Amy. But is Steph obsessed with a schoolgirl vendetta or closing in on a deadly killer?

Pact of Silence

A fresh start for a new life
Newly pregnant, Emma is startled when her husband Luke announces they're swapping homes with his parents, but the rural idyll where Luke grew up is a great place to start their family. Yet Luke's manner suggests something odd is afoot, something that Emma can't quite fathom.

Too many secrets, not enough truths

Emma works hard to settle into her new life in the Yorkshire countryside, but a chance discovery increases her suspicions. She decides to dig a little deeper...

Be careful what you uncover

Will Emma find out why the locals are behaving so oddly? Can she discover the truth behind Luke's disturbing behaviour? Will the pact of silence ever be broken?

Be Sure Your Sins

Six people
Six events
Six lives destroyed
What is the connection?

Detective **Melissa (Mel) Cooper** has two major investigations on the go. The first involves six apparently unrelated individuals who all suffer inexplicable life-altering events.

Mel is also pursuing a serial blackmailer but just as she's about to prove the link between this man and the six bizarre events, she's ordered to back off.

So why are her bosses interfering with her investigations? Who are they trying to protect? And how far will they go to stop her?

The answers come from a totally unexpected source.